A PACT WITH
THE SAVAGE HEALERS

"Wait!" Melissa said, "I know a way for you to get Readers. I will aid you in this battle if you will do what I ask."

Lord Wulfston studied her. "And what," he said finally, "do you ask?"

"In a room off your dungeons," she said, opening to Reading for their reactions, allowing Torio to Read her hope, her sincerity, "there are twelve bodies. Seven are Readers. Use your sorcery. Bring them back to life. Bring back only one of them and I promise you I will do anything you ask, Lord Wulfston—anything!"

By Jean Lorrah

SAVAGE EMPIRE
DRAGON LORD OF THE SAVAGE EMPIRE
CAPTIVES OF THE SAVAGE EMPIRE

. . . with Jacqueline Lichtenberg

FIRST CHANNEL
CHANNEL'S DESTINY

CAPTIVES OF THE SAVAGE EMPIRE

JEAN LORRAH

BERKLEY BOOKS, NEW YORK

CAPTIVES OF THE SAVAGE EMPIRE

A Berkley Book / published by arrangement with
the author

PRINTING HISTORY
Berkley edition / February 1984

ISBN: 0-425-06465-4

The entire *Savage Empire* series is dedicated to the person who got me into professional sf writing and then encouraged me to start my own series:

Jacqueline Lichtenberg

I would also like to thank the many readers who have sent comments about *Savage Empire* and *Dragon Lord of the Savage Empire*; I hope you enjoy this third book in the series.

If there are readers who would like to comment on this book, my publisher will forward letters to me. If you prefer, you may write to me at Box 625, Murray, KY 42071. If your letter requires an answer, please enclose a self-addressed stamped envelope.

All comments are welcome. I came to professional writing through fan writing and publishing, where there is close and constant communication between writers and readers. Thus I shall always be grateful for the existence of sf fandom, which has provided me with many exciting experiences, and through which I have met so many wonderful people.

Jean Lorrah
Murray, Kentucky

Prologue

THE LEGEND OF THE FIRST READER

Before there was an Aventine Empire the world was broken up into little kingdoms. In one of those kingdoms lived a young man who had the power to Read—to know what was in other people's minds—but he was the very first to have such power, and he did not know what to do with it, so he remained a poor honest laborer.

In this kingdom the king had no sons, but he had one very beautiful daughter; all men who saw her wanted to marry her. Since she did not know how to choose among her many suitors, she declared a contest: Whoever could give her her heart's desire would have her hand.

So men brought her gold and jewels, fine horses, musicians and dancers to entertain her, perfumes and spices—and always she declared that their gifts were not her heart's desire.

The young Reader, though, was able to Read what was going on in the princess' mind as her suitors displayed their treasures and were rejected. The king grew angrier and angrier as the girl refused one after another of the fine, strong, wealthy men. The Reader knew that the king wanted his daughter to marry a king . . . but the daughter did not like the powerful men who tried to claim her hand.

Watching the princess each time there was a public ceremony for another suitor, and Reading her true desire, the Reader fell deeply in love with her. At length, despite the fact that he was a common laborer with no property to give her, he decided to risk pressing his suit. When he stepped forward, the people laughed to see a poor man with no troop of servants carrying treasures, marching forward empty-handed to the foot of the throne.

The king, however, was curious enough to allow the Reader to offer his gift. The young man drew himself up, and addressed the princess. "All your life," he said, "you have had gold and jewels, slaves, furs and perfumes, horses and falcons, treasures from all the lands of the world. All these your father can provide for you—yet you say you do not have your heart's desire. Thus it cannot be any worldly treasure that you long for. What you desire is the love of a good man—a man who is not bent on accumulating treasure or making war on his enemies—a man who will place you above all things as the greatest treasure of his heart. This I can give you, as no man else."

Never before had the princess met a man who understood her deepest desires. "Yes!" she cried. "That is my heart's desire! I shall love you above all men!"

But the king, who had thought the young man comical until his daughter's response, was maddened with anger. "You lie!" he roared. "No daughter of mine would be so foolish as to forego power and wealth for such frivolity! You are a liar, young man, and will die for daring to say such a thing about a member of the king's family! And you," he added, turning to his daughter, "will deny what he has said, or I will have you killed, too!"

"But I can prove it!" cried the young Reader. "I can tell you what is in your heart—I can hear any man's thoughts! You are thinking that you want a strong and powerful man to marry your daughter and be king after you—someone who will give her strong sons who will capture many lands and accumulate great treasures. But if you could Read what was in her heart, you would know as I do that these things mean nothing to her.''

Now the king knew that the Reader spoke the truth about what he was thinking, but he also thought it nothing but common sense, such as any man ought to think. He had the young man hauled off to the dungeon, threatening to cut his tongue out if he continued to tell lies about the princess. That night, however, another suitor for the princess' hand arrived—a great and powerful warlord from a neighboring land.

Languishing in his dungeon, the Reader Read the plans of the warlord. He had brought with him an army, claiming it was his gift to the princess, for surely it must be strength of arms that was her heart's desire. But he was also prepared for rejection—in which case his army, thus smuggled into the heart of the kingdom, would turn on the people. They would kill the king, and the warlord would take the princess by force and make himself king of all the land.

Knowing this, the Reader begged and pleaded with his guards to arrange an audience for him with the king. As it happened, the king had planned to test the young man's claims, for he could see great value in someone who could tell him his enemies' secrets . . . if such an impossible claim proved true. So the next morning he had the Reader brought before him, and the Reader told him the plan of the warlord. The king had his own army, disguised as common people, surrounding the warlord's army when he made his offer to the princess. She rejected him, of course—and he turned and shouted to his men, ''To arms!''

Just as quickly, the king's men threw off their disguises, and in a battle at the king's feet they slaughtered their enemies. The Reader was elated—he had proved his value, and was sure the king would change his mind and allow him to marry the princess.

But the king saw only danger in a man who knew what was in people's minds—he immediately envisioned his son-in-law plotting to kill him and take the throne, and no reassurances would make him trust the Reader, nor would the pleadings of the princess mitigate his decision.

He knew, of course, that the Reader was a double-edged sword: If he did not like the way the king treated him, he might run away to work against him with one of his enemies. Therefore he had the young man hamstrung, so he could not run away, and he tortured him to force him to Read for him.

In less than a year the king had conquered all the neighboring lands. He always knew the size of the enemies' armies, where they were located, all the battle plans. He also captured the fine, strong, warrior son of one of his enemies—a man who saw opportunity in ingratiating himself with a king he could not conquer. Soon plans were underway to marry the princess to the warrior—for she had learned well the lesson her father had taught her. The Reader might have been willing to give her her heart's desire, but he had not the strength to win her and then protect her. So she gave up her desire for someone to love her in exchange for someone who would be very much like her father, shower her with presents, and protect her against her enemies.

On the eve of the wedding, while the bridegroom and his prospective son-in-law were drinking themselves into a stupor with the wedding guests, the Reader was of course left alone in his room in the castle—what need to chain him in the dungeon once he was lamed? The treatment he had received for revealing his gift had worked on his mind in the past year—and he had learned to walk again, if with a hideous limp. When the revelers were thoroughly drunk, he set fire to the castle, went to the room where the princess lay guarded only by women, whom he killed, and carried the girl off into the night.

In the morning, the king and his would-be son-in-law were found dead, along with most of their guests. The princess was found in the woods nearby—she claimed to have been raped by the Reader, and nine months later she bore a son.

The princess ruled the land as her father had before her, for she had his army and she knew his methods. Her son turned out to be a Reader like his father . . . and it is said that all the Readers of what would become the Aventine Empire are descended from him. His father, however, disappeared without a trace. Here and there were heard tales of a strange lame man who could tell people's most secret thoughts, but no warlord ever held him again, and no one knows what finally became of him. Perhaps, bitter and disillusioned at the fate of his offer of true love, he is wandering still.

Chapter One

Where do I belong? What should I be doing with my life? Certainly not healing!

Magister Jason was wrong to encourage me. He should have let me quit the first time I lost a patient— then I would not be about to kill my best friend's son!

Looking down at the fretful child, Melissa wished she were anything else but a Reader in the hospital at Gaeta. Alethia trusted her to cure Primus, but how could she? The boy's appendix was inflamed; all their herbs, compresses, and cold packs had failed—and now she would have to try surgery as a last resort. What if Primus died?

She Read within the boy's body, wanting to moan with his pain and fever, studying the swollen, throbbing organ. If this went on, it would burst, spilling poisons throughout the child's system. Then there was no hope at all of saving him. She *had* to cut out that infected bit of intestine!

For the first time, she was sorry she and Alethia had been reunited. This was why a Reader still in training, like Melissa, was discouraged from keeping up associations with childhood friends who had dropped by the wayside.

Alethia, too, was a Reader, but she now wore the Sign of the Dark Moon, the badge of a Reader who had failed to achieve one of the two top ranks, and for whom a marriage had been arranged. Alethia and

Melissa had been fast friends at the Academy. Melissa would never forget the day Alethia, aged seventeen, had been told that her powers had shown no increase in more than a year, and it had been determined that she would go no further.

Alethia had spent the evening sobbing on Melissa's shoulder. Her life was over—both girls were quite convinced of it. She would be married off to a similarly failed male Reader, to breed children who might have the talents they lacked. The loss of her virginity would diminish what powers she had; her badge—a black circle on a field of white—would be the only sign that she was a Reader . . . a failed Reader.

Melissa had absorbed Alethia's agonized fear that day, and applied herself thereafter with the greatest diligence. Never, she vowed, would she be taken like Alethia, to spend her life producing the children of a stranger and using whatever Reading power she retained to show non-readers where to dig wells or locate their lost sheep.

At eighteen Melissa passed her preliminary examinations and was sent to Gaeta for training in healing. She had arrived in fear, knowing that more than half the Readers who completed the medical training still eventually failed and were married off. It would be better to live as a healer than as a message service and finder of strayed children—but Melissa's heart throbbed to the vibrations of the great hospital. There was pain and suffering here—pain she shared with the patients when she Read them—but Reading the easing of that pain because of something she had done was the most satisfying use she had ever made of her talent.

Her primary teacher was Magister Jason. They never met face to face, of course—no male and female Reader could unless one or both wore the Sign of the Dark Moon. Celibacy was the rule and the necessity for the upper ranks and those still in training; temptation was to be avoided.

But the touch of Jason's mind was an inspiration to

Melissa. Disciplined yet vibrant, he Read with her as she examined patients and learned to interpret the data she gleaned. Medicines, bonesetting, manipulations of joint and muscle—these she learned from the other healers. Jason taught her to look deep within the human body and, when no other means would suffice, to cut into it and make repairs. She quickly progressed from sitting entranced while her mind looked through Jason's eyes, her hands feeling what his were doing, to the day when she herself held the knife, and Jason's mind guided her.

She never wanted to give up the experience of his mental touch. There was only one way to manage that: She must become such an expert healer that she would be invited to stay at Gaeta for the rest of her days, as Jason did. She dreamed of their spending hours each day in deep rapport, healing the sick and injured together. Her skills improved rapidly under his tutelage. She was happy.

And she remained happy . . . until the first time she had a patient neither medicines nor surgery could cure. They had had no choice—none of their medicines, no applications of herbal packs, nothing would reduce the ulcerating tumor blocking the girl's intestine. All the surgeons hated abdominal surgery, for more than half the time they could not prevent an infection that killed the patient within a few days of gruesome agony.

Melissa had administered the herbalist's latest concoction to the girl. For the next few hours her patient's body temperature would rise dramatically—possibly enough to kill the organisms introduced by surgery. But such high temperatures often caused convulsions that killed the patient more efficiently than the infection.

That was the first time Melissa faced the possible death of a patient. She was still in training; the teachers examined her patient hourly, but none of them offered any advice beyond what she had already tried. She had done everything right—and still her patient would probably die. It was the first time she questioned her desire to spend her life as a healer . . . and that day brought the reunion that would soon make her question it again.

The girl had drunk the new medicine in total trust, then, in exhaustion and hope, fallen asleep. Melissa left her sleeping, not knowing where she was going, but having to get out of that sickroom for at least a few minutes.

"Melissa, there's a visitor for you in the family room," one of the aides told her.

Melissa cringed. Probably the girl's father again. She gritted her teeth and prepared to face him.

But it was not a man waiting for her. It was a young woman—a very pregnant and obviously happy young woman who wore on her cloak the Sign of the Dark Moon.

"Alethia!" Melissa cried, running to embrace her friend. "Oh, how good to see you again! What are you doing here? There's nothing wrong—?" Automatically she Read Alethia, finding to her relief nothing but a perfectly normal pregnancy, advanced approximately seven months.

"No, there's nothing wrong!" Alethia laughed. "I'm happier than ever in my life, Melissa. My husband and I were just transferred here to Gaeta. I thought you might be taking your medical training by now."

Alethia's pregnancy was her second, it turned out; she had a son almost two years old, who was being cared for by a neighbor while she went visiting. "I can't work now, anyway," she explained. "After about the fourth month, my range is severely limited—but it comes back, Melissa. By the time Primus was six months old, I was Reading as well as I ever could—at least so far as I can tell. Well enough to be wonderfully happy with my husband."

"You are happy? The man the Masters chose for you—?"

"Oh, Melissa, I am so fortunate! You must meet him. When do you have a day off? Come spend the day with me, and meet Rodrigo when he comes home in the evening. He's a navigator for the fishing fleet—finds the schools of fish for them, too. He's good at it—they usually come in with a full catch by the middle of the afternoon."

And how insensitive he must be, Melissa thought, *to be able to shut himself off from the deaths of all those captured creatures.* Readers occasionally ate fish—but they rarely caught them themselves.

"I'm glad you're so happy, Alethia," Melissa said cautiously. "I have an occasional afternoon off—never a full day. My next afternoon is the day after tomorrow—but I have a very sick patient, and if I cannot leave her—"

"I understand," said Alethia. "Melissa, I cannot Read to the hospital now, to contact you. I'll show you on the city map where our house is. I can still receive perfectly well from a stronger Reader—thank the gods for that, as it allows . . ." She lowered her voice, and drew Melissa to where they could not be overheard from the hallway. "I want to tell you what it's like for two Readers to be married. If it should happen to you, you mustn't have the blind terror I had—and that Rodrigo had, too. You'll probably be a Magister—even a Master one day. But . . . they're failing so many Readers . . . you should know it's not terrible at all to be married. You can Read me; you know I'm really happy, not lying to you. We'll talk when you visit me, Melissa."

Melissa expected to cancel that first afternoon with Alethia, for her patient grew progressively worse, until all they could do was dull her pain with opiates. She died just before noon, her father and Melissa on either side of the bed, Jason Reading with Melissa. When the child slipped from unconsciousness to death, it was Melissa's task to tell the father. She wished that he would rage, strike her, do anything but thank her for her efforts in a voice gruff with tears, and leave her to her own inadequacies.

But Jason was there, his mind calming hers, telling her, //It happens to all of us, Melissa. There was nothing more you could have done.//

//There has to be more!// she told him. //Why did you give me this patient if you thought I couldn't save her?//

//Because no healer could have . . . and you needed to learn that we cannot work miracles. Melissa, you were born to be a healer—but you must accept your limitations if you are ever to be one of the best.//

//How can I accept the deaths of children! We must find some way to stop infections so when we save some-one's life with surgery we won't be killing him with the organisms we admit with the knife.//

//Good—let the experience lead you to seek answers, and you will make a fine healer one day. Meanwhile, you are now off duty. Find something to keep you from brooding.//

//I am going to visit a friend.//

But even Alethia could not cheer Melissa. Her house was a lovely cottage surrounded with a flower and herb garden; her little boy was a tow-haired charmer—but all Melissa could think of was the girl who had died.

She picked at the lunch Alethia served, and tried to be polite . . . until finally, seeing the dismay in her friend's eyes, she confessed, "This morning one of my patients died. It's the first time, Alethia, but I know it won't be the last. I'm no good as company today."

"Oh, Melissa, how terrible! I understand—but you shouldn't go back to the hospital. Why don't you go down to the beach for a while? I'll bring Primus down to play in the sand after you've had some time to your-self."

It was a hot summer day, but the breeze along the shore made it pleasant to stroll. For a while Melissa lost herself in the sound of the water, the screech of the gulls. Approaching no one, she watched pelicans dive for fish, and children build castles. Her unadorned white tunic marked her as a Reader in training; no one approached her.

The solitude didn't help much; her mind went back over every step of the treatment she had given her patient. First she had tried medicines. The herbalist had advised her at every step—but should she have accepted his concoctions routinely? She had had training in herbs . . . but he had spent his life studying them. Had she decided on surgery too soon? Too late? Jason had agreed with her decision—because it was the best decision, or because it really made no difference?

She felt sticky. Her bare arms were beaded with sweat, and freckles had sprung out on them in the heat of the sun. Her skin was turning pink; she would have a nasty sunburn if she didn't get off the glaring sand.

She wasn't ready to go back to Alethia's, but she saw deep shade under the pier. The rocks would be awash at high tide, but it was out at the moment, leaving a pocket of cool shade there. The sand was damp in the cavelike space, but the rocks were dry. She climbed up, using physical activity to tire herself out, as if she could thus tire her mind out from its ceaseless circling.

Her climb brought her up close to the pier, the boards just a short distance over her head. She leaned back in an unexpectedly comfortable niche in the rock, and watched the striped patterns shift as clouds passed overhead, birds swooped by, and occasionally a person walked above her, unaware. At the end of the pier some people were fishing.

Then someone stopped, almost over her head. She could not see through the cracks in the boards, and she didn't want to Read. Perhaps the person would go away.

But no, the person sat down on the edge of the pier, legs dangling over the side. Male legs, and just the edge of his short summer tunic, white, bordered in black. A Reader! From the hospital, no doubt; someone in the two top ranks. No cloak in today's heat to tell her whether he was Magister or Master . . . and she hesitated to Read him, to tell him she was there. They were not exactly face to face—but she was not sure what the rules would say even about face to feet!

Go away! she willed without Reading, but the man

lifted one foot at a time out of her sight, and returned them to her view bare of his sandals, wriggling his toes in the sea breeze. She was trapped; she could not get down from her perch without coming into his view.

"I know you're there, Melissa," he said. "Why are you not Reading?"

Magister Jason!

She had never heard his voice before—only the "voice" he projected when Reading. Often a Reader's physical voice and his Reading "voice" were far different from one another; not so in Jason's case. His calm baritone exactly matched the reassuring tone she had known so often in her mind in the past few months.

"I didn't really think about it," she replied, "but I suppose I knew that if I were Reading you would Read how depressed I was, and make me come back to the hospital. I wanted to be alone."

"Melissa, you have every right to be upset. I did Read for you. When I could not find you, I contacted Alethia, and she told me where you had gone. You seem better."

She knew he wanted her to open to Reading, but she did not want him in her mind just then. "I am better," she told him. "I think I can go back to Alethia's house and be a sociable guest. You are not canceling my afternoon off?"

"No, of course not. Alethia is worried about you, though, and rightly so. She can give you what I cannot, Melissa: a shoulder to cry on. There are times when even Readers need another person's touch, you know. If you are to be a successful healer, you must learn that some things must be treated in other ways than with medicines and surgery." He took a deep breath of the fresh sea air. "I had forgotten myself how cleansing to the spirit the sea can be. Thank you for reminding me." He pulled his feet up, preparing to leave, but remained sitting for a moment so she could hear him over the surf and the bird cries. "Go back to Alethia, and let her help you." He got up, picked up his sandals, and walked barefoot back along the pier.

Melissa stayed where she was, giving Jason time to be well out of sight. He hadn't scolded her for not Reading as she walked along the beach—Gaeta had so many Readers that they had to Read constantly when moving about the town, lest male and female encounter one another by accident. She should not have forgotten that simple precaution.

How strange that Magister Jason should venture to talk to her this way. There were special rooms at the hospital where Readers as yet unable to reach the plane of privacy could talk; no Reader ever Read into those rooms, the only way to eavesdrop on a conversation. A mental discussion, though, was "overheard" by every Reader within range who happened to be Reading.

She looked up at the boards of the pier over her head—they were as effective as the screen placed between male and female Readers using a privacy room. She had never done so. She talked with nonReaders all the time—but talking with Magister Jason, so formally, without the mental intimacy she was accustomed to. . . . *It's your own fault,* she told herself. *He was willing to Read, but you weren't.* And he had been concerned enough about her to leave his duties to search for her.

She put the thought out of her head, and walked back up the beach, Reading dutifully. Near the path that led up to her street, Alethia was sitting on the sand, watching Primus digging with a shell. "Did Magister Jason find you?" she asked as Melissa approached.

"Yes, he found me."

"You must be very important to him if he left his patients to search for you," said Alethia. "You didn't—?"

"We didn't see each other."

"But he risked it," Alethia said in a peculiar tone, and tried to Read Melissa. But her poor powers could not penetrate the barrier Melissa felt around her reactions to the meeting at the pier—a barrier hiding something Melissa herself was not sure she understood.

The little boy could not stay out in the sun for long; soon his mother gathered up the protesting child, and both women went up to the cottage. Melissa helped cut up vegetables for dinner, while she and Alethia laughed over memories of hiding from the cook at the Academy when it was their turn to wash dishes, and how they had cajoled extra sweets out of her. Melissa's sorrow dissipated. She never did get around to crying on Alethia's shoulder.

Rodrigo arrived home smelling of salt air and fish, kissed his wife and son openly, and went apologetically off to the public bath so as to be presentable for dinner. Melissa was hard-put to account for Alethia's infatuation; her husband was quite ordinary in appearance, hardly taller than she was, slightly overweight, hair faded from salt and sun, eyes disappearing into leathery wrinkles that marked the man of the sea.

But when he returned, clean and dressed in a fresh tunic, she Read the rapport between husband and wife —and the deep, abiding love beneath it. Physical appearance was nothing to them; their minds met and twined in an endless dance. Their powers might be small, but they were beautiful—and for the first time in her life, Melissa felt left out of a gathering of Readers.

She returned to the hospital that evening, her mind at ease. Spending hours in the presence of people living life fully, caring for their child and awaiting the next with joyful anticipation, Melissa had lost her gloom. She would work toward positive solutions—and that meant first doing so well in her medical training that she would be chosen to stay here at the hospital. She would complete her training, and then devote her life to finding a way to prevent the infection that had killed her patient.

Before she could even begin, however, she was faced with another hopeless patient—and this time it was Alethia's little tow-headed son. Now, as Melissa left the sickroom to find Alethia, she was still Reading Primus. She had insisted Alethia lie down in her own room, promising to call her if anything happened . . . but she could not merely Read for the mother now. She would have to hold her friend as she told her the truth. They had to attempt surgery.

Alethia, though, was sound asleep on Melissa's bed. The strain of her child's illness along with her advancing pregnancy had finally exhausted her. Perhaps it would be best if she didn't know when they took her son into surgery. She certainly needed the rest. Melissa tiptoed away, and returned to Primus' side, trying to judge the moment when she could have no more hope that the medicines would take hold, but before there was danger of the appendix rupturing.

Jason was wrong. I wasn't born to be a healer. He should have known when I couldn't learn advanced Reading.

After her earlier patient had died, Melissa had driven herself to perfect her surgical skills, becoming fanatical about boiling everything in the sickroom, not just the surgical tools, attempting techniques to keep incisions as small as possible and to shorten the time the patient was exposed. But medical skills were not all she was here to learn.

She was expected to continue her lessons in Reading —and those did not go well at all. She had barely managed to learn to leave her body behind while her "self" went out of body. She hated the feeling, fearful that she would lose herself, never to return to the physical. And she was completely incapable of leaving the simple plane in which another Reader might perceive her for one of the planes of privacy. She must learn to do that before she could become a Magister Reader, and be safe from being married off as Alethia had been.

She saw Alethia often, and knew that there was absolutely no pretense to her friend's happiness. She began to understand more clearly the joy of Readers united both mentally and physically, and sometimes—especially when she had failed again at one of her Reading tests—she thought she might not mind being married off . . . if it were to the right man.

Facing surgery on Alethia's son, she almost wished that she *had* been failed by now, and thus could avoid this responsibility. Hers were the best techniques anyone had for abdominal surgery; she could not ask another surgeon to perform the operation or she would be denying the child his best chance to survive, small as that chance was.

It was time, Melissa decided. She sent an aide she trusted to scrub the child with the precious soap smuggled in from the savage lands while the authorities looked the other way.

She supervised the preparation of the surgery herself, the swabbing of the table with alcohol, the boiling of the instruments. She and her assistants scrubbed themselves with soap and rinsed their hands in alcohol—but it was not enough. Their hands were where the infection clung, in their pores, to sweat out as they worked. And they could not boil their hands.

Primus was brought in, drugged with opiates. He was unconscious, his pain gone for the first time in days. Melissa breathed a prayer to the gods to assist her. She worked rapidly but thoroughly, Reading to be sure she cut out every bit of infection, and sewed up the wound with greatest care. Then she just stood there, wishing, willing, that the wound remain clean. She concentrated so hard that her Reading blanked out for a moment, and she became dizzy. But that would accomplish nothing. There was nothing to do but wait.

Alethia woke to the news that the surgery had been done. She sat by her son all night, while Melissa slept only fitfully. In the morning Primus was awake and crying at pains in his abdomen, but they were only gas, and Melissa did not want to drug him again. The herbalist gave him tea, and they placed fresh compresses over the incision. It was still too early to know what organisms might be breeding in the child's intestine—but Melissa could not Read anything that seemed dangerous. She slowly let hope creep up on her. As the hours passed, her hopes grew. The second morning Primus asked for breakfast—and hope became certainty.

Melissa asked Magister Jason to Read Primus before she would believe it—but the boy was healing. There was no infection. She turned to Alethia, who had been Reading with them, and the two women embraced, tears running down their faces. "Oh, Melissa," Alethia sobbed, "how can I ever thank you? No one else could have saved my little boy." And for a moment Melissa felt as if Magister Jason's arms were around her, too.

The next morning she was called for the first time into one of the privacy rooms. The screen was set up— Magister Jason wanted to talk with her.

"Melissa, yesterday I was so proud of you that I went to Master Florian to recommend that we keep you here at the hospital. I have never seen a healer progress so rapidly! You have more than a year to study; by the time you finish, there will not be a more skillful surgeon in the empire."

"Thank you, Magister," she said, blushing under his praise . . . but something in his voice warned her that he had not called this conference to congratulate her.

He sighed, part sorrow, part exasperation. "Do you know what Master Florian told me?"

"Probably that my Reading skills are not progressing as they should." She wished she could see him, and resisted the temptation to Read through the screen.

"You have made almost no progress since you came here. Soon you must go on to the healing of minds rather than bodies—and you cannot do that if you have not advanced much further. We should not be using this clumsy apparatus—by this time you should achieve the plane of privacy with ease. I am removing you from hospital duty three mornings each week. You will spend that time improving your Reading."

"But Magister—!"

"Be prepared in your room immediately after breakfast tomorrow. I have been remiss—I assumed that you were doing as well in all your studies as you are in surgery. I do not want to lose you, Melissa."

And with that she was dismissed.

That afternoon she told Alethia of her problems. "It's obvious you love your work," her friend said. "How important is it to you that you learn the healing of minds, when you are so successful at the healing of bodies?"

"I cannot imagine anything more satisfying than saving Primus' life . . . but then, I have never yet been involved in trying to save a patient's sanity."

"I think you had best resign yourself, Melissa," said Alethia. "The word is that since a Master Reader turned renegade, all tests have been tightened immeasurably."

"A Master Reader—? Alethia, what are you talking about?"

"Master Lenardo, from the Adigia Academy."

"He was exiled last spring. Yes, I know about that."

"But he came back! Sneaked into the empire, right past all the Readers along the border—claimed to be a savage lord! They say he's learned their sorcery."

"That's nonsense. They'll execute him, and that will be the end of it."

"They can't execute him, because he escaped. They say he took two young Readers with him, right across the border at Adigia—made the gates open by magic!"

"If this is so, why haven't I heard anything about it?"

"It's all the gossip along the Path of the Dark Moon. I would think that *all* Readers would have heard about it."

The next morning, Melissa prepared for her lesson with Magister Jason. After a light breakfast, she returned to her room, smoothed the bedclothes carefully, and lay down, taking care that her light summer dress had no wrinkles to irritate her helpless body. When Jason's mind touched hers, she left her body behind with an effort. He was already out of his, feeling light, free, joyous. That was how it was supposed to feel; for her it had gone from terrifying only as far as uncomfortable.

Jason Read her feelings. //You are still afraid that something will happen to your body while you're out of it. Look back, Melissa. Read your own body as if it were a patient's. You are breathing regularly, your heart is beating strongly. Your body could stay for a day or two like that with no harm done—in fact, it can be left that way for survival if you should ever be trapped without enough food, water, or air.//

//I know that.//

//No, you don't. You can parrot it back when you are being examined, but you don't *know* it, Melissa, and that is why you fear to leave your flesh behind.//

//You're right,// she said—and did as he told her, deliberately Reading into her own body as if it were that of a stranger. She was in perfect health, merely in a coma. If that were one of her patients, she would be satisfied to leave her alone without fear that she would suddenly die.

Feeling more secure, Melissa tried to follow Jason's next instructions, but to no avail. She Read him as he tried to show her what could not be described in words: how to make the transition to another plane of existence. In deep rapport, she felt him take his bearings and then—disappear! The shock was as great as if he had died—she had to fight her instinct to return to her own body and go in search of his!

Moments later, he was back. //You did not follow.//

//I couldn't. I don't know where you went.//

//Try it again. Read *with* me.//

She tried . . . but did not succeed. She simply could not Read "where" his consciousness disappeared to. They spent a frustrating hour in futile attempts, and then Jason told her, //That's all for today. I have patients to see. Master Florian will work with you tomorrow.//

//Magister—//

He did not retreat to his body. //Yes?//

For a moment she did not know why she had tried to keep his presence with her. Then she remembered: //Is

it true that there is a renegade Reader who has gone over
to the savages and learned their magical powers?//

//Where did you hear such a thing?//

//Alethia told me. Is it true?//

//How could it be? Two Readers have been exiled.
The savages kill Readers—they are terrified of us. This
is some half-truth blown all out of proportion along the
Path of the Dark Moon. The failed Readers have little
accuracy, Melissa. They often get even important messages wrong—always check such information carefully.
I will find out the truth of this matter.//

It was nearly ten days before Jason worked with Melissa again. She had made no gains; it was as frustrating
as the last time. Before they returned to their bodies,
however, she asked him, //Did you find out about the
renegade Reader?//

There was mental silence for a moment. Then, //The
tale is partly true. Master Florian is reluctant to discuss
it. There is no truth to the story that Master Lenardo
has learned savage sorcery—but he has broken his Oath,
and taken a wife among the savages. There is some
garbled story about his having a daughter, which is
simply not possible, as he has even now not been out of
the empire nine months. He seems to have made a pact
with the savage Adepts, to Read for them against the
empire. He came back to Tiberium recently, and stole
away one of his former students—but not by magic.
They fought their way to the border, and the boy was
killed at the gates. Lenardo escaped, but he has broken
his Oath in every possible way. His powers cannot but
be diminished severely. The Council of Masters is
watching the situation closely, fearing he may lead an
attack against us.//

This was bad news indeed. The savages had been driv-
ing back the walls of the empire for many years now, led
by Adepts with powers of sorcery unknown in the empire. They could throw thunderbolts, make buildings
topple, kill people—all with the power of their minds.
But they could not Read—they had to see what they

were attacking. With a Reader to be their eyes at a distance—

Jason followed her train of thought easily. //Yes—it could mean the end of our civilization. Please do not discuss this with other trainees, Melissa. We must wait and see what the Council of Masters decides.// He added, //We should not discuss it, even here. It is unlikely that anyone else is out of body just now, and might intrude on us—but it is always possible. You must learn to achieve a plane of privacy. There is no other way for us to discuss anything that we do not want another Reader to know about.//

When Melissa returned to her body, she discovered to her horror that it had moved! Her head was turned to one side, and her left arm was tight against her body, the right flung out, elbow bent. What had happened?!

She was unharmed, although the panic of fitting her "self" back inside a body that was not as she had left it gave her a ringing headache. She found the hospital in the throes of recovery after a small earthquake. It had been only a minor shock, but it had frightened many of the patients. There was broken crockery and glassware to clean up, but otherwise no damage.

Melissa went through the wards, reassuring patients, and was soon back to her daily routine. Just before noon, she received a message she had been expecting for days: Alethia was in labor. Her pregnancy had been perfectly normal; any midwife would do, but Alethia wanted Melissa, and her teachers had given permission. Despite the morning's excitement, her duties for the day were covered, and she went off to her friend's house.

It was an easy birth. Rodrigo was home in time to witness his daughter's entrance into the world, and Melissa watched the family with great pleasure. The neighbor who cared for Primus brought him home, and he looked curiously at his little sister, then demanded supper. By the time Melissa left, Alethia was sleeping with the baby by her side, safe in a world in which earthquakes were minor matters. *I could be happy in a mar-*

riage like that, Melissa thought.

The earthquakes continued, minor but annoying—perhaps ten days would pass, perhaps almost a month, and again the ground would shake beneath them. Aventine history recorded nothing like this; there had been major earthquakes, even volcanic eruptions from time to time, spaced generations apart, but never such a series of minor shocks. Eventually, though, people became used to them, and hardly noticed when they happened.

Autumn passed and winter brought cold rain. Melissa spent her time off in Alethia's cottage, thoroughly enjoying that happy family. Primus was back to full health. The baby grew and prospered. Life was good.

Melissa's life at the hospital, though, was not so good. She still had not achieved the plane of privacy—which meant that she could not learn the difficult task of maneuvering on the varied planes of existence. Without that ability, she could not begin the second part of her medical training: ministering to sick minds.

Some part of her was content with what she had achieved. She was an excellent healer of sick bodies; surely that would be enough to keep her here at the hospital . . . with Jason.

//That is your problem,//he told her. //You have not made a commitment. One day you want to be a healer, the next you want to be a wife and mother like Alethia. One day you are satisfied with surgery, and the next you want to be a Master Reader—until you try the exercises again.//

But she could not tell him that he was a major part of her problem. If she could only detect any certain sign, beyond the interest he took in her as a student, that he really wanted and needed her—

Then one day, as she was walking toward Alethia's house, a boy came up to her. "You Melissa?"

"Yes," she replied.

"Here." He shoved a note into her hand, and ran off. She read it: "Meet me at the quay." There was no signature. Yet she had no doubt who had sent it.

//Alethia.//

//Melissa! I've been expecting you!//

//I'm sorry—I've been called away. I'll come back if I can. Hug the children for me.//

Today she huddled up in her woolen cloak against the sea wind, sharply different from the breeze last summer. Jason was already there, in her spot on the rocks under the pier. So she went up into the street and out onto the pier, kneeling above him, drawing her cloak about her. Now she was not Reading, and neither was he. "What's wrong?" she asked.

"I'm not certain," he replied. "A number of things. A date has been set for my testing, although I did not request it."

"Testing?"

"For the rank of Master."

Glad they were not Reading, she considered why she was startled. She had always thought of Jason as permanently fixed, a healer at the hospital. Few Readers became Masters, and testing for that rank was usually done when they were between thirty and thirty-five years old, at the peak of their powers. It suddenly occurred to her that she had no idea how old Jason was.

For just one moment she allowed herself to Read—to "see" him. She had never done it before; she had never allowed herself to think of his physical being. He was sheltered on the rocks as she had been last summer, his cloak pulled about him—not an official black Magister Reader's cloak, but a plain heavy brown wool cloak such as everyone wore in the cold weather. As Melissa was bundled up the same way, the boy who had brought her the note probably had no idea they were Readers.

She could not judge Jason's height, nor much of his build without probing. But she observed his face—a dignified face, younger than his graying hair suggested. The hair was thick and crisp, cut short in the prevailing style. His eyes were brown, like her own, and troubled. His mouth was meant to smile—its grim set now belied both the prevailing upturned lines and the tone she "heard" most of the time when she Read him.

"Don't you want to be a Master Reader?" she asked, realizing that he was, indeed, of the right age for testing.

"It would never have occurred to me to request testing, nor has Master Florian suggested it to me. I am a good Reader, Melissa, well worthy of the rank of Magister. However, my powers are not exceptional. The word is that only the most exceptional Readers are being accepted into the Council of Masters now—so why have they called for me?"

"Your healing skills—often they are allowed to compensate for other Reading powers."

"At Magister rank, yes, but not Master. I . . . wonder if this testing is somehow related to the other matter—the reason I wanted to speak with you privately today."

She realized that, indeed, nothing he had said so far warranted this strange, uncomfortable meeting. Why could he not have called her into a privacy room? "What is the other matter?"

"The renegade Readers."

"Readers? More than one?"

"It seems that Lenardo may be in contact with Readers inside the empire—may have corrupted them. A plot is feared—an attack, with Readers aiding the enemy."

"But . . . Magister, they can't think *you* would—?" She wanted to call back the words, and only made it worse by adding, "We're so far from the border; how could—?" Then, "Forgive me. They cannot be thinking any such thing."

"They can, and no doubt they are," Jason replied. "I brought it on myself, with my curiosity. What need has a healer to know about renegades and politics? The Council of Masters, in this time of peril to the empire, has a right and a duty to discover whether my curiosity is just that . . . or whether I am spying for the savages."

"Oh, no! I know you're not!"

He laughed. "So do I—and so will the Council of Masters when they test me under Oath of Truth." But his next words were sober indeed. "Melissa, I have no fear for myself. I am concerned about you."

"Me?"

"Even if I wished to, I could not conceal from the Masters that you provoked my curiosity. You are no spy, either—but that is not what they will tell you the testing is about. If I am tested for the rank of Master, I will probably fail, but that will make no change in my status here. If they test you, though, for the rank of Magister, you will fail. I will try to persuade them that you belong here, at Gaeta, but your chances so long as you cannot pass the tests for Magister rank are very slim." His voice became tightly controlled as he added, "I don't know if they will even send you to one of the smaller hospitals to work . . . but I do know that they will arrange a marriage for you, and you will lose your powers, not develop them further."

Midwinter was near; Jason was to travel to Tiberium for his testing, but severe weather postponed his journey. Snow filled the passes in the hills, and had no time to melt before another storm laid further layers on it. Weeks passed, and he worked even harder with Melissa, determined to ready her to pass her testing. She became more and more at ease outside her body—especially when Jason was with her. Still, neither he nor any of the other healers could teach her to move to other planes.

Alethia reported further rumors among the failed Readers—reports from those who had recently joined their ranks that the testing had become harsh, unfair —that almost no one was passing into the top two ranks, and that it seemed to have little to do with their Reading skills, more with the answers they gave under Oath of Truth.

"But don't you think their stories are prejudiced?" Melissa asked Alethia. "Doesn't every failed Reader feel he has been treated unfairly?"

"I didn't," said Alethia. "I knew full well that my

skills had not improved for months. I have been on the Path of the Dark Moon for three years, Melissa, and never before have I heard such a series of complaints. Nor have there been so many failures—or so many testings—before. Something strange is going on in Tiberium.''

And a few days later, after another fruitless lesson but before they returned to their bodies, Jason told her cryptically, //The pier. After supper.//

She was there first, shivering despite her warm cloak, so she climbed onto the rocks, sheltering from the bitter wind. Jason came and sat above her. ''I leave tomorrow, Melissa. I do not know whether I will return.''

''Not return?! But you said even if you failed—''

''They may decide an error was made in elevating me to the rank of Magister. Master Florian warned me today. The Council of Masters does not usually test any but Master candidates; the Academy faculties are considered to have all the knowledge and power to decide who is worthy of Magister rank. Now there is a rift in the Council between the Masters of Academies and those Masters who do not teach—but the latter outnumber the former. Once this matter of renegade Readers is settled, we may see much retesting, with stricter standards.''

''Magister Jason, surely you could not fail a retesting.''

''I do not think I could, after years of experience. Yet . . . Master Florian told me that they retested and failed one of his former students, a man of unquestioned powers, the head of the hospital in Termoli. He had been a healer for twenty years and more. They declared him unfit, and ordered him married off. He took poison rather than accept such dishonor to his work. Master Florian is heartsick. And . . . he did not deliberately tell me, but I caught his thought: I am not so skilled as the healer they failed.''

''Magister . . . you would not—?''

''Kill myself? Who can say what a person would do?

At one time I would have said yes—if the Masters decided that I was unworthy of the work I have been doing for ten years, I would have seen no choice but suicide. But through you I have learned these past few months what your friend Alethia knows about joy and love within an honorable marriage. I do not know, Melissa. May the gods not force such a choice upon me . . . for I truly do not know what I would do."

He gave a sad little laugh. "A teacher always learns from his students, but you have made me think about things no other student ever has. I will do my best to protect you, but I cannot promise anything. I wish I could promise always to be there to protect you—"

He stopped, as if afraid he had said too much, and got up. "Magister Jason!" Melissa called after him, but he turned and walked back along the pier, not even pausing to say goodbye.

And in the morning he was gone. Melissa prayed for his safe return . . . although she knew they were selfish prayers. All day she did her duties by rote, hardly Reading lest one of the other healers perceive the turmoil in her mind. "I wish I could promise always to be there to protect you," Jason had said. He had spoken of learning from her about "joy and love within an honorable marriage."

It was like the day she had suddenly discovered that she could Read beneath the surface of things, to see what was inside. An ordinary tree had become a treasure trove, insects crawling beneath its bark, squirrels nesting inside a hollow portion of the trunk, sap flowing —a whole community of life she had never known was there, although she had passed the tree every day.

So, suddenly, she discovered the interior of her relationship with Jason . . . and knew that she loved him. She had learned from Alethia what a beautiful experience the marriage of two Readers could be. If the Masters failed Jason . . . and then they failed her . . . was there any chance that they would be married to one another? Surely Jason could arrange it—oh, *surely* he could have the woman he loved. He must love her—he had risked much to speak with her, even those few times. He had warned her about the testing—why had she not declared her love? He didn't know she loved him! He must know. He *must*.

Her thoughts circled endlessly, constantly shoved to the back of her mind in the face of her duties and lessons, only to come forward each time she had a moment's peace. Finally she lay in her lonely bed, thinking it all out one more time before she would allow herself to sleep.

Reading outward, Melissa's restless mind met Phoebe's. The motherly woman who cared for the female trainees was making one last check of her charges before going to sleep herself. //Still awake, Melissa? Is anything wrong?//

//No, Magister Phoebe,// she lied. She didn't know if Phoebe accepted that, or merely respected her right not to discuss a personal problem.

//Then go to sleep, dear. You don't want to be tired for your lessons tomorrow.//

//Yes, Magister.//

She closed her mind to Reading again, and in her internal privacy, remembered. There was so little to remember—long talks, but how many statements that she could interpret as intimations of love?

Her bed began to shake. Another of those annoying tremors—nothing to worry about.

The shaking got worse—the floor heaved, and Melissa was tossed into the air, landing back on her bed in a tangle of bedclothes, her left wrist suffering a harsh blow against the wooden frame. As the bed bucked again, she grasped the frame and was thrown sideways, the bed toppling over on her. There was a terrible roaring, pierced by screams. She started to Read, but found the stark terror of the hospital patients too much to bear. But neither could she bear not to know what was happening. She Read again, and was bombarded with pain—suffocation—the roof had collapsed in the east wing, crushing the patients on the top floor and bringing them and their rooms down onto the orthopedic ward below.

Melissa Read but could not move—no one could. The shocks kept coming, one after another, throwing her hither and yon. There was no way she could scramble to her feet. A heavy wooden wardrobe crashed to the floor, missing her by a hand's span, but heaving a splintered section like a spear into her leg. She screamed in pain, and tried to pull it out as her bedroom turned into a battleground, pieces of wood and shattered crockery flying all around her. The best she could do was try to wrap herself in the bedclothes.

The door of her room burst open with a sharp CRACK! and banged against the wall, slammed shut again, bounced open, and was wrenched off its hinges as the building heaved in a new direction. Smoke sailed in from the hallway—it was winter; there had been fires throughout the building to keep the patients warm—the hospital was on fire!

Melissa began to cough and choke, her own body's heaving so distracting that she missed the point at which the ground stopped billowing beneath her, and everything settled into pain and fire and smoky haze. Finally she realized that the earthquake was over—but she was trapped! Her room had no window. Smoke was pouring through the door. Pulling the blanket over her nose and mouth, she dropped to the floor, where the air would be best, but there seemed to be no good air. She tried to crawl, her leg stinging where the splintered wood had pierced it. It was not a severe wound . . . but that did not matter. She could not escape the smoke. Her eyes burned. Her lungs burned. The whole world was burning—and then it disappeared into blackness.

Chapter Two

A satisfying rumble shook the ground beneath Torio as he Read this section of the fault settle into a more stable configuration. "Perfect!" he said aloud, and Lord Wulfston dropped his concentration and became Readable as a human presence once again. He could not be Read further, for he was a savage Adept, capable of causing the earth to shift—with proper guidance.

The two men were seated cross-legged, hands joined, on the floor of an abandoned house several miles inside the Aventine border. For winter travel they were dressed in heavy woolens and furs, but even so Torio shivered . . . no . . . *he* was not shivering—the ground was moving again, only moments after their successful effort!

He Read the fault, but it was secure—and the shock waves were coming toward it, not away from it. Not the minor quake they had just set off, but a major one somewhere farther away—could it be the very catastrophe they were seeking to avoid?

The ground they were seated on rose and fell, as if they rode a boat over the wake of another. "It shouldn't be that severe!" said Wulfston, not knowing the effect was not the settling they had triggered.

"It's a distant quake!" said Torio. "I can't Read that far." Torio's Reading range, without leaving his body, was approximately three miles. It was a good range for a

Magister Reader, an excellent range for one as recently exalted to that rank as Torio. Nonetheless, it was frustrating to know that Readers could go far beyond the good or excellent, and not know how the breakthrough was made.

Only one person had thus far made that breakthrough. //Master Lenardo!// Torio shouted mentally.

For once Lenardo did not correct his title. //I'm here, Torio. Let me Read for you—the Masters will be looking for you and Wulfston.//

"Lenardo is investigating," Torio told Wulfston, and Read with his former teacher. Lenardo was not with them in person, but was Reading them from Zendi, deep in the savage lands. He no longer had to leave his body to Read over such distances—but even more important under the present circumstances, Lenardo had the power to Read without allowing other Readers to Read him. No Reader had ever developed that ability before, or most of the vast range of Lenardo's powers.

Not allowing himself to comment or question mentally, Torio followed Lenardo's perceptions, tracing the shock waves of the earthquake backward, south and west to their source. Gaeta!

Torio had never been there, but he recognized the city where he would have been right now, taking medical training at the great hospital, if his life had followed a Reader's normal path. It had not. Inside the empire he was considered a renegade. If he were caught he would be examined by the Council of Master Readers, using whatever techniques they deemed necessary to bring into his mind information that would aid the empire against the savages. Then he would be executed as a traitor.

Outside the empire, though, in the savage lands, he was a lord by virtue of his powers, with lands set aside for him to rule when he was ready. Could he ever be ready for such a role?

Lenardo had focused on Gaeta. The last shocks were

still pounding the seaside town as the two Readers observed. As the earth's heaving ceased, people began pulling themselves up from wherever they had been thrown. There were fires all over town—it was winter, and in every home people were trying to keep warm. But most fires were just scattered coals, quickly shoveled back into place, flaming hangings or other items stamped out. Here and there small buildings had fallen, garden walls collapsed in spots, but most of the town had only minor damage that would be set right in a few days of work.

The hospital was another story. It was the largest building in town, set on a hill overlooking the sea—and part of that hill had fallen, sending the seaward wall of the building tumbling down into the road below. Under such stress, the second story of a newer wing had collapsed onto the rooms below, trapping both the patients and the many Readers who lived and worked at the hospital. People were hurt, stunned, trapped under rubble—they were in no condition to put out the fires spreading through the halls!

As the fire blazed up atop the hill, people in the town below realized that the hospital was in trouble, and every uninjured person hurried up the hill to help. First they had to unblock the road—but willing hands set to work, and everyone with shovels, buckets, anything that might help, quickly dug through the fallen earth. Soon buckets of water were being passed from nearby wells up to those fighting the fire—but it was slow, so impossibly slow! All those able to move inside the hospital were already pulling people out as best they could. There were plenty of Readers—no one would be left to die because his presence was undiscovered—but people were dying throughout the building, dying in agony of burns, or, less painfully, of smoke inhalation or suffocation because they could not be reached in time. Others were bleeding to death, trapped where no one could reach them to staunch their wounds.

And every Reader suffered the agony of the wounded and the dying. Torio and Lenardo suffered with them, even more so because they could do nothing to help . . . and because it was entirely possible that their manipulations had unintentionally caused this tragedy.

Lenardo withdrew his attention from the scene of chaos, and sought the point that had been the center of the earthquake. Here the rock levels beneath the earth were freshly slanted—a secondary fault no one had realized was there. Torio felt Lenardo's remorse, regret—but concentrating on the major, unstable fault they had been trying to ease, who could have guessed that their small tremors would shake loose this other instability? If it had been any distance from the hospital, or if the hospital had not been such a mixture of additions clinging to the top of that hill. . . .

But it had happened, and it was their fault. Torio was glad he dared not "say" anything to Lenardo through their mental linkage. He would not know what to say at the moment to the man who had led him out of the Aventine Empire into a new way of life, only to have their best intentions erupt into death and destruction.

They brought themselves back to the abandoned house. Torio came out of the trancelike state in which he had been Reading Gaeta, and found himself gripping Wulfston's hands convulsively.

"I'm sorry," he said in a choked voice, releasing his grip.

Wulfston paid no heed to Torio's unnecessary apology. "What happened?" he asked as he stretched his hands, wincing as circulation brought pain—followed immediately by the warmth of Adept healing.

"Gaeta," said Torio. "The hospital. The quake destroyed the *hospital*, Wulfston—patients, healers, everyone dying—"

"Torio!" Wulfston gripped the younger man's shoulders despite his sore hands, at the same moment that Lenardo told him, //Not now, Torio! Get out of the empire—then we'll talk about what went wrong.//

"We were not aiming at Gaeta," Wulfston said firmly. "It's nowhere near the fault we activated. It was coincidence."

"No. All the minor quakes we set off along *this* fault activated *that* one."

"Lenardo?" Wulfston asked.

"He's still Reading us," Torio replied. "He wants us to leave."

"I was about to suggest the same thing," said the Adept, climbing to his feet and stretching his legs. "Lenardo, we'll see you in a few hours. Come on, Torio."

Torio also rose and stretched. Both Readers and Adepts were accustomed to using the stable, cross-legged position for periods of concentrated effort; even in this cold weather, neither man was cramped.

Their horses were tethered outside, saddled and ready. They rode at a normal pace, not a gallop—they had not yet been Read, and did not want to call attention to themselves.

"If they think we deliberately destroyed Gaeta," Torio said, "they'll be Reading for us all along the western coast. No one will look for us here."

"If they think we would deliberately attack a hospital," Wulfston said grimly, "how will we ever make them trust us enough to negotiate a treaty?"

Both men fell silent. It was a dark, moonless night; Torio took the lead, guiding the horses by Reading. Trying to deny his aching guilt, he reminded himself, *We did not activate the fault, Drakonius did. We are simply trying to repair the damage before Tiberium is destroyed.*

The capital city of the Aventine Empire sat directly on the unstable fault line. A major earthquake there would mean thousands of lives lost—and Lenardo had had a series of precognitive flashes showing that very event. With the mysterious increase in his Reading powers, that odd talent had also increased—and Torio had no doubt of Lenardo's accuracy. What he doubted was whether anything they did could prevent the prophecy from coming true: thus far, every one of Lenardo's visions had come to pass.

Despite having left the Aventine Empire for good, Lenardo did not want harm to come to his homeland. Both Lenardo and Torio had life-long friends in Tiberium; Torio had no qualms about helping to prevent the destruction of the capital. What he had observed in his few months in the savage lands made him certain that Readers and Adepts had to learn to work together.

Unbidden, the scene of horror at the Gaeta hospital rose in his mind—that was the result of a Reader and an Adept working together. Yet, had there been Adepts in Gaeta, the fires would have been out as fast as an Adept could see them—or a Reader tell him where they were. An Adept could lift walls off people by the power of his mind, and as to healing powers. . . .

Torio's first experience in the savage lands had been at the hands of one of their miraculous healers. Casting his lot in with Lenardo and his daughter Julia, he had fought his way with them out of the empire in a long, harrowing ride. They had reached the gates of Adigia unharmed—but just as they escaped across the border, Torio had been struck by an arrow. They had had to ride on, the arrow grating and tearing at the flesh of his shoulder while he clung desperately to Lenardo, trying not to fall off the galloping horse.

In the Aventine Empire, had Torio been tended immediately he would probably have lived. But he might have died from loss of blood; he might have died from infection; he would certainly have had a long, painful recovery and an ugly scar. If an Aventine healer had gotten to him only when the savage healer had, after he was faint from blood loss and the arrow had wrought great damage to the bones and muscles of his shoulder, he would have had a much lesser chance of surviving, and if he had, he would certainly have had restricted use of his arm.

Under the care of the savage healer, Torio's wound had healed within a few hours to the point at which he could use his arm without pain. Within a few days no one could have known the wound had been there; there was not even a scar.

Raised an Aventine citizen in constant fear of the encroaching savages, Torio had never realized that they used their powers for anything but destruction. Ever since he had discovered what good they could do, he had been as eager as Lenardo to find ways to bring their two powers together. What he was unsure of was the right way to do it.

Wulfston rode silently, not intruding on Torio's thoughts. They had crossed the border by breaching the wall earlier today—Wulfston had simply brought a portion of it down in a neat mound over which they had easily ridden their horses. There were other ways, Torio had learned—an Adept could walk in at a gate if he chose a time when few guards were about, by first planting the suggestion in their minds that they had orders to let him in, and then that the event had never happened. Nowadays, though, every gate was heavily guarded and that technique could not be used on more than one or two people at a time.

That Adepts, with no Reading power, could manipulate minds as well as bodies, was one of the more terrifying discoveries Torio had made on the other side of the border. It was a wonder that the empire had not been destroyed generations ago by people with such powers. Lenardo said that the only reason was that up to now the Lords Adept had spent so much energy fighting one another that they had been unable to concentrate their powers against the empire. But now. . . .

Now there was peace in all the savage lands along the Aventine border. Lenardo, Aradia, Wulfston, and

Lilith held what Aradia claimed was the largest territory ever united in mutual agreement. Twice their alliance had been attacked by other savage lords, and twice they had won—the second time with Torio in the midst of the fighting. The lands of the Lords Adept who had attacked and been destroyed had increased the territory they held; it now seemed, as their numbers had increased with the addition of Torio, Lenardo's daughter Julia, and Lilith's son Ivorn, that the alliance of Readers and Adepts was perceived as too powerful and dangerous to try to attack. Besides, as Aradia was fond of saying, their enemies probably thought that if they just waited long enough the members of the alliance would begin to fight with one another, and leave themselves vulnerable.

Torio was automatically Reading their way through the woods that grew wild all along the border—a sort of no-man's-land on either side of the wall where no one wanted to live. Restricting his concentration to an area directly ahead, he narrowed the possibility of another Reader's homing in on him and reporting their whereabouts to the Aventine guard.

Restricting his Reading that way, though, meant that he could not let himself be wide open to anything within his range, or to the relays of powerful Readers who might be sending messages related to their escape. It was probably true that the search for whoever triggered the earthquake was centered near Gaeta, two days' ride away—but someone was sure to report that there had been a quake in this area just before the major one, and then. . . .

Sure enough, Torio felt the touch of another mind. Instantly, he stopped Reading. "Wulfston—they've found us."

"It's all right," said the Adept. "I know the way from here." He rode up beside Torio and took his horse's rein. "We're still an hour from the border—

don't Read, and perhaps they won't be sure of where we are. I can handle anyone they send against us—but I'd rather not."

Torio let Wulfston lead him, feeling again the frustration he had left behind for many years before crossing the border into the savage lands: the frustration of being truly blind. The feeling came on him now only when they had to hide from other Readers, something unheard of in the life he had known before. Privacy, yes —there were times when Readers wanted to shield their thoughts or conversations—but then they used techniques which did not leave them helpless and dependent, led by someone else through a world suddenly unfamiliar and dangerous.

Torio had been born blind; darkness and dependency had been his heritage until his Reading abilities woke when he was six years old and he had been taken to the Academy at Adigia. It was there that his life had become inextricably entwined with that of Lenardo— Master Reader, renegade, and now savage lord.

Lenardo had been teacher, mentor, and father to him ever since the day his Reading had forever dispelled Torio's darkness. The boy had never known light, associating it only with the warmth of the sun on his skin, and even after he had been discovered and begun training as a Reader he had still not understood what "seeing" was. It was normal enough for a small child just beginning to Read to "hear" only those thoughts broadcast strongly by trained Readers, and to sense only the vague forms of the world about him; still, within a week of his first experience of Reading, Torio walked confidently in the world without bumping into things. What he could not understand as the months passed was that his teachers insisted that what he was doing was not "seeing."

Master Clement, head of the Academy at Adigia, had told him not to worry about it—visualization would come later. Lenardo, though, had understood the boy's confusion. Never having seen, Torio had no motivation to visualize. He was so perfectly delighted with the independence that Reading gave him that he could not imagine anything more. So one morning just at dawn, Lenardo had taken the sleepy child up to the top of the Academy tower. There, he had turned the boy to the east, so he could feel the first rays of the sun on his face, and Read the sunrise for him. Shape and color burst into Torio's mind for the first time—a whirl of uninterpretable data, but beautiful. More beautiful than anything he had ever experienced before! With Lenardo's mind guiding him, he understood: this was light. This was seeing. This everchanging panorama was what everyone who could see experienced constantly. //How can they do anything but stop and watch it?// Torio had asked.

//Too few ever stop and watch,// Lenardo replied. //You don't understand yet how much you have just made *me* appreciate what I can see, Torio.//

Torio had been barely seven years old then, and Lenardo about the age Torio was now, newly established as a teacher at the Academy. From that day Torio learned more quickly from Lenardo than from any of the other teachers—and over the years, as the boy grew up, the student-teacher relationship turned into a deep and abiding friendship.

Thus it was that Lenardo had chosen to trust Torio with the knowledge of his secret mission into the savage lands last year—branded as a traitor and exiled, to all public appearances—so that he could seek out Galen, the renegade Reader, and prevent him from aiding the savage Adepts intent on destroying the Aventine Empire.

And thus it was, when Lenardo had to all appearances turned traitor in his turn, Torio had fallen under suspicion. He had not really understood last summer what he was fleeing *to* when he joined Lenardo in that crazed flight across the border—he had been fleeing *from* the decree of Portia, the Master of Masters among Readers, who had declared Torio unfit without testing him, and decided to marry him off to weaken his powers and prevent his becoming a threat to the empire.

Overnight—literally—he had gone from candidate for testing for the top ranks of Readers, loyal citizen of the Aventine Empire, to savage lord with lands held for him against the day when he had learned enough about the wielding of power to be able to rule them. Barely two seasons had passed since that precipitous change in his life, and he had not yet adjusted to it. He was not sure he could.

Everything he had ever known was turned topsy-turvy. The savage Adepts were power-mad monsters with no motive for living except to destroy anyone and anything that came in their way—but Aradia and Wulfston and all the other Adepts Torio had met were trying to build a peaceful amalgam of lands, an alliance too strong to be readily attacked, so that their people could live in health and safety. And, although the hope had been postponed by the events of the winter, they still wanted eventually to try to make peace with the Aventine Empire.

Marriage severely weakened the powers of either a Reader or an Adept, Torio had always been taught. But Lenardo was married now to Aradia—and both their powers had increased dramatically.

And, most significant, both Readers and Adepts had always believed that their powers were separate—mutually exclusive. No Reader had ever learned Adept powers, and no Adept had ever learned to Read . . . until now. But only last summer, Aradia, Adept and adult, had somehow through her association with Lenardo developed the ability to Read. Even more astonishing, Torio had been witness when, to save Aradia's life, Lenardo had somehow found within himself the Adept power to spark a fire with his mind—thus setting off the explosion that destroyed the Lords Adept who were attacking the city of Zendi.

He had witnessed it . . . and still Torio found it almost impossible to believe. Lenardo's Adept powers were minor—nothing compared to what Aradia or Wulfston could do—yet every time Lenardo would casually light a candle without touching it, or move a small object without getting up to fetch it, Torio felt as if his old friend and teacher had become a stranger.

For that reason, Torio had agreed to work with Wulfston, whose lands were to the west of Lenardo's. In Wulfston, Adept powers were not disturbing—it was only when a Reader exhibited such powers that a chill crawled up Torio's spine.

Closed within himself because he dared not Read, Torio found his mind cycling the same thoughts over and over. What was he doing here? Where did he belong? Could the tampering with nature he and his colleagues were doing—causing earthquakes, attempting to raise Adept powers in Readers and Reading in Adepts—result in anything but ultimate doom? Was Gaeta a warning from the gods?

"Torio!" A sharp whisper from Wulfston as he pulled the horses to a halt. "Listen!"

Torio listened—but he did not have the usual heightened senses of the blind. Like any Reader, he had neglected his physical senses, relying on the sense that brought him so much more information. Thus it took him a few moments to sort out what Wulfston had heard from the normal sounds of the winter woods.

Beyond the sighing of the wind and the call of some night bird there was a distant rhythm—felt more than heard, as if it came through the ground and up their horses' legs to pound softly like the blood in their arteries. Men marching.

"You couldn't have heard that while we were riding," Torio whispered. "Did you Read it, Wulfston?"

"You know I cannot. Besides, I am braced to use my

Adept powers. I heard it. Where are they?''

Torio dared to Read again, directly ahead. A band of perhaps a dozen Aventine guards were marching along a small section of road that paralleled the wall—and if they had not made the mistake of falling into step when they reached that bit of smooth surface, they might have succeeded in the ambush they were obviously planning at the fallen wall. They were closer to it than Torio and Wulfston, and led by a Reader—a young man wearing the Sign of the Dark Moon. It should be possible for Torio to Read such a failed Reader without being noticed—provided he controlled his thoughts and impressions with the greatest care. Alone, it might not have been too difficult; relaying verbally to a nonReader made it extremely hard to avoid thinking something to let the other Reader know he was there.

''They're headed straight for the fallen wall,'' he told Wulfston. ''That means a better Reader than they have with them scanned along the wall until that point was found. I suppose they're counting on my not daring to Read, if they think they can ambush us there.''

''We'll go around them'' said Wulfston. ''They probably have no idea how little energy it takes to start an earthquake, and think I'm too exhausted to make us another entrance. They're wrong.''

So Torio and Wulfston moved off at an angle that would bring them to the wall behind the guardsmen, actually taking them across the border closer to the road to Zendi. Torio continued to Read cautiously ahead of them—

And felt something.

They were being Read! Not probed for thoughts, but being scanned as Torio had Read the Reader with the guardsmen, just for identity and position. A better Reader than Torio was observing them, but had slipped just enough to let him sense . . . her . . . attention. Portia.

The Master of Masters was an old, old woman who

never left Tiberium. She had to be out of body to be Reading the border, but her physical presence was not necessary to relay their whereabouts to—

There was no use trying to hide anymore. Torio let himself Read on every side to his full range, and found the army closing in on them from every angle except directly ahead.

"We're surrounded!" he told Wulfston. "Run for it!"

The two men kicked their tired horses, and plunged through the woods. Portia began to relay strongly, //They've Read us! Hurry! Close in before they cross the border and set other sorcerers on us!//

//It's too late,// Torio told her with grim satisfaction. //None of your guards are close enough to stop us now.//

//Torio! It *is* you—have they resurrected you from the dead? Is that in their powers?//

So the guards at Adigia had reported that they had killed him? It might have looked that way, and their Reader had been unconscious—Torio himself had seen to that.

Some perverse impulse led him to tell her, //Yes, they resurrected me, Master Portia, when my own people would have destroyed me. Call off your dogs—you have no idea of the powers we can wield, working together!//

The Readers who led the Aventine troops "heard" the exchange, of course—and Torio felt the superstitious fear it planted in them. They hesitated. "Wulfston—do something—anything! Scare them off!"

Wulfston pulled his horse up, the animal rearing in protest at being pulled off its pace. He controlled his mount with one hand, pointing with the other. They could hear the guards approaching now on every side— close enough to see the flash of lightning that appeared to come from Wulfston's outstretched hand. He turned his horse, his cloak billowing behind him, and fire described an arc in front of the approaching army, trees blazing up just paces before them in the white heat of a savage funeral pyre, consumed to ashes so rapidly that the nearby trees and brush did not catch fire. A smoking, scorched arc lay before the soldiers, who had glimpsed through the trees the savage sorcerer using his powers.

Torio Read their fear with glee. "Now!" he shouted, and he and Wulfston pounded for the wall. It loomed ahead of them, half again as tall as the tallest man, nothing a horse could leap, although with the aid of Adept power . . . but he could not ask Wulfston about that now, in the midst of their dash for safety. Again they halted, as Wulfston examined the wall before them, hardly able to see anything in the darkness, seeking the weakest point. Dry brush before the wall burst into flame, illuminating and revealing a crack—and Torio Read the stones beneath the flaw give way. The wall came tumbling down, neatly, Wulfston guiding the falling rubble as he had before, to give them a smooth pathway.

Almost before their bridge to freedom was built, they were galloping toward it. Behind them, the Aventine army gave chase. "They won't follow far!" said Torio as they reached the savage side of the border.

"They won't catch *us*, but they might harm some of our people if they come upon them," answered Wulfston. He halted again, looked back, and concentrated strongly. Trees creaked, branches dropped—and then two huge trunks fell with a mighty crash, neatly closing the passage Wulfston had made in the wall. "There," he said—but the strength was gone from his voice, and he swayed in his saddle, becoming Readable emotionally. The emotion was exhaustion.

Torio understood at once what had happened. All the spectacular Adept tricks Wulfston had performed this night might appear to the uninitiated harder than felling a few trees, but for all of them the Adept had either been working with nature—seeking the fault in the earth, the flaws in the wall, and letting gravity do the rest—or performing very basic tricks such as the control of fire. Throwing thunderbolts had used up some of his energy, but Wulfston was a fully empowered Lord Adept approaching the prime of life. Those powers were easy for him to control. His last act, however, had been directly against nature—breaking down the substance of huge, healthy trees. Torio knew that he had chosen it only because the other way of closing off the wall—raising the fallen stones back into their places—was even more difficult, possibly beyond his powers. His choice had meant that once he had started the trees to falling, gravity came to his aid.

But now Torio had an exhausted Lord Adept to get back to Zendi, a ride of several hours yet. "Can you ride on for a while?" he asked. "If they can Read that we're nearby, they might think it worthwhile to try to break down your plug in the wall—or burn it."

"I'm all right," Wulfston said, although he was breathing shallowly, his heartbeat far too rapid. They were still in overgrown woodlands, and would be for several miles yet. When Torio took his horse's reins now, Wulfston did not protest, but concentrated on staying awake and in the saddle—for an Adept's natural response to using his powers for extensive work was to fall into a deep, restorative sleep.

"Hang on," Torio urged. "Portia is Reading us—I can't hide your weakness from her. If we don't keep moving, she might send the troops through to try to take us."

Wulfston sat up straighter. "You tell Portia," he replied, "that I still have energy reserves—and that it takes far less effort to kill men than to stop them *without* killing them."

Torio Read Portia absorb the truth of that, and call back the guards. Then he and Wulfston rode on toward Zendi.

It was mid-morning before they reached the city.
Zendi lay in a plain, with well-traveled roads approaching from all four directions. Patches of snow lay in the
fields about the city, but inside all was clear and dry.
From a distance the walls appeared impregnable, but
the gates stood open in welcome to one and all. Zendi
appeared prosperous to an external glance—but Torio
knew what was inside. Twice last year Zendi had been
the scene of devastating warfare. The walls stood, the
gates had been repaired, and the crater Lenardo had
blown to destroy the enemy had been filled in. There
were empty places along the streets, though, like missing
teeth, where buildings had been destroyed in one battle
or the other. The whole northwest section of the city
was rubble, awaiting spring for rebuilding.

Zendi might put on a fine face for strangers, but the
buildings were almost bare of furnishings. The city's
carpenters and cabinet makers were spending the winter
producing necessities, but most people still slept on
pallets and hung their clothes on pegs.

Despite the primitive conditions, the people of Zendi
were happy: For the first time in most of their lives they
were warm, well fed, clothed, and secure. The marriage
between Lenardo and Aradia had strengthened their
alliance—and if that one held, the others would.

Wulfston and Torio were well known to the people of
Zendi. Shouts of greeting went up as they passed, and
people stuck heads out of windows to see, waving cheerfully. They knew nothing of the mission the two men
had been on, but Reader and Adept together were the
symbol of their new and hopeful life.

There were other signs—happy, healthy children
playing in safety in the streets, and Arkus, Lenardo's
chief architect, in front of a dilapidated building, going
over restoration plans with a stonesmason. "Welcome,
my lords!" he called as Wulfston and Torio passed, and
Arkus' wife Josa, heavy with child, came out onto the
front steps to greet them. Lenardo had given this young

couple a structurally sound house, but it was up to them to make it livable.

When Wulfston and Torio reached the large house that was now Lenardo's home, he and Aradia came out to greet them. "Oh, you are exhausted, my brother," Aradia said to Wulfston as he climbed down from his horse. "I should have gone with you."

He managed a weary smile. "There's nothing wrong with me that food and sleep won't cure. I know we need to counsel, but I'm afraid I'm in no conditon to join you."

Lenardo said, "Torio can tell us everything, and we won't make any decisions without you. Come in and eat."

The dining table in the large hall was also council table when all the Readers and Adepts gathered. It was the only place they had where four Adepts and three Readers could sit together in comfort. All three Readers were there today, but two of the Adepts, Lilith and her son Ivorn, were in their own land. "I sent her a message this morning," said Aradia. "If we need a formal council, she will come—but have we enough information to make decisions yet?"

"I don't think so," said Torio, picking at the food Cook had set before him. Wulfston ate heartily of the roast meat, bread, wine, and vegetables, as Adepts always did when they used their powers. It was Wulfston's second meal that day, as they had carried bread, cheese, and wine with them, but to watch him one would think he hadn't eaten in days.

Readers were vegetarians, for red meat seemed to inhibit their powers—no one really understood the mechanism. As usual Lenardo was an exception to all the rules. Nothing seemed to limit his Reading. He and Aradia ate a modified diet including some meat, but more fish, cheese, and eggs. Torio stayed with what he was familiar with—there was so little familiar in his life these days.

Lenardo's daughter Julia came bouncing in in the middle of the meal, curls windblown, cheeks rosy from the cold. In unReaderlike manner she hugged Torio, then hugged and kissed Wulfston, saying, "Sorry I'm late. I was helping find some strayed horses, and I couldn't Read that you were back till I got inside the walls." The apology was in part a boast—Julia was not yet ten years old, and to be able to Read from any point of the city walls to Lenardo's house at her age was exceptional. Torio wondered how much she knew, for she had undoubtedly slept through last night's disturbance.

She sat down next to Lenardo, asking, "May I have some meat today, Father?"

"No, Daughter. We will have nothing inhibiting your Reading."

"But how can I learn Adept powers if I don't have the strength?"

"Show me an Adept trick, and you may eat anything you please," Lenardo replied.

They were so natural together that they actually seemed father and daughter—they even looked alike. But the dark-eyed, dark-haired child had met Lenardo only last year, when her budding Reading powers would have caused her to be murdered by her own people had Lenardo not rescued her and then adopted her. There were no Academies here; he was teaching her himself, using the apprentice system favored by the savage Adepts. It was obviously working well; Julia's abilities were growing so rapidly that Torio saw distinct improvements on each of their frequent encounters.

Adoptions of heirs were common here. Used to not seeing, Torio rarely Read anyone's physical appearance on first acquaintance. He had known Wulfston for several days before he discovered the Adept was black. It was only then that he had realized that Wulfston and Aradia were not blood-related as he had assumed, since they addressed one another as brother and sister and had the normal love/annoyance relationship of siblings.

Wulfston, it turned out, had been born in the Aventine Empire. When his Adept powers manifested, he would have been killed by outraged neighbors had not Aradia's father, Nerius, stolen the little boy away and smuggled him across the border. Then Nerius, a most powerful Lord Adept, had adopted the boy as his son and raised him together with his daughter—and by some miracle they had reached adulthood as friends rather than rivals.

Amid the family atmosphere, Torio's qualms lessened. Up until a year ago there had been no place on either side of the border where Readers and Adepts could be friends—where a child was safe even if he developed the wrong ability. Surely this kind of cooperation was right!

Nonetheless, when Torio met with Lenardo privately after Wulfston was in bed, more unconscious than sleeping, he still had uncertainties. "I feel," he explained aloud, for to assure privacy they were not Reading, "the way I felt the day Decius was wounded because of what I said and did."

Decius was one of the young Readers in training at the Adigia Academy, now moved to Tiberium. The day of the savage attack which had resulted in the move, Lenardo had allowed Torio to give Decius his lesson in swordplay. Blindfolding the boy, so he would have to reply on Reading as Torio did, he had accomplished more in that one lesson than Lenardo had in a month. Torio had congratulated his pupil warmly—and then forgotten him as the alarm went up: The savages were attacking the Academy!

But Decius, basking in the praise of the acknowledged best swordsman in the Academy, had not gone to hide with the children as he should have. Only thirteen, he had joined the battle—and sustained a wound to his leg so severe that there was nothing the healers could do but amputate. Knowing that the boy would never have tried to fight if he had not just been praised, Torio was stricken with remorse.

"You didn't do anything wrong that day," said Lenardo. "Decius misinterpreted what you said—he heard what he wanted to hear."

"This time it wasn't misinterpretation," Torio said grimly. "I was defiant to Master Portia."

"She has been a teacher for many years," Lenardo replied. "The defiance of young Readers should come as no surprise to her."

"But I lied to her." Lying to another Reader was a breach of the Readers' Oath.

"She didn't know you were lying?"

"It . . . wasn't exactly a lie. She thought I had been killed when we escaped last fall—and she asked if the Adepts had raised me from the dead. I said yes."

"That *is* a lie, Torio."

"I know. I meant I didn't make it up—Portia did. I just thought it was so ridiculous—"

"I understand," said Lenardo. Torio heard him get up and move—to the window, heavily curtained now against winter drafts. They were in the room Torio always used here, sparsely furnished with a bed, a chest, and a chair. Torio was on the bed, fighting physical weariness because his mental state would not let him relax and sleep. "Did your lie serve a higher purpose?" Lenardo asked.

"No. It was something I said in anger—Master Portia refused to give me a fair chance last fall, but I was more angry at myself, and all of us, for what we did to Gaeta."

"Good," said Lenardo.

"What do you mean, good? I was angry and I did something stupid."

"But you understand *why* you did it, Torio—that is what is good. And if you understand why, then you will not do it again. Remember what you said about Galen

—that he did wrong for the right reasons?''

"That's what we did last night," Torio said grimly. "How can we ever know we're doing the *right* thing?"

"We will never do such terrible damage again as we did at Gaeta, once we find out how the one fault set off the other. I must study not just the main fault we have been trying to relieve, but the faults under the entire empire before we try again. I still foresee a terrible catastrophe. I only hope we have time to prevent it. Your lie might help us, Torio. Even though they now know we are causing the earthquakes, and have no idea it is for their own good, the Aventine government will think twice before attacking if they believe we have the power to raise the dead.''

But Lenardo's precognition failed him in that hope. Two days later, Torio was packing his few belongings to return to Wulfston's land when Lenardo contacted him. //Torio, leave your body and join me.//

He did not question, but lay down on the bed and composed himself. A Reader of Torio's age would normally have used this technique only a few times in practice exercises; but with all the communications over long distances he had performed in the past few months, it had become almost commonplace to Torio. He and Lenardo were the only ones in their small community who could do it; Julia was far too young, and Aradia had not the skill.

When he left his body and joined Lenardo, Torio found a third presence. //Master Clement!// He allowed his joy to suffuse the atmosphere; the old man had been teacher to both Lenardo and Torio, and Master of their Academy.

Warmth flowed from Master Clement at the contact, but he told them, //I cannot stay long. Join me on the plane of privacy.//

//There is something wrong,//Lenardo said when they had made the peculiar change of "position" that took them completely out of contact with the physical world. Not even the best Reader who ever lived could spy on them here without making the move with them and thus revealing his presence.

//Aye,// Master Clement replied without prologue. //The Aventine Senate is preparing an army to attack you—but not along the border. They are commandeering every sailing vessel they can, to travel up the coast, land the armies, and drive you south into a trap laid at the border. Portia has told the Senate the savages set off the earthquake that destroyed the Gaeta hospital. Lenardo, you should have known that such a target—//

//The hospital was not the target—there was no target. You know what we intended, Master Clement.//

//I know what *you* intended, Lenardo, but perhaps one of your Adept allies—?//

//No!//Torio interjected. //It was Lord Wulfston working with me that night, Master Clement. He would not do such a thing! And even if he wanted to . . . you know my abilities are not great enough to guide him to a target so many miles away, nor are any Adept's powers strong enough to move a pebble, let alone a rock face, at that distance.//

//You would not lie to me, Torio? I know you did to Portia, and I dare not contradict you without revealing that I know much more of what is happening on the other side of the border than I am supposed to.//

//I'm sorry,//Torio said penitently. //I didn't think.//

//The impetuosity of youth. You must learn to curb it, son. What you said is not the reason the empire is preparing to attack you—but it is a cause of their great haste. Portia has convinced them that you are growing together in the powers of darkness. She also fears the ancient prophecy: When the moon devours the sun, then the earth will devour Tiberium. There will be an eclipse just before Summer Festival. Portia fears that if we do not stop you by then, you will destroy the empire.//

Despite their bodiless state, Torio could feel tension from Lenardo. //We cannot allow the Aventine army to attack us. Master Clement, without Adepts they will be powerless against us. I will not have good men slaughtered—for that is what it would be. Can you not persuade Portia—?//

//Do you think you could, Lenardo? Or the Senate? Even if it is a foredoomed effort, they must do something—and I have told you of their sneak attack to give you the opportunity to plan. I am trusting you—and you, too, Torio—to find a way to prevent a battle in which all too many lives would be lost. I must return now—I cannot allow myself very much time in which no one can contact me. The Council of Masters meets frequently these days—and our work is not at all pleasant.//

The old man's presence was gone. Torio and Lenardo remained on the plane of privacy for a few moments more. //The attack will come against Wulfston's lands,// said Lenardo. //You will have to Read for him, Torio.//

//I know—but what will he do? Sink the ships? Drown all those people? Readers will be navigating the ships. It wouldn't be a mistaken thought flung in a moment's anger—it would be deliberately using my powers against other Readers! Master Lenardo, how can I?//

//Stop clinging to the past—here I am a lord, as are you. Master your powers instead of restraining them. You never question defending your life with your sword—why do you question defending it with your powers?//

Powers. Unrestrained powers, used to gain control over other people. He couldn't go home again, Torio knew—but how could he adapt to living the way people did here?

Chapter Three

For three days after the earthquake Melissa was patient rather than healer. It hurt to breathe. Her throat was so raw she could not talk, and she could hardly Read beyond the confines of her room. The healers placed poultices on her throat and neck, and kept a pot boiling over a brazier, producing steam. Although she knew what they were, it was the third day before she could smell the vinegar in the poultices, the sage in the steam.

She was wakened by Magister Phoebe with comfrey tea laced with honey—and for the first time it was not sheer agony and force of will to drink the fluid her body desperately needed. "Very good, Melissa," said Phoebe. "You're going to be just fine."

"I know," Melissa managed, her voice between a whisper and a croak. //How badly was Gaeta hit?// she asked.

Phoebe replied with the mental intensity used in training children, //The town had very little damage. The hospital received the worst of it.//

//Were other Readers hurt?//

//Yes, dear, but there are healers enough for everyone. You rest. I'll bring you some soup later.//

Melissa was not in her own room, but in a much smaller one that probably belonged to one of the non-Reader workers at the hospital. She remembered the fire in the wing where her room had been, the smoke, trying to crawl out. . . .

She was not burned. Smoke had choked her—her throat and lungs were damaged but healing. She had no memory of how she had gotten out. Her leg had been hurt . . . yes, there was a wound, now stitched up and bandaged.

She tested her Reading power, and found that this morning she could Read the corridor outside, and along that to the kitchen, apparently undamaged. She could reach no farther—but that was better than yesterday, which meant she was healing. When she was strong enough, a period of fast and meditation would bring her powers back to normal.

That afternoon Alethia visited with her baby, and Melissa was happy to hear that they had suffered little damage from the quake. "But you should hear the rumors!" Alethia confided. "They say that the savages set off the quake, all the way from the border."

"They couldn't have," Melissa said through the pain in her throat.

Alethia insisted, "They finally did what they wanted to. That's what all those tremors were: They were trying to make a big earthquake by starting little ones."

Melissa considered that, remembering how the minor tremor had been followed by the huge one—and how she had been flung in two different directions. If the savages had that kind of power, though. . . .

Alethia saw the expression on Melissa's face. "Don't try to talk," she said. "You mustn't strain your voice. I'll tell you all about it, Melissa." They were not Reading because the intensity they would have to use would have had the effect on nearby Readers of a shouting match in Melissa's room, but at that moment Melissa was glad of the excuse for another reason: Although they had not planned it for privacy, not Reading allowed Alethia to tell her all the news that came in on the Path of the Dark Moon without Melissa's being scolded for gossiping.

For what amazing gossip Alethia had today! "There are *two* renegade Readers aiding the savages now—but one of them is a ghost!"

Before Melissa could get out a denial of such nonsense, Alethia continued, "Remember Master Lenardo from the Adigia Academy, who went over to the savages last year?"

Melissa nodded.

"That's old news. The latest is about the boy he stole away last fall—a magister candidate of great promise. Nobody knows how he made the boy go with him, but he did—only at the border the guards caught them and killed the boy. But Lenardo carried off the body . . . and the savage sorcerers brought the boy back to life!"

Melissa shook her head, and croaked, "No!" Jason was certainly right about how garbled the information was that came by the Path of the Dark Moon.

"Yes," Alethia insisted. "After all, Melissa, a Reader can get lost trying to negotiate planes of existence, out of contact with the physical world. His body can be left to die. This is just the opposite—if the savages have the power to make a body live again, maybe Master Lenardo could have guided the boy's mind back to it. Although how they could make his heart work after an arrow was shot through it—"

Melissa shuddered and shook her head. "Alethia, no," she forced out. "No one could do that." She swallowed, trying to ease the pain in her throat. "I'm a healer. I *know* better. And you have had enough training to know better, too. Either the boy is dead, or he was not hurt as badly as the guards thought, so he recovered."

"I'm sorry," Alethia said contritely, as Melissa coughed from her exertions. "I mustn't make you excited. Let's discuss something else." And she began to tell Melissa about her children's latest exploits.

Melissa, though, was only half listening. There must be some kernel of truth in such a frightening story—the earthquake part was almost certainly true, and if the savages could attack the empire that way once, they could do it again. What little peace and security they had known behind their walls could now be gone forever. She wished that she could discuss it with Jason, but she dared not ask whether he had contacted anyone. She was certain he would have, the moment news of the quake reached him, but she would have been unconscious or too sick to contact then . . . and no one knew how much she cared about Jason and wanted news of him. He could be having long conversations with the Master of the Hospital every day, and she would never know it!

Her frustration gave her incentive to heal quickly. The next day she could Read the whole wing of the hospital she was in—and discovered the makeshift accommodations, the harried healers trying to treat the worst injured of the patients—the ones who had been kept together here—and also to find time to go off to treat the sick and injured taken in by townspeople since half the hospital complex had been demolished. Over Master Phoebe's protests, she spent the morning helping the herbalist, and after some rest went back to work that afternoon. The next day she picked up her healer's routine as best she could, even though there were times she had to stop, lean against the wall, and gasp for air for her protesting lungs.

Melissa was not the only healer who had been trapped by the earthquake. There had been eight rooms in her wing; five other healers had been in their beds when the quake came. Three of them had crawled out or been found in time, but two had died.

A healer in the orthopedic wing had been crushed to death. Another, pinned under fallen debris, had bled to death before he could be reached. Half a dozen other healers were now patients—the hospital was desperately short handed.

Days and nights flowed together as Melissa pushed herself to be healer to those hurt more severely than she was. She did not develop pneumonia, thanks to the herbalist's constant attentions, or perhaps to the will of the gods. Healers from other hospitals arrived to take some of the burden, and one morning Melissa awoke with no pain in her chest or throat, and realized that she had had a long, full night's sleep and actually felt normal. When she stepped outside she found the sun shining, and saw tender green shoots of spring growth pushing up through the soil.

Her Reading seemed to have returned to normal. Students at her level had been treated like any other healers during the emergency. Now that she had experienced the community of healers working together, she dreaded even more the possibility of being sent away.

She checked her patients and found no one who needed her physical presence immediately; she had time to breathe fresh air in what was left of the hospital garden. It was still too cold to stay out long, but sunshine and the fresh sea breeze had been unattainable luxuries for too long.

Melissa had been Reading automatically, to avoid encountering male Readers, but now she stood at the newly repaired wall overlooking the town and the sea, closing her eyes and Reading as far as she could in every direction. Behind her, inside the building, she touched a familiar presence. //Jason!//

Some of her hurt that he had returned and not contacted her must have flowed through that unguarded moment, for he replied, //I arrived only last night, Melissa, after you were asleep. You seem well. I have heard nothing but praise for you.// He was stiff, formal, without even the friendly communication they shared when other Readers might pick up their conversations.

//Yes, I am quite well,// she replied. Did he even know she had been injured? //And you? Were you tested?//

//I was tested.// He allowed no feelings to show—she did not have to be a Master Reader to know he was holding something back. //I have a new assignment.//

//A new—?//

//Not now, Melissa. As soon as you can resume your lessons we will discuss it. Go in and eat breakfast now. You have a full day's work.// And he stopped Reading.

Melissa survived the next two days in a ferment of curiosity—but every time she met Jason's mind he gave her a curt reply and shut her out. Finally, the third day, she was scheduled to resume her lessons with him.

It was weeks since she had left her body—she wasn't sure she could do it. When it worked, she decided she must be nearly well, as a Reader's powers were directly related to his or her health. Savage Adepts, she had been told, weakened their bodies when they used their powers —the only reason the empire had any hope at all against them.

Since she had been thinking about the savage attack, the first thing Melissa blurted out when she met Jason's mind that morning was, //I must tell you what Alethia's been telling me. All kinds of wild rumors are coming down the Path of the Dark Moon. What did you learn in Tiberium?//

//We are not here to gossip,// Jason chided her. //Have you mastered the move to the plane of privacy?//

//I haven't even tried since you left,// she told him. //First I was hurt, and then I was too busy. Didn't Master Florian tell you?//

//You've had no lessons at all?//

//No. There hasn't been time.//

Despite their bodiless state, something like a sigh of exasperation came from Jason. Was he angry at her?

He caught the thought she had meant to keep private, and replied, //No, I am not angry with you, Melissa. I am . . . concerned about your progress. However, your experience may have worked to ease your anxiety. You were badly hurt. You passed out—but you didn't die.//

//What has that to do with moving to another plane of existence?//

//When you Read that you could not get out of the building by yourself, why did you not leave your body and direct one of the other Readers to it? You stayed, passed out, and could have died. The smoke damage to your throat and lungs, the days of pain, were unnecessary. Because of your fear of leaving your body, you caused it harm. Never would you leave your surgeon's tools in the rain to rust—yet you left the most important implement of your skills, your physical self, for others to rescue. You became a liability, a patient instead of a healer. I commend you for working so hard as soon as you were able—but you would never have been hurt in the first place if you had used your skills to save yourself!//

Melissa was stunned. The last thing she had expected was a scolding for being hurt! Guilt stabbed, for Jason was right; she should have been willing to let go of her physical being before it overclouded her mind and made her unable to function. //I . . . didn't think,// she said contritely.

//Nor did the other teachers expect you to,// Jason told her. //Do you realize what their unwavering praise for you means? They didn't *expect* any better of you! I expect more, Melissa. Can you give it?//

For Jason? //I can give it.//

//Then make certain that your body is safe . . . and know that *you* are something separate from it. You know where your body is. We are going only to a plane of privacy for a lesson—you are safe with me, Melissa. Perhaps one day you will feel secure enough to make the twists and turns a Master Reader must know—but there will be none of that today. No way to get lost. A simple move—//

Adrift on the hypnotic flow of Jason's reassurances, Melissa for the first time released her attention from the physical world to concentrate *only* on his essence—and together they . . . moved . . . to another plane.

Suddenly the entire universe consisted of nothing but Jason and Melissa!

As far as she could Read, Melissa perceived nothing —nothing as an actual entity, it seemed, rather than as the absence of something. It pulled at her, wanting her to spread to fill the void. Jason was there, allowing her to experience without interference—but she knew that if she did not resist the pull he would draw her back. With that reassurance, she was not afraid.

When Melissa had more or less settled into equilibrium, she asked, //Does anything else happen?//

//No—and that is the danger here, the desire to *make* something happen. Never seek this plane alone, Melissa; without another mind as an anchor, the desire to find the something you *think* must be beyond the emptiness can become too strong to resist.//

//Something beyond the emptiness? I don't sense anything like that.//

The essence of a tolerant smile warmed her. //That is my impression. You perceive it another way?//

//A void, wanting me to fill it.//

//Aye—equally dangerous. On one hand, you must become accustomed to the sensation, so you can ignore it and do the work you came here for, but on the other you must not get so used to it that you allow it to slip up on you and draw you away, unaware. Another reason never to come here alone.//

//Why would anyone come here alone? A Reader alone can have privacy just by not Reading.//

//There are . . . other uses for the plane of privacy. However, they are not a part of your lessons for Magister rank. Congratulations, Melissa. You have just passed the crucial test—you will do with the Masters exactly what you have just done with me. Your continued role as a healer will be assured.//

She had not even been thinking of that! Perhaps that was why she had finally been able to do it? It didn't matter; she was here, alone with Jason. //What do I do now, Magister? Or . . . are you Master Jason now? No one has told me.//

//No, I am not a Master,// he replied. //All we are

going to do today is remain on this plane for a brief time, and then return. Each time you will be able to stay a bit longer without fear of being seduced into remaining here. But today we have only a little time, and there *are* things I must tell you, lest you destroy your life as a healer.//

//What?//

//I will be going away soon, Melissa. That is good, for otherwise, as my student, you might come under suspicion just as Master Lenardo's student, Torio, came under suspicion when his teacher and close friend defected to the enemies of the empire.//

//Suspicion of what? You haven't done anything wrong!//

//I asked the wrong questions. I asked about Lenardo, because of the things you told me—but I kept the Council of Masters from finding out that you were involved. To do so . . . I had to refuse Oath of Truth.//

And thus, Melissa knew, he had forfeited all hope of being elevated to Master rank. //But why? What I told you is known all over the empire. It was all gossip along the Path of the Dark Moon.//

//Which everyone in the upper ranks dismisses. Until you resumed your friendship with Alethia, you knew nothing of such gossip, nor did I. I had always been taught that the failed Readers invariably garble information. But what I learned in Tiberium corroborates Alethia's story. There is more, and much more serious.//

//The earthquakes,// said Melissa. //I know about the savages causing them—they kept on setting off quakes until they finally caused a really big one.//

//We should have realized they could do that—at least once they had Readers to tell them where the fault lines lay. No—what is so frightening is a new power, which could only have been developed by Adepts and Readers working together. Melissa . . . I learned this from the Council of Masters. Master Portia herself was witness to the fact. The boy, Torio, Lenardo's student—//

//No! It can't be true—I told Alethia it was nonsense!//

//You've heard? It's been reported on the Path of the Dark Moon?//

//He was killed . . . and then brought back to life by the savage Adepts.//

//Yes. And it is true, Melissa. I suppose there is no way to keep such an astonishing fact secret among Readers—each Master undoubtedly told some other Reader he thought should know, as I am telling you—//

//But it's true? How could they do such a thing?//

//I do not know. Torio was killed the day Lenardo took him out of the empire—but the night of the earthquake, Portia discovered him guiding the savage Adepts. He admitted to her that the Adepts had raised him from the dead—you don't think a boy who had not even achieved Magister rank could lie to Master Portia, do you?//

//Then . . . what hope have we? If they have the power of life and death—//

//There is only one hope: to strike first and quickly. The empire has been on the defense for generations. Now we must attack—and we must kill both Lenardo and Torio. If there are other, younger, Readers, we will be able to handle them once the two strong Readers are not available to guide the Adepts. That is my new assignment, Melissa.//

//You are supposed to go into the savage lands and kill—?//

//No—oh, no, there will be no more individual Readers sent beyond our borders! The Adepts have little trouble subverting them, it seems. The mistake was in ever exiling Readers in the first place. There should have been a different law for them—but then how many Readers have ever turned traitor? Generations pass between such incidents. It was inevitable, though, that eventually an exile would be discovered by a savage

Adept capable of making a Reader work for him. We were fools to think the savages would *always* kill Readers! Now we will pay dearly for our stupidity, if our desperate effort does not work.//

//And what is the desperate effort?//

//The empire is preparing a fleet of ships, the largest fleet ever known. Warships, fishing boats, merchant vessels—many will gather here at Gaeta in the next weeks. We are gathering the largest army ever. We will sail up the coast, out of range of the most powerful Reader, and put ashore west of Zendi, which is reported to be the seat of government of the savage lands. It will be a hard three-day march from the coast to Zendi—but three days will not give the savages time to gather an army anywhere near large enough to counter ours. Since it is unlikely that either of their mature Readers will be near the coast, they may not even know we are coming the first day or two. If our own Readers do their work we can prevent runners from escaping ahead of our army to spread the news.//

//But you will be fighting people with Adept powers.//

//Aye. The first minutes of battle will mean many deaths—until the savage Adepts use up their energies. After that, the savages will have nothing but ordinary soldiers—and although their warriors are fierce and well-trained, our troops will outnumber them. We will kill the Readers. We will kill the Adepts if we can, although they always save one last bit of their power for escape. If we take the Readers from them, though, they will be blind—and we will push the empire walls beyond Zendi, and perhaps go on to win back all the lands the Aventine Empire once ruled.//

//What is your role in this plan, Magister?//

//The fleet requires navigators. I have been assigned to direct the five Magister Readers chosen for that task.//

//But—you're a healer. You should be directing the medical corps!//

//Certainly I will work with the healers after the fighting has begun—but until that time there will be little need for healers except to dole out herbs for sea-sickness. Now, Melissa, you should not remain on the plane of privacy any longer. The troops will begin arriving soon. I will have no time to give you further lessons. Let me say goodbye to you now.//

//Goodbye? But—//

//It is best this way. Until I have proven myself in battle, I will remain under suspicion—and I do not want that suspicion to fall on you. Do not let any of the other Readers know anything you learn from Alethia. Work hard with Master Florian and Magister Puella. I expect to return to find your skills much further developed.//

//What if you don't—?//

//It is time to go, Melissa,// Jason told her firmly. //The same way we came—with me . . . now—//

Melissa had no choice but to follow him. They were still in their bodiless state, though, and she tried once more, //Magister Jason, what if—?//

//Melissa, you have done beautifully!// he overrode her anxious question with his powerful mind. //Just remember what you have learned today, and you will excel as both Reader and healer!// And then he left her, returning to his own body so that she could not communicate with him without having every Reader in range privy to their conversation.

As soon as Melissa reached her body, it responded to the emotions she brought with her. Her stomach churned, her eyes welled with tears, and she turned her face into the pillow to muffle her sobs. Jason was going away to die! She had no precognition, but she knew the reason for his abrupt farewell: he did not expect to return from his mission into the savage lands.

He had made light of his assignment. Navigator, healer—it sounded safe enough; as safe as any assignment in an army heading out to war. But in this war the enemy would be seeking out Readers, exactly the way Jason had described the mission of the Aventine army.

Now the savages *had* Readers to pick out their fellows —and only the savages had the Adepts who could kill at a distance with no weapons but their minds. The better the Reader, the easier the target . . . and Jason was a very good Reader.

It's my fault, Melissa realized. *My silly, childish gossip with Alethia gave Jason the questions to ask in Tiberium that put him under suspicion. He could have just told them about me, but he wanted to protect me.*

She mulled that over. It was a strange reaction on Jason's part, to protect her at the expense of his own promotion to Master rank. He admired her as a healer. He had made certain she would be able to go on to higher ranks. But why? She had done nothing wrong— shouldn't the Council of Masters be told that things they thought were secret were traveling the Path of the Dark Moon? If they *had* called for Melissa, under Oath of Truth she would have been exonerated of gaining wrongful knowledge.

But she would stand self-accused of gossiping, of spreading rumors—and if they had called her to Tiberium before today, she would have failed the Reading test they might have given her, and been relegated to the Path of the Dark Moon herself. And Jason did not want that.

Jason had assured her that if he survived the war, they could be together—colleagues at the hospital at Gaeta. A lifetime of mental intimacy—surely the purest form of love two people could know. He must love her. Otherwise it made no sense for him to take such risks on her behalf.

She could not let him take them alone!

In battle, no injury would require greater healing skills than Melissa already had. More healers would be needed—the call would certainly come for volunteers. She dared not volunteer before that call, but she would be ready when it came! Now that Jason had let her know, once and for all, that he wanted them to be together, she would see that they were not separated, even for the length of the war.

Her decision made, Melissa went about the rest of her day's work in a glow of happy expectation, secure that whatever the future held, it would be with Jason.

As the days passed, the army gathered in Gaeta. The demolished section of the hospital was leveled, and a temporary barracks built. Every home in town took in a soldier or two, and still they came. Tents blossomed on the hillsides surrounding the town, where flocks of sheep usually grazed at this time of year. The shepherds had to move early to the higher elevations, but everyone knew that an important battle against the savages was being prepared for, even if they did not know the events that had precipitated it. Somehow, the word got out to the nonReaders that the savages had caused the recent earthquake—at that, people became even more responsive and eager to aid the army.

Troops exercised in the streets and in the hills; mock battles charged across the meadows, and the healers at the hospital spent many hours treating sprains and strains that were anything but mock as soldiers who had not fought for years renewed their battle skills. There were sword wounds, too, among those who practiced too enthusiastically, knocks on the head, and even the occasional arrow gone astray.

When the number of such injuries diminished, although the maneuvers did not, the healers knew the army was ready for battle. The generals knew their work —ships were already in the harbor, waiting for these troops; every other port in the empire had a part of the fleet waiting, and a part of the army preparing in its environs. All would gather here at Gaeta on the first day of spring.

At last the call Melissa had been waiting for went out: healers were needed for the army. She had been bubbling over with enthusiasm for the war effort since her last lesson with Jason—no one was surprised when she was first in line to put her name on the list.

Melissa had tried several times since that last lesson to contact Jason, to tell him she understood what he had done and that she would not let him go into danger alone. He was rarely in the hospital, however. He spent much time with the ships' masters, comparing maps and knowledge of the coastline above the border of the Aventine Empire. Merchants who would not say how they got them quietly contributed current maps. Melissa tried not to allow herself the childish thought that Jason stayed out of the hospital to avoid her.

But he would not communicate with her. When she tried to contact him, he told her he hadn't time, or he was busy with someone else. Knowing that she would attract attention if she kept trying, she finally gave up.

Thus it was that on the day she boarded ship with the other female healers, and watched Gaeta becoming smaller and smaller as the ship swayed its way out to sea, she felt Jason's astonishment to meet her mind as the Readers aboard all the ships reached out mentally to identify themselves. The bulk of the fleet was passing Gaeta to the west, having sailed up from the south. There were many Readers whom Melissa had never met before—she had not realized that there were so many Readers that all of these could leave the empire and still leave it with plenty of healers and other Readers to rely on.

In that crowd of eager, curious minds, there was no privacy for Jason and Melissa—she could not tell him why she had come, nor could he scold her, as she could sense he wanted to. The whole journey, she realized, would be equally frustrating. She should have known there would be no privacy—but at least they were sailing into danger together.

The first day's sail was a pleasant adventure. The sun shone, the sails swelled with a fresh breeze, and the ships moved swiftly and easily. Two ships besides the one Melissa was on carried female Readers, all healers. Some of the male Readers were also healers, but they would be expected to fight if it became necessary. As the eyes and ears of the army, the Readers would be protected as much as possible, but they would also have to defend themselves.

Most of the Readers wore the Sign of the Dark Moon, but neither Alethia nor Rodrigo was among them. Alethia, with two small children, had never been considered, but Melissa's friend had confided her intense relief when her husband had been told to stay in Gaeta and continue the work which kept food on the tables of the empire.

Both soldiers and sailors were accustomed to Readers guiding them, but most of them had worked only with men before. On Melissa's ship, a converted whaling vessel called the Western Sun, the crew fell all over themselves in their attempt to do and say the right things, knowing that these women could, if they chose, Read every thought they had. The embarrassment level reached a high Melissa had never known before—and she suddenly realized that these men were trying not to show that they reacted to the healers as attractive women. In trying to be friendly and put the men at ease, the healers only increased the tension . . . until what was happening dawned on them, one by one, and they withdrew into a restraint that quickly eased the situation.

How strange, Melissa thought. It had not occurred to her since her normal adolescent turmoil several years ago to think of her physical attributes, other than her skills as a healer. Now she realized that all the Readers on this mission were physically attractive people. The old, the infirm, and the out of condition had been left at home where only their mental powers mattered. Every Reader on this journey was in the prime of life and the glow of health—no wonder it made the sailors uneasy to be suddenly surrounded by pretty young females not only forbidden to them, but capable of knowing their thoughts!

As soon as the women realized what was happening, things settled down to a smooth, uneventful journey. Melissa learned how boring the life of adventure could be. After she had explored the ship, there was nothing to do but sit around and talk with the other Readers, or listen to the sailors tell tales of other journeys, other battles. The third day out they sailed north of the empire's border, well out of sight of land and range of any Reader not out of body and specifically looking for them.

The seas became rougher, and a few Readers had to take their own medicines for seasickness. Melissa wanted to stay on deck, but the lurching swells made it too difficult for someone unaccustomed to sailing to stay on her feet. Half-stumbling, half-crawling, she found her way back to her hammock, and rode out the rough weather safe in its coccoon.

When the seas smoothed, the sailors laughed at the women for referring to what they had been through as a storm. "That was nothing!" they were told. "You'd better get your sea legs before we go much farther!"

But there was no time for that; the fleet turned and headed toward land. The maps showed a harbor large enough to accommodate about a third of the fleet—they would disembark in shifts, provided they dared enter the harbor at all. They were still out of range of the most powerful Readers—which meant their own Readers could not Read the shore. Even in calm seas, leaving one's body in a moving vessel was not recommended; one of the four Master Readers traveling with them would do it when they were closer in, with other Readers carefully monitoring him.

The gentle breeze dropped to a calm; the fleet slowed to a crawl. The sun set without any great glory, for there was not a cloud in the sky. The waves settled into gentle rocking. Apprehension rose from the experienced sailors at the unnatural calm.

In the tense atmosphere, every Reader was Reading, seeking for a clue to their being stalled here. Then, "Lower the oars!" shouted the captain of the Western Sun—almost half the fleet were equipped with oars—and soon they were moving forward again, leaving behind those ships equipped only with sails.

Jason's ship also had oars—even though she could not communicate with him among the mass of Readers, Melissa could use the mental clutter as a mask to watch him. She had noted carefully during the whole journey just where his ship was in relation to hers and what his responsibilities were. He was guiding them now, transmitting the proper heading to the Readers in all the other ships.

Melissa Read ahead, trying to sense the land. Nothing. The ship moved as smoothly as a chariot on a main road, no waves to interfere with the skilled oarsmen's efforts.

Suddenly every Reader in the fleet Read a new mental voice, strong and vibrant and commanding. //Stop. Turn your ships around and return to the Aventine Empire, and no one will be harmed.//

Although the voice was calm, it struck fear into Melissa's heart. They were discovered. What could have prompted a Reader to leave his body and seek them out here? How could he have known?

//You are helpless against us,// the voice continued. //We are Adepts and Readers working together. We will stop you before you reach our shores. Turn back, lest you come to harm.//

The Readers conferred with one another. No one transmitted the message to the nonReaders, and the oared vessels continued smoothly onward.

//We do not fear you.// Jason transmitted to the mysterious renegade. //We far outnumber you. Read the size of the army proceeding against you, and surrender before *you* come to harm.//

There was a pause. Then the renegade responded, //Your army will never reach shore. Behold!//

A fresh breeze rose, and howled into a biting north wind. As the ships rocked and shook, the oarsmen broke rhythm in surprise. As fast as it had come, the wind died. //Behold your weakness,// Jason told the renegade. //A little wind like that cannot stop us.//

"Keep moving!" he called to the captain of his vessel. It was an unnecessary order; the men had already taken up their smooth pulling again.

Every Reader in the fleet was Reading to full capacity —it was not Melissa's own powers, but the range of one of the Master Readers that suddenly brought the land ahead into their minds. As the ships sped over the calm sea it took form as hills and a harbor—and on one of the hills overlooking the harbor three people, almost unReadable. Two men stood, facing the sea; the third lay on a spread cloak on the ground—his body was there, but not his mind, which roved among the fleet of ships. That explained the pause—he had had to return to his body to speak the the others, the Adepts who had then raised the wind.

Three people—only three people against the greatest army the world had ever known! Relieved laughter raced through the minds of all the Readers. Search as they might, they found no one else, no army to ambush them. So they had been discovered by accident, and these people had come out to try to stop them—but surely the entire Aventine army was not to be stopped by two Adepts and one renegade Reader! The Master Readers transmitted the information to the officers, and the fleet sailed on.

As the ships proceeded, the renegade tried again, this time less certain, more pleading. //Go back. You do not realize our strength. You do not understand Adept powers.//

//Prepare for Adept attack,// Jason transmitted to the Readers on the other ships. //There are only two of them—a few thunderbolts and they'll have worn out their powers.//

But there were no thunderbolts. No ships caught fire. No men were thrown overboard. They sailed on, into sight of the hills, although by now it was full dark and they could not make out the figures on land. Nor could the Adepts see them—the Reader would have to describe where they were. Melissa Read him return to his body—they had now come within his ordinary range. That must be what the Adepts had been waiting for. She braced herself for fires, thunderbolts, anything—and still nothing happened.

Melissa had never been in a battle in her life, but she had heard tales of the destruction caused by savage Adepts. Was it a bluff? Were these perhaps apprentices who could do no more than cause a bit of wind, trying to scare the army off to buy time for master sorcerers to join them?

The wind rose again. It howled and whirled, twisting the sails of the ships—and this time it didn't stop. The ship heaved. Memories of the earthquake flinging her around made Melissa grasp the ship's railing with all her strength. Eyes closed against the flying spray, she Read the oarsmen give up fighting the bucking ship. Sailors were herding the passengers belowdecks before they were swept overboard. The gale went on and on, gaining in strength, tossing them one way and then another— pure wind from a cloudless sky.

The Western Sun was a fine, strong vessel. Melissa knew it must have weathered many such storms; she would be safe if only she could get belowdecks, but she knew better than to try alone. If she hung on to the railing long enough, one of the sailors would come and help her. For a moment she wished Jason's strong arms would rescue her, but he was on another ship, his attention on the conference of the Master Readers and the officers trying to decide how to handle this strange situation.

Jason was also on deck, caught as Melissa had been when the wind rose. He was stronger, however, and began to fight his way toward a hatch. Each time he lurched from one handhold to another, Melissa's heart lurched with him, but he was in the center of the deck now, unlikely to be thrown overboard—

A wave swept across the deck, knocking him down

and drenching him, but he grasped a rope and pulled himself to one of the masts, gasping for breath. He clung, gathering strength, waiting for a lull—but as his concentration was on the wind and water, he missed the stresses accumulating above his head.

One of the sails came loose from its moorings, flapping in the wind. It caught and billowed full—the ship was thrown over onto its side, but sluggishly righted itself, once.

Jason hugged the mast as another wave washed his feet out from under him. He heaved himself upright again as the ship righted—but the buffeting wind shifted to another quarter, twisting the mast with its unfurled sail like a twig in a child's hands.

//JASON!// Melissa screamed and sent intensely— he Read her, and what was happening, but there was nothing he could do. The twisted mast splintered with a crack so loud Melissa was sure she heard as well as Read it—mast, sail, crossbars, and rigging fell on Jason, crushing him—she felt his pain, and then nothing as he blacked out.

//Jason! Jason!//

No reply. He was unconscious. Was he dead? Melissa forced herself to Read calmly, all the while maintaining her own precarious hold on the railing of the Western Sun. He was alive, but badly injured. She had to— No, a healer had to get to him at once!

She broadcast the message to the Readers in Jason's ship, and immediately two healers started for deck—but they could not get the hatch open against the wind, while outside the fallen rigging was tossed to and fro, Jason with it, his limp body hitting spars and tackle, suffering more damage with every blow.

The broken mast swung off Jason and swept against the taller center mast of the vessel, already weakened from the strain. It gave—and in its fall crashed through the deck. Water poured into the ship. Jason, released from the rigging, was swept overboard as everyone else became far too busy trying to hold the wallowing vessel together to try to reach him. He was unconscious! He would drown!

Without a thought, Melissa jumped into the sea. Cold water enveloped her, and her waterlogged cloak threatened to pull her under. She struggled out of it and kicked off her sandals, managing to stay afloat despite the waves washing over her head. Finally she was swimming, if it could be called that, and was able to Read for Jason.

She expected his mind to answer hers—but the cold of the water had not brought him conscious! Despite her dread fear she Read in every direction, thoroughly disoriented. Finally she located him, still unconscious but alive. She tried to swim toward him, but the waves pushed her back. She cursed them as she struggled, refusing to give in and let Jason drown.

The sea began to settle; the waves resumed a more normal pattern. Melissa swam strongly now. At last she reached Jason, pulled him up and held his face out of the water while she Read around them. They had been blown far from either ship—and Jason's ship was coming apart, spilling people into the sea. As she Read, the "voice" of the renegade Reader broadcast clearly, //Swim for shore! We'll help you! Don't be afraid—we won't hurt you.//

It was not directed specifically at Melissa and Jason, but at all those floundering in the sea. Two other ships were sinking, passengers and crew swimming for their lives. The waves washed them toward shore—but many tried to reach the other ships, fearing what would await them in the savage lands. To her horror, she Read one Reader run out of strength, flounder, and drown—then another. Even if she tried, she could not shut out a fellow Reader's agony. She could not waken Jason. What was she to do? They were farther than any of the others from the surviving ships—she could not swim that far, towing Jason. Neither, though, would she submit Jason or herself to the mercies of the savages!

As she floated, indecisive, her feet scraped bottom.

She Read a sandbar, leading away from the harbor toward a stretch of rocky beach. It was hopeless to try to reach the ships now—both she and Jason would drown. If she could get him ashore and hide him while he recovered, perhaps they would be able to make their way through the savage lands on foot, back to the empire. Perhaps. But that was a problem for later. Right now she must save Jason's life.

In moments she could walk the sandbar, pulling Jason with her. She got him onto the beach and left him, searching for a safe haven where she could get to work at healing him. If only she dared broadcast to the departing Readers where they were—but that would tell the renegade, and their enemies would be upon them.

Stumbling in the dark, she risked Reading directly ahead of her, hoping the renegade Reader was distracted by what was happening to the Aventine fleet. Soon she found a series of caves in the cliffside, and searched until she discovered one above the tide line with access from the beach. Jason hadn't stirred, but he was still alive. She dragged his dead weight a few paces, rested, and hauled some more, Reading his injuries. He had a concussion, which was probably why he was still unconscious, but he would recover from that. The much more serious problem was a ruptured spleen—unless that bleeding stopped by itself, he would die, for Melissa had no way of performing the surgery necessary to stop it. She wanted to stop and weep out her frustration—but she had to get him into shelter before daylight.

Exhausted from tension and the battle against the sea, Melissa found herself in a kind of nightmare trying to heave Jason's helpless form up into the cave without doing him further injury. It all ran together—she surprised herself when she was finally there, Jason still and cold beside her. She wrapped her body about his to try to keep him warm, and Read him. He was still alive, but his internal bleeding continued, slow but deadly. *An Adept could stop it,* she thought. *But what price would he extract? And then he would have two Readers to force to work for him or to kill in the attempt.*

She risked Reading and found the renegade directing people who had joined the triad on the shore, helping those who had survived the shipwreck to dry ground. There were no Readers among them—all had either gotten to the surviving ships or drowned in the attempt. Could she pretend she was a nonReader and go for help? The soldiers and sailors didn't seem particularly afraid—just glad to be alive. They would worry about what happened to them later; there was no hope if they were dead. The same applied to Jason—Melissa had to save his life first, and worry about the consequences later.

Shivering in her sodden garments, she had just made up her mind to go for help when Jason came to with a groan. "You're safe," she told him. "Lie still, Magister, please!"

He opened his eyes, but it was dark in the cave. Then he Read her. //Melissa?//

She didn't have to warn him not to broadcast strongly; his injuries had made his Reading weak as a child's. "Yes, I'm here," she told him, not daring to transmit at the intensity it would take for him to Read her words. "You were swept overboard in the storm. You have a concussion and some broken ribs. I'm going for help."

//No!//

"I have to—I don't have any medicines, bandages, instruments—not even herbs. We'll pretend not to be Readers, and nothing will happen to us worse than to the other prisoners."

//Melissa, I'm not so badly hurt I can't tell I'm dying. Child, why did you do this to yourself? You can't save me, and now you have destroyed your own life. Not that—// He stopped a thought in midstream, and she felt him battling pain as well as a host of conflicting emotions. Then he decided. //Since you are in danger of falling into Portia's trap when you return to the em-

pire, I must tell you all I know. At least then you will
have a chance.//

Portia's trap? Was he hallucinating? His mind
seemed clear as far as Melissa could tell, but this did not
make sense. "I must get help for you!" she protested,
but Jason continued as if she hadn't spoken.

//In Tiberium I was under constant scrutiny from the
Council of Masters. They questioned me about Lenardo, Torio, other renegade Readers. Melissa, the
Council is living in fear. The empire is falling to the
savages year by year, and the Readers cannot stop it.
Already we are denied political power—and there is talk
in the Senate of removing autonomy from the Readers,
making nonReaders responsible for the Academies.//

"What do we care?" Melissa asked. "They can't possibly know what we really do—or even what we think of
them."

//That is precisely why they fear us. Three Readers
have gone over to the savages in the past few years—and
until Lenardo stole Torio away, with many nonReaders
involved in the chase, *the Senate did not know*. Portia is
supposed to keep the Emperor and the Senate informed
of anything the Readers learn that is of importance to
the government—and she did not tell them of the defec-
tion of Readers to the enemy!//

"No wonder they're angry! That was *wrong*, Jason.
How old is Portia? Has she become senile?"

//It may be. But she is crafty, and she has power. The
Council cannot depose her—a majority of their mem-
bership agree that the government should be left unaware of matters dealing only with Readers. They are
actually threatening to retest and demote Masters who
have been Council Members for years! I talked privately
with Master Clement, Lenardo's teacher. He says the
Council is trying to prevent a split that might give the
government an excuse to disband it—that is why those
who disagree with Portia are not joining together
against her. The worst thing that could happen now
would be public knowledge that the Council of Masters

are fighting among themselves.//

"I understand, Magister Jason. Still, I must get home, and how can I do that without your help? There are people out on the beach, helping the survivors—"

He grasped a fold of her tunic as she got to her knees. //No, Melissa. Listen to me. The savages have gotten three Readers into their hands in the past three years. *All three have been Read working for the savages.* Lenardo, I'm told, even styles himself a savage lord. No Reader has escaped from them, and none have died, it seems—at least not resisting the savages. What do these facts suggest?//

Melissa sank back to her knees beside Jason. "You think . . . the Adepts have ways to force the Readers to work with them?"

//They have learned how to twist the minds even of Master Readers. The savages feared Readers only until the Adepts learned to control them. If they can turn a Master Reader against his homeland, to help destroy it with earthquakes, what hope is there for you or me? I do not want them perverting my mind, or yours. Wait till everyone is gone, Melissa, and then use your best Reading skills to get away, to go home. I do not know what you will be going home to, with our fleet returning in defeat, but we must fight these savages as long as we can. If only the Readers were not turning on one another—//

His thought trailed off in a wave of pain, but he brought it under control. //Melissa, when you return the Council will probably marry you off. I deeply regret your futile attempt to save my life—but you will be unable to hide this incident under Oath of Truth.//

"In an emergency—"

//At any other time, of course. But now, returning from the savage lands, you will be suspect, and they will seek to render you harmless. I wish . . . you and I—//

She ached with grief. If only they could both go home, perhaps they could always be together—but for the Council to give her to someone else— "Why? If I do manage to get home, it's proof that the savages couldn't hold me.''

//Proof of your strength. They will want to dilute your strength . . . but—// Another wash of pain obscured his thoughts. He was growing weaker. Melissa could Read the numbing cold coming over him.

"Jason," she whispered, "leave your body. Don't suffer such pain.''

//Not . . . until I have told you. Alethia is right.//

"Right? Right about what?''

//Right to be happy in marriage. It doesn't . . . really weaken . . . abilities.//

" . . . what?''

//Treating patients with sickness of the mind. It's possible to make them . . . believe things we want them to . . . so they can live normally. Only healers, under supervision, ever do it—only if there's no other way. The Council—Portia—they—//

Jason was approaching unconsciousness; Melissa could Read his mind clouding, although he fought it valiantly. He seemed to be confusing the Council with the savages. "Rest, Jason. Save your strength." She cradled his head in her lap, trying to lend him strength, refusing to let herself cry. He was still alive. There had to be something she could do—

//Melissa!// His hand fumbled for her, and she took it, squeezing the cold fingers, trying to will warmth into him. //It's a lie, Melissa. Marriage doesn't . . . only if you think it— Don't let them make you think it will impair your powers. You are a healer. You are worthy to be a Magister Reader. Don't believe—// He ran out of the frail strength he had rallied.

"Jason?''

There was no response. His mind was beyond her Reading. She gathered his body into her arms and sat through the night as the life slowly left it—long after Jason had left her, forever.

Chapter Four

Torio sat at the long table in the great hall of Wulfston's castle, hot cereal turning cold before him. Wulfston sat to his left, cereal bowl long empty, consuming eggs and meat with thick slices of fresh hearty bread. They had spent a long night directing rescue efforts and then healing the injured. Wulfston was no more tired than Torio this morning, though a good deal hungrier.

The castle dungeons were full of Aventine prisoners, being served a good meal and bedded down with warm blankets. They would not be harmed, Torio knew; the nonReaders were not what disturbed him.

It was the first moment he had had to think since the storm, intended as a show of power to frighten off the approaching fleet, had broken up three vessels, drowning eleven people—six of them Readers.

Wulfston finally noticed Torio's silence and lack of appetite. "Eat your cereal," he said. "I don't want to have to heal you, too, Torio."

"I'm not sick—just disgusted."

"Disgusted? You'll have to explain your feelings—I can't Read you."

That's a good thing, Torio thought, for he found himself taking a new view of this Adept he had come to trust. "It's happened twice now, Wulfston. Twice our attempts to prevent disaster have created it instead."

"I felt as bad about the earthquake as you did," said

Wulfston. "We initiated it—and even though our intentions were good we must take responsibility for the consequences. This time, though, we were attacked. What do you think we should have done—let them land and kill us all?"

"You said you'd just blow them off course!"

"That's all we *did*. Torio, you cannot hold me responsible for some of the dilapidated ships the Aventines sent! Moreover, we were dealing with the forces of nature—and no matter how much we may know about it, loosing such forces is always dangerous."

"Then perhaps we should never loose them. *Readers* died at Gaeta, and *Readers* died last night. And it's my fault!"

There was a long pause. Wulfston pushed his chair back so he could turn and study Torio. "Are the deaths of Readers more important than the deaths of other people?"

"No, of course not," Torio said frustratedly. How could he explain to a nonReader? "I may be able to shut out a nonReader's pain or fear, but rarely a Reader's. But that's not the important thing. My Oath binds me to all Readers. To turn against another Reader is as if . . . as if you turned against your sister."

"I have no trouble understanding that," Wulfston said patiently. "What I do not understand is why you feel you turned against those Readers. You were trying to help them—if they had cooperated we could probably have saved them *and* the five nonReaders who drowned. *They* turned against *you*."

"Why would they trust a renegade?" Torio got up. "I'm sorry, Wulfston. I know you see everything from a different perspective. I'm going out for some fresh air before I try to sleep. I'll make a final check to Read if we missed anybody."

Wulfston let him go, saying only, "Don't hesitate to send for me if you need me."

It was dawn, but the castle was settling down to rest after last night's activities. "Good morning, my lord," people said as Torio passed, and he tried to hide the fact that each such greeting felt more like a blow.

The stable boy jumped to saddle a fresh horse for the young Lord Reader, and soon Torio was cantering along the road to the harbor, his cloak thrown back as the morning sun warmed his chill away.

The fishing boats were late starting out today, as they had been used in last night's resue effort. Torio Read them leaving the harbor as he topped the hill and stopped, concentrating on the scene below. He had Read all around the area hours before, and found no stragglers within his range. It was not likely that any more survivors could have reached shore. To his relief, he Read no more bodies washed ashore, something he had feared he *might* find.

The ride had not settled his mind. From the savage point of view, he had done nothing but help defend his new ally. But Torio had trouble thinking of himself as a savage. *I don't know what I am.*

He had joined eagerly in Lenardo's plans for making peace between the savages and the empire—but if the empire sent an army against them, how could they seek peace?

The sea breeze stirred his hair, throwing an overgrown lock down across his forehead to tangle in his eyelashes. It could not interfere with the vision he did not have, but it annoyed him anyway, and he pushed it back with an impatient hand. A mark of the savage, long, unkempt hair. He would cut it, he decided, and stop attempting to conform to the fashion of people he didn't belong with. *But if I cut it short, people will just think I'm imitating Wulfston*, for the Lord of the Land wore his wiry hair close cropped as any Reader's.

Shoving the recalcitrant hair back angrily, Torio wondered, *How can I decide what to do about my life when I can't even decide how to wear my hair?*

He was tired, he decided. After a few hours' sleep, things would look different. But first he must make a Reading search of the shoreline in both directions.

Just as he reached for the reins to guide his horse toward the north, Torio Read a brief start of fear, followed by sharp sorrow and a sense of devastating cold. It cut off as abruptly as it had begun, but not before Torio had located its source as somewhere along the rocky beach outside the harbor, more than a mile away.

A Reader! At that distance no nonReader's feelings would have come through so clearly. He easily guessed that a survivor of last night's storm had hidden among the rocks, not Reading so as to escape notice. In sleep, the Reader had automatically shielded his thoughts—but Torio had caught the unshielded moment of waking, cut off as soon as the Reader realized where he was.

He urged his horse forward, skirting the harbor and taking the trail down to the beach, picking his way through the rocks as he Read the area. The Reader was in a cave—a woman, huddled beside the dead body of a man. Both wore the plain white tunics of Readers, the man's banded in black. He had been a member of the upper ranks; the woman was still in training.

Torio felt sick: a seventh Reader dead. But the woman was alive—unhurt so far as he could tell, except that she shivered in her damp garments as the morning breeze entered the cave.// Come out in the sun, where it's warm,// Torio projected at the most intense level, but the woman was holding tight against Reading, lest she be Read. *I'd have found you anyway*, thought Torio. *If you hadn't given yourself away it would just have taken a bit longer*.

The woman tensed and looked up as she heard Torio's horse approach. The cave was shallow—she could not retreat. He dismounted and climbed the rocks, calling, "Don't be afraid. No one is going to hurt you."

When Torio reached the cave entrance the woman was crouched at the back like a trapped animal, her fear escaping the hold she kept on Reading.

They were no more than a few paces apart, the body

of the dead Reader between them. Torio said, "There's really nothing to fear. You are in Lord Wulfston's lands. My name is Torio . . . Magister Torio."

It was the first time he had claimed aloud the rank Lenardo insisted he was entitled to, although he wore the robes of a Magister Reader on ceremonial occasions. He had meant to reassure the woman, but instead her fear grew, her heart pounding wildly. "Then it's true!" she gasped.

Even as Torio was trying to fathom what "truth" frightened her so, her fear was shoved aside by desperate hope. "Can the savage sorcerers bring Jason back to life? The way they did you?"

No! Oh, no—his lie come to haunt him! No wonder this girl was terrified if she thought Torio half a ghost.

"I was not dead," he said gently. "The guards were wrong. I was wounded, and healed by Adept power—but no one has the power to return life to the dead."

"You're lying," she spat. "Take us to the savage Adepts who saved you. Let *them* decide!"

Maybe Wulfston could persuade her—everyone seemed to find it easy to trust him. "Come with me. Lord Wulfston will tell you it's not possible. And do not fear to Read—I am the only person in this land capable of intercepting your thoughts."

When she began to Read him, Torio found it easier to Read the woman before him—hardly more than a girl, somewhere near his own age. She was numb with cold, but instead of moving toward the inviting warmth outside she bent to the body on the cave floor, saying, "Please help me—"

"I will send someone at once to take his body to the castle. He was your teacher?" he asked, although the girl's attitude suggested more than that—some relationship not possible between a male and a female Reader in the Aventine Academy system.

"Yes," she answered his spoken words. "Magister Jason. We were at Gaeta together—"

Torio's stab of guilt made the woman look up at him.

"You caused the earthquake, didn't you? You almost killed me that time, and now you've killed Jason. If you don't bring him back, the gods will exact retribution, Torio."

The gods did not concern him; his conscience did. "The earthquake was not meant for Gaeta—"

"Tiberium, I suppose," she said resignedly. "Now that you've destroyed our fleet, you think you'll go back and wreck the rest of the empire. But we'll fight you. You won't be able to twist the minds of *all* Readers. How many more will you have to kill?"

"We do not want to kill *any*," he said, knowing that her mind was wandering in shock. "You are cold and tired. Let me take you to a safe place. At least come outside, where it's warm."

It took much persuasion to get the young woman to leave the body of the dead Reader, but finally Torio put her up on his horse, wrapped his cloak about her, and climbed up behind her. "You haven't told me your name," he remembered.

"Melissa."

"Melissa, Read with me, please. I am searching for other survivors. If we encounter any more Readers, you may be able to help me persuade them we want to help."

"I don't know that you do," she replied, but she Read with him along the shore. He felt her surprise at his range. "You're so young—and you have misused your powers. How can you Read so far and so accurately?"

He didn't tell her that he was not Reading at his best this morning, tired after being up all night. Instead he suggested, "Perhaps my abilities will persuade you that I have *not* misused my powers." It was the reassurance he clung to himself: he had not lost any of his abilities since throwing his lot in with the savages. Rather, they had improved—faster, Lenardo judged, than they might have if he had stayed in the empire's Academies. Faster than Lenardo's had at Torio's age, the Master Reader insisted.

Torio and Melissa found no more survivors, and so, after stopping at a sailmaker's cottage to ask him to send his apprentices for Magister Jason's body, he turned the horse back toward Wulfston's castle. Melissa had grown warm and sleepy in his arms, as Lenardo's daughter Julia had once done riding thus with Torio. But Julia was a child, and Melissa a full-grown woman . . . something Torio became keenly aware of as her weight settled drowsily against him and her scent tickled his nostrils.

She had made no protest at his touch, although this was hardly an emergency. He did not know which Reader had tried to save the other from drowning in last night's storm, but under such conditions the restrictions against male and female Readers being together were definitely suspended.

Perhaps, despite his assertion of his rank, Melissa regarded Torio as a failed Reader. Portia had, after all, declared him such. But she had declared Lenardo failed as well—Lenardo, whose powers exceeded those of any other living Reader, including Portia herself.

Portia was a frail old woman—she must be beyond the peak of her powers. She had even believed Torio's lie. It hadn't been delivered under Oath of Truth, of course, but even so, no Master Reader should have been fooled by a Reader as young as Torio.

He wished he could talk to Lenardo. Later today he would have to report events in Wulfston's land to his teacher; perhaps he could discuss his own uncertainties as well. Not that these were really anything new; this was the same indecision he had felt ever since he had first come into this land on the spur of the moment, without any thought to how he would fit in here.

Wulfston's castle was quiet when they arrived, the servants alert, but no one else stirring. Torio Read Wulfston sleeping—but not the sleep of total exhaustion, bordering on coma, that Adepts went into when they had used their powers to the limit. Wulfston could be wakened if he were needed, but Torio saw no reason that his introduction to Melissa could not wait a few hours. She, too, should rest.

He took her to the kitchen, where food was available any time, day or night, and left her eating soup while he sought out the seamstress, a motherly sort who quickly took Melissa in hand. Then he went upstairs to his own room.

As he passed the open door to the room next to his own, a voice called, "Torio?"

"Yes, Rolf, I'm back," he replied. "I found a Reader who survived the storm. Hilda's taking care of her."

Rolf sat up. "Another Reader? Good. Do you think she will help us?"

Torio stood in Rolf's doorway, Reading the boy—he was only a year younger than Torio, but at moments like this he seemed impossibly naive. "After we killed seven of her fellow Readers and almost drowned her, why would she?"

"Oh." Rolf leaned back on his pillows, although Torio could Read he was rested enough for the moment. The boy had used his talent to its full last night, for he was not a fully empowered Adept like Wulfston. Rather, he had a single Adept talent, the ability to control the weather—he and Wulfston together had created the storm, and then held the seas calm for the rescue work. Afterward, Rolf had barely made it back to his own bed before falling into exhausted slumber, while Torio, Wulfston, and several minor Adepts with the power of healing worked on until early morning.

"Melissa—the Reader—is down in the kitchen now," Torio offered, knowing Rolf would be hungry.

The boy got up at that, pulling on slippers and robe and feeling for the stick leaning against the wall by his bed.

For Rolf, like Torio, was blind.

Illogically, Torio always felt uneasy around Rolf. Perhaps it would not have bothered him so much if Rolf were not exactly what Torio would be were he not a

Reader. He felt guilty to have escaped the world of darkness when Rolf could not—an absurd feeling, for it was not as if Torio were withholding something he could have shared with Rolf. No one could give another person Reading ability.

Rolf and Torio were one of Wulfston's experiments. The Lord Adept had long theorized that Reading and Adept powers were two functions of the same ability. Then his own sister, Aradia, had proved him right by learning to Read. Later Lenardo confirmed that Aradia's double talent was not unique by developing Adept powers. Wulfston wanted desperately to learn to Read, but he had made no progress, nor could he teach Torio even the simplest Adept trick.

Since Aradia had learned to Read only after falling in love with Lenardo, and Lenardo had first conquered Adept powers to save Aradia's life, Wulfston now theorized that motivation was a prime force in manifesting a new power. Hence his bringing Rolf and Torio together. They were close in age, and both were blind from birth with the same defective nerves from eye to brain.

Torio knew Wulfston had another motive for wanting Rolf to learn to Read. The black Adept had been Lord of the Land for barely a year, but he felt an obligation to right the wrongs Drakonius, the former lord, had done to his people. Rolf's blindness was one of those wrongs—a sin of omission, for Wulfston claimed that any Lord Adept could have made those defective nerves regenerate in an infant.

Born in the Aventine Empire, Torio had never had the opportunity to be healed by a Lord Adept, but once he developed Reading skills his blindness hardly mattered. Most of the people Torio had met in Wulfston's land had no idea he was blind. Wulfston hoped that Rolf, motivated by Torio's abilities, would quickly learn to Read. Given the facts—and Torio had witnessed the dual abilities of both Lenardo and Aradia—it made perfectly good sense to the young Reader. Thus he became more and more frustrated that he could not help Rolf learn.

Rolf moved past Torio and down the hall, completely at home in the familiar castle. Torio went into his own room, undressed, and went to bed. He was tired enough by now not to risk leaving his body to report to Lenardo until he had slept—but just before he withdrew from Reading, Lenardo contacted him. //Torio—why did I have to hear about the battle in your land from the watchers?//

//It's all over,// Torio replied. //I've been up all night—I was going to rest before trying to contact you.//

Lenardo could not miss the fatigue that had finally caught up with Torio. //Very well—tell me anything I need to know, and then sleep. I can Read most of what is going on there for myself.//

//Seven Readers died,// Torio told him. //One survived—a girl, Melissa. She may Read you if you're not careful. Not that it matters, I suppose.//

//It doesn't. But I think I shall let Wulfston make friends with her first. We can certainly use another Reader, if it's possible to get her to trust us. Oh—one more thing. Master Clement seems to have lost Portia's trust. He was not able to find out when or where the fleet would land. If I had known, I would have been there, with Aradia.//

//It was more effective as it happened,// Torio replied, //although I've spent so much time outside my body the last three days that I'm almost surprised I have one to return to!//

//You did a fine job. Give Wulfston my greetings, and assure him that we will come at his call. Sleep now.//

For a moment Torio felt that same feeling he had known as a little boy at the Academy, when he had wakened screaming from nightmares in which his ability to Read had disappeared, leaving him blind and helpless. Either Lenardo or Master Clement would come to comfort him, holding him and Reading with him until he was reassured, and dared let go of the world he Read, to sleep.

How absurd those childish fears now seemed. Today he had no lack of confidence in his powers—only in his judgment of what to do with them.

Torio woke at mid-afternoon, gathered clean garments, and went to the castle bath—a far different device from the Aventine baths he had been accustomed to. Cisterns on the roof of the castle gathered water, some of which went into a tank above a small stone room. By opening a tap like the one on a keg of ale, he would be showered with water—effective, if not luxurious.

If I ever have a castle, Torio thought, *I will install a real bath.* But he could not imagine himself building a castle, ruling a land, although Lenardo and Wulfston assured him that that was his destiny.

The spring sunshine had warmed the water in the tank. Torio lavished the pleasant soap that was the unexpected invention of the savages all over himself, including his hair—a luxury he had seldom known at the Academy. As he scrubbed his face, he decided he needn't shave again for a day or two. He wasn't quite sure whether he shaved to keep some small link with his appearance as an Aventine Reader, or because his beard was still so sparse that he could not achieve the full growth that Lenardo and Wulfston wore.

When he had toweled off with fine linen, Torio put on the garments Wulfston's seamstress had provided him—the clothes of a savage lord. He wore a silk shirt and hose, and an embroidered tabard cut full enough to disguise the fact that his body was not yet filled out to a grown man's musculature.

If he had to wear such outfits, he was glad his legs were not thin, like Rolf's. Torio had had the enforced exercise of the Academy, the body expected to be as healthy as the mind—and in a sort of perverse insistence that his blindness should not keep him from any activity he chose, he had spent many hours turning himself into an expert swordsman.

But it was not just the regimen of exercise that had given Torio a healthier body than Rolf's: the young savage still bore the scars of malnutrition in childhood, as did so many people in these lands that had for generations been ruled by a series of Adepts all calling themselves by one name: Drakonius. Although everyone was now well fed and cared for, even Adept healing could do little for adults with bowed legs, missing teeth, crooked backs. Still, the children were thriving, and after Drakonius Wulfston was having little trouble gaining the love of his people.

Torio started downstairs to the main rooms of the castle, restricting his Reading to just ahead of himself as he always did indoors, to avoid breaching someone's privacy. As he crossed the hall to the main stairs, though, a door opened. Melissa Read him, and ducked quickly back into her room.

//We don't segregate male and female Readers here,// he told her. //There are not enough of us, and no Academies.//

//That's not it,// she replied sheepishly, reopening her door. "I . . . don't understand what you intend to do with me," she explained as Torio approached.

"I don't know—Lord Wulfston doesn't even know you're here yet," Torio replied. "But we're certainly not going to hurt you."

"But I am your captive. You turned me over to Hilda. She fed me, helped me bathe, put me to bed—and when I woke up I found clothes laid out, and the door not locked. No guard. It doesn't make sense."

Torio grinned. "If you want to run away, go. If Wulfston wants you, we'll have you back here in a few hours."

"You're not *that* good a Reader," she said, "and you're the only one working here, aren't you? I could leave while you're asleep. You'd never find me if I got out of your range before you woke up."

This time he laughed—for he had been as astonished as any other Aventine citizen to discover that the savages had ways of communicating over distances that did not involve Readers. Lenardo had often told the story of being caught by watchers when he had once escaped from Aradia's castle—how foolish was the empire to assume that just because they had no Readers the savages could not invent other ways of transmitting information. "Try it. You won't get far."

She tried to Read him, and he deliberately thought of swordplay exercises until she gave up. "I'll find out from someone else," she said.

"Invade the privacy of nonReaders?"

"If they're my enemies. But I think first I should meet your Lord Wulfston—I would not want to anger him before I have the chance to ask him to use his powers to revive Jason."

"Melissa, I told you—"

"Why should I believe you? How do I get to meet this savage Adept?"

"I'll wake him—he's probably hungry again by now anyway." He called down the stairs for a guard to take Melissa to the great hall, warning her, "They'll try to feed you again. Everyone thinks Readers have the same requirements as Adepts—if you don't learn to say no, you're likely to get very fat!"

Somehow, his encounter with Melissa made him feel better, even though she had raised again the issue of his lie to Portia. He went to Wulfston's room, and Read through the door. The Lord Adept was still asleep. Torio knocked. No response. That meant there was only one safe way to wake him.

Torio entered Wulfston's room and approached the bed, where he carefully touched the Adept on the forehead, between the eyes. Wulfston woke immediately. "Torio. Is anything wrong?"

"No. If you are not rested, it can wait."

"I'm fine," Wulfston replied, sitting up and stretching. "What happened while I slept?"

"I reported to Lenardo, who sends his greetings. And I found a surviving Reader."

"Good . . . I think. Who is he? Any chance of winning him to us?"

"It's a young woman. She has passed her preliminary testing, for she was doing her medical training at Gaeta. She almost died in the earthquake, she told me."

Wulfston frowned. "Then she will be difficult to persuade, unless you can show her *why* we were setting off the quakes, and why we have to do it again and again until we relieve the pressure on that main fault. Where is she?"

"Downstairs. She wants to meet you."

"Certainly. Go on down and keep her company—I'll be with you in a few minutes."

When Wulfston joined them, he was dressed as the Lord of the Land, in an outfit similar to the one Torio wore, but much more richly embroidered and made of materials in the same dark brown color as his skin. He even wore a small gold crown—and Torio told Melissa, //Lord Wulfston honors you by arraying himself to meet an equal.//

//Or to impress someone he hopes to use,// she shot back, but rose as Torio made the introductions.

"Lady Melissa," Wulfston greeted her. "You are most welcome here. I trust you have been made comfortable?"

"Yes, thank you," she replied. "I haven't been treated like a prisoner at all."

"But you are not a prisoner! Please sit down. You are my guest. Before you leave us, though, I hope we may show you what we are attempting to do here."

" . . . leave you?" Melissa asked as they took their places at the dining/council table in the great hall.

"We will send you home, of course, unharmed—as soon as we can arrange a meeting with representatives of the Aventine government. That was the one positive effect of your attack: It provided us with Aventine citizens to trade for such a meeting.''

//I can't Read him!// Melissa complained to Torio, while aloud she said, "You have never traded prisoners before—you've always killed them. Or perhaps twisted their minds to make them work for you."

"*I* have never before held Aventine soldiers, my lady. Do not judge the alliance of Adepts and Readers who now hold these border lands by the actions of Drakonius. He was the one who constantly attacked your land, seeking to take it all. Drakonius is dead, and my allies and I seek peace with the empire."

//He is telling the truth,// Torio supplied, and Melissa suppressed an angry accusation. Torio felt her force herself to be calm.

"You speak the Aventine language very well, Lord Wulfston," she said.

"I was born in the empire," he replied.

"Then you are an escaped slave?" Melissa asked sweetly. Torio wanted to kick her under the table, but settled for projecting annoyance. Melissa knew as well as he did that although black Nubians, like the pale blonds from the far northern lands, usually entered the empire against their will as slaves, most of them earned freedom and the same rights of citizenship as anyone else.

But Wulfston took no offense. "My parents were freedmen, and I was born a free citizen. Not that my status would have mattered when I began to show Adept powers—our neighbors were perfectly willing to murder a citizen. However, I was rescued and adopted by Lord Nerius, who made certain that I remained fluent in my native language."

"And now you make all your people learn it? Everyone seems to speak to me in Aventine," observed Melissa.

"You haven't met very many people here yet," said Torio, "but the reason so many speak at least some Aventine is that a generation ago these lands were part of the empire. It's fortunate for me—I've been here long enough to understand most of what is said in the savage language, with the help of Reading, but I'm still not fluent at speaking it.''

Melissa stared at him. ''If you've gone over to their side, why do you still call them savages?''

Wulfston chuckled. ''It's what we call ourselves, as our alliance has chosen no formal name yet. Lenardo started the habit. Who knows—we may end up calling ourselves savages by default: The Savage Alliance.''

''This . . . alliance. It includes the renegade Lenardo?''

''He made it possible,'' Wulfston replied. ''Until we had a Reader, we dared not defy Drakonius. Even our attempts to maintain peace in our own lands were interpreted as treachery—if Lenardo had not been there to guide us last year, Drakonius would have destroyed us. By now he would have carried his conquests even further. Has no one noticed that for a whole year there have been no attacks against the walls of the Aventine Empire?''

''Of course we've noticed. We've also noticed your *new* strategy: cause earthquakes to destroy our cities —then you can walk in and take over without a fight.''

Wulfston said, ''We know that is how you interpreted the accident at Gaeta.''

''Accident!'' Melissa scoffed.

''Yes, accident,'' said Torio. ''We did not mean to harm Gaeta, or any other city. We are trying to relieve the pressure on the main fault under Tiberium. We don't *want* the capital of the empire to fall, Melissa.''

''We seek a peace treaty with the empire,'' explained Wulfston. ''Once we succeed in neutralizing the fault, thus preserving your capital, it should not be difficult to demonstrate that our intentions are peaceful. Gaeta was a major setback in our plan.''

''If you think I would try to persuade other Readers that what you say is true, you are greatly mistaken,'' said Melissa. "There is only one thing—"

At that moment one of Wulston's guards burst into the hall. "My lord! The watchers report an attack!"

Torio Read the man, then out into the passageway where a runner waited, panting, to tell his story. Wulfston had him brought in at once.

The report was short and clear: the Aventine fleet had not simply given up and returned home. The entire fleet, including those temporarily becalmed vessels that had been unable to participate in the first attack, had sailed south and landed, still in Wulfston's lands. They were now setting the army ashore, about two days' march to the south.

Rolf entered the hall as the watcher was telling his story, and stood near the door. "A good muddy rain will slow their march and dampen their spirits," he said. "I'll take care of it, my lord."

"Thank you, Rolf," said Wulfston. "That may buy us some time—I want the battle down there to the south, not here where my people have made such progress rebuilding and planting. Torio, notify Aradia and Lenardo. They'll come to help—but how do we hold the whole Aventine army off until they get here? Gevin," he said to the watcher, "send for everyone with Adept powers—we'll try to maintain a holding action. Lilith is so far away . . . but have her notified anyway, Torio, and hope she arrives just in time for a victory celebration."

As Wulfston issued orders, more people entered the hall. Messages were passed; riders and runners left the castle grounds. Men from the village near the castle converged at once, drawing weapons from the armory.

Torio felt Melissa's astonishment at the instant organization. "How can you manage all this without Readers?" she asked as the hall cleared, leaving them a center of calm at the core of a bustle of activity.

"We managed without Readers before Lenardo came," said Wulfston. "However, Torio cannot do everything. I could certainly use the help of another Reader . . . but I cannot ask that of you, Melissa. I'm afraid, as a precaution to keep you from reporting our moves to the Aventine army, I must put you to sleep until the battle is over."

"Wait!" she said, closed tightly to Reading. "I know a way for you to get Readers . . . or certainly one more Reader. I will aid you in this battle, Lord Wulfston—I will take Oath of Truth to Torio to bind it—if you will do what I ask."

Wulfston studied her. "And what," he said finally, "do you ask?"

"In a room off your dungeons," she said, opening to Reading for their reactions, allowing Torio to Read her hope, her sincerity, her burning desire to persuade the Adept, "there are twelve bodies. Seven are Readers. Use your sorcery. Bring them back to life as you did Torio. If the others won't serve you out of gratitude, *I* will. Bring back only one of them—Magister Jason—and I promise you I will do anything you ask, Lord Wulfston —anything!"

Wulfston's shock was so great that he became emotionally as Readable as any nonAdept: disbelief, revulsion, horror at the very suggestion. "Melissa . . . where did you get such an idea?!"

The girl looked to Torio, her last hope collapsing. "But you—"

"I *told* you it was a lie!" he said wretchedly. "It never happened, Melissa. I will give you Oath of Truth—"

"You don't have to," she said dully. "Lord Wulfston just did." Tears burning, she rose and fled from the hall.

Wulfston stared after her, his usual unReadable self once more. "What lie, Torio? What could you have told her to make her think—?"

"I didn't know Master—Lord—Lenardo hadn't told you. I was too ashamed to." And he told Wulfston how he had let Portia think her assumption was true.

"That's why they're attacking now, Wulfston—they're afraid to let us develop our powers together any further. It's my fault."

"It's nobody's fault. Torio, there is one lesson you must learn before you can be any good to yourself or to anyone else: Mistakes are to be learned from. Instead of berating yourself for a mistake in the past, determine never to make the same mistake in the future. Use it for growth, not to keep yourself from growing."

"Yes, my lord. I'll go and find Melissa."

"Leave her for now. If she conquers her grief enough to contact the Readers with the Aventine army, there's nothing she can tell them except that we are preparing to move against them. That can hardly be unexpected. Go contact Lenardo. I will deal with Melissa later."

"Yes, my lord."

"Torio—stop that! You are not a chastened apprentice. You are a Lord Reader, allied with other lords to fight off an attacking army. *We* are the ones being attacked. I am relying on you—I *must* rely on you. If you do not accept your responsibilities, many people will die in this battle who should not. And if that happens, Torio, this time it *will* be your fault."

Chapter Five

The sun was setting as Melissa ran out into the court-yard of Wulfston's castle. It was jammed with horses, wagons, people preparing for battle—against Melissa's friends and country. Her shock and grief made her whole body ache . . . but her duty shored her up. Before Wulfston caught her, she must find a safe place to leave her body—then he could do nothing except kill her physical being. Death of a body left behind happened to Readers sometimes. No one was quite sure where the consciousness went when that happened—no living Reader had ever found the way to the plane of the dead, and returned.

If they kill me, I'll be there with Jason.

Somehow, though, she did not think Wulfston would kill her. What she had Read in that totally unguarded moment had shown her a man of open honor—a clean conscience combined with the firm purpose and respon-sibility of a leader. He would act only in ways that he considered right.

However, she had no way of knowing what Wulfston considered right. She merely assumed that murdering the helpless would be unacceptable even by savage stan-dards. His intent to "put her to sleep," on the other hand. . . .

Surely that was a euphemism; if she allowed him to use his powers on her, she would wake up a loyal savage. He had obviously done it to Torio, although the young man was a skilled Reader. Since she now knew it was not gratitude for restoring his life, why else would he work for the savages?

Melissa left the courtyard and walked through the village. No one paid attention to her—people were too busy, and she did not look out of place in the linen dress Hilda had given her. She was accustomed to an unfitted ankle-length tunic; the tight bodice and sleeves of this dress seemed to bind, and the mass of material in the pleated skirt felt heavy—was it meant to slow her down if she tried to run away?

No, it was similar to the dresses she saw on the village women, although their voluminous skirts flowed without pleats, and were of rougher material than Melissa's. She had simply been given something appropriate to a guest of the Lord Adept.

As she reached the edge of the village and saw plowed fields ahead, Melissa realized that she had no idea where she was going. Back to the cave? But it had taken over an hour on horseback to get here from there—she didn't have time to walk it.

She had Read all through Wulfston's castle when she woke up; perhaps she should go back there—the last place they'd look for her! But Torio—

Cautiously, trying not to project, she Read the sleeping rooms. Torio was just lying down to leave his body. Still in hers, Melissa could not follow him, but he was supposed to be reporting the Aventine attack to Lenardo. His consciousness would be many miles away.

Melissa scurried back through the village and into the castle, avoiding anyone she knew had seen her earlier. Safe in her own room, she prepared carefully, knowing that it could be hours before she would dare reunite with her body. Lord Wulfston had a battle to fight, many miles away; once he left his castle, he would soon be too far away to do anything about Melissa. Although some things on this side of the border did not fit what she had been taught, it must be true that an Adept's powers diminished with distance. If not, surely the empire would have been destroyed many generations ago.

It was the first time that Melissa had attempted this feat alone—always before it had been with one of her teachers for a lesson. *This is what those lessons were for,* she told herself, and floated free, carefully orienting herself.

As always, outside her body, her Reading became sharper and clearer. Torio's presence was nowhere to be felt—she did not pursue him to the east, where he would be contacting the other savage lords in the city of Zendi. Instead, she Read the castle again. Wulfston was entering his own room, a few doors away. He took off his crown, exchanged his heavily embroidered tabard for a plain woolen over-tunic, and slung a heavy cloak over his arm. Then he climbed the stairs, past the bathing-room and up to the castle's watchtower. There were two men up there already, one the watchman, the other Rolf, the blind boy who claimed to have the power to change the weather.

"The watchers have found some clouds," Rolf reported, "but I cannot reach them from here. Will you help me, my lord?" The boy had a map unrolled on the ledge before him, his hands tracing the coastline as if he felt it.

"Where are the clouds?" asked Wulfston.

"Here, my lord." Rolf's hand circled an area on the map that represented the sea several miles to the west of the coast.

"And the enemy?"

The watchman replied, "A new report, my lord—look!"

Melissa followed the direction the man pointed, and "saw" from a hilltop beyond the fields a light flash on, off, on again for a longer time, then off . . . slowly it dawned on her that it was a code. This was the way the savages, without Readers to transmit their messages, told what was happening at a distance.

Melissa was Reading Rolf, for all three savages spoke

in their own language, which she did not know at all. Rolf was the easiest to Read—but he could not see the flashing light and hence could not interpret the code. As Wulfston read it aloud, though, Rolf assimilated it—and so did Melissa. "Enemy moved three miles inland, ten miles south of nearest community. Still marching northward."

Wulfston took Rolf's hands in his. "Here we are," he said, laying the boy's left hand on the map where the castle was marked, "and here is where our enemy is now." He laid Rolf's right hand on the area described in the watcher's message. Then he turned to speak to the other man. "Glyn, acknowledge that message. We're going to try to let foul weather encourage them to make camp. I don't want them to reach *any* of our villages if we can stop them."

The watchman picked up a lantern, turned it toward the hillside where the other light had shone, and began to open and close the cover in rhythm. Melissa turned her attention to Wulfston and Rolf—but both were concentrating now, and had become unReadable.

She studied the map, then allowed herself to "move" southward, farther than she had ever been from her body before. As she had been taught, she noted landmarks, refusing to be afraid. By the time she reached the marching Aventine army, storm clouds were already gathering overhead. Could the Adepts work at that distance? The clouds compacted until the air could no longer hold their moisture, and a steady rain began to fall. Although the army was spread out over several miles, the rain was centered on them . . . it moved with them as they marched, turning the sandy earth to mud, sucking at their feet.

As long as they kept moving, none of the Readers with the army could leave their bodies; they would not notice Melissa unless she deliberately contacted them. They were all Reading, of course, so she easily located them, spread through the line of march, a Reader with every unit. At the back of the army she found the

medical personnel—the women Melissa had been traveling with. With relief, she met the motherly mind of the
woman who cared for the trainees at Gaeta. //Magister
Phoebe!//

Surprise, relief, and welcome. //Melissa! Can it be?
Where are you, child? We thought you had drowned!//

//Melissa! Are you all right?// from the other
women, her colleagues and friends.

//I'm fine, alive and—if I can stay out of my body
long enough—relatively safe.//

//Did anyone else survive? We felt Celia die—//

//No,// she replied sadly, //only nonReaders survived, except for me.//

Other Readers, those she knew only from having
touched minds with them on the sea journey, fixed on
her. //You were with Magister Jason,// interrupted
Master Amicus. //He was badly injured—do you know
if he survived?//

//No . . . he died,// she told him, unable to hide the
sting of her grief. She felt the Master's suspicion—out
of body, she should not feel such strong emotion, and
while it was natural for a student to grieve at the loss of
a teacher and mentor, she knew her feelings were too far
beyond that to hide. //He died rather than be captured,// she told them. //The savages might have been
able to save his life, but he would not risk letting them
twist his mind.//

//If they hadn't already.// This from Master Corus.
//And you, Melissa—where are you?//

Two Master Readers were focused on her—she could
never get away with a lie. Why did she feel she *ought* to
lie? //I am . . . in the castle of one of the savage lords,//
she replied—and instantly knew why she should not
have said it.

//Traitor!// Master Amicus projected. //You felt it,
Masters—she would have lied to us, but realized we
would detect it. Jason corrupted her, as we feared!//

//No!// How could they distrust her? //No one cor-

rupted me! Listen to me! Lord Wulfston is alone here—
his allies will take hours, perhaps days, to come to his
aid. They're sending the storm to slow you, so they will
have time to gather their armies—//

//Listen to yourself!// Master Corus cut off her attempt to give them vital information. //First you say
there is only one Adept to fight us, and then you say
they are causing the rain. As to gathering an army—
when has the savage army not been prepared and ready?
You have been sent to deceive us, woman.//

//Foolish child,// said Master Amicus. //If there
were Adepts close enough to cause the rain, do you not
think Master Readers could detect them?//

//If there were Adepts close enough to cause the
rain,// added Master Corus, //they would already have
attacked.//

//Maybe . . . maybe they can only manipulate something like clouds at this distance,// Melissa said uncer-
tainly. //I don't know—I'm only telling you what I saw
here. I'm trying to *help* you! Masters, ask me under
Oath of Truth.//

//While you are out of your body? What would that
prove?// asked Master Corus.

//I did not believe it.// Great sadness from Master
Florian, one of Melissa's teachers at Gaeta. //I thought
Portia was grown overly suspicious in her old age—but
now I see she was right. Melissa, how could you turn
against your own people like this?//

//I haven't turned. Master Florian, make them
believe me! There is one Lord Adept in the castle, and a
boy who can control the weather. He's blind, but—//

//Oh, child, they have twisted your mind indeed if
you think Torio can control the weather,// said Master
Florian.

//Torio? No—he is working for Lord Wulfston as a
Reader. This other boy, Rolf—//

//Could they confuse her that much in one day?//
asked Master Corus.

//It must have been Jason,// Master Florian said miserably. //I trusted him completely—I never understood why Portia suspected him. Now I see what he did to this girl, a fellow Reader—his student. By the gods, I was wrong. Portia knew what she was about, making Jason chief navigator for the fleet. He had to lead us to the enemy—and with so many other Readers—better Readers—in the fleet, there was no way for him to warn them.//

//They killed him for betraying them,// said Master Corus.

//No—// Melissa began. Torio had been broadcasting to the Readers in the fleet to turn the ships, not telling Wulfston where a particular Reader was. Then she realized the implications of what Master Florian had just revealed. //Portia made Jason chief navigator—to *test* him?//

//Maybe he did warn them,// mused Master Amicus. //He was on deck—and so was this girl, on her ship. They may have meant to jump ship and join the savages. Jason may be guiding them against us at this very moment.//

//No!// Melissa protested. //No—Jason never did anything wrong. He died because Portia put him in that lead ship! She killed him!//

//We must make camp,// said Master Corus, and began to broadcast that to the other Readers.

//No!// Melissa told them. //Keep moving. They *want* you to stop! They'll have time to gather their army—//

//Ignore Melissa,// Master Amicus told the Readers. //She has betrayed us. Our enemies want us tired out when we meet. Make camp. The Readers will keep watch.//

Melissa could not believe what had happened. her consciousness drifted above the Aventine army making camp in the mud while warm, dry pallets were prepared for the Master Readers so they could leave their bodies.

If they discovered that Melissa had told the truth, what would that mean to them? To people who could callously send a fellow Reader to his death because they distrusted him. . . .

The Council of Masters had killed Jason. They—Portia foremost, but all of them who had agreed to her plan—had placed him in the forefront of that fleet expecting him to betray himself or die. But he had remained loyal. And what had it gotten him? Death, while those who were supposed to be his friends and protectors gleefully assumed his guilt.

Oh, Jason!

If only the Readers were not turning on one another, she seemed to hear his mental voice. *You will be suspect,* he had told her. *They will seek to render you harmless.* He had meant that they would marry her off, to blunt her powers. How innocent he had been—he would never have dreamed that, without evidence, they would call her traitor. But he had known they would distrust her. How could Readers, of all people, distrust one another?

She had no place to turn now. Jason was dead. Home was closed to her. The Master Readers had no interest in rescuing her—if they thought her mind had been tampered with, why did they not want to take her back to Gaeta, where sick minds could be cured? Obviously, she wasn't worth the effort!

Shock and despair slowly melted away before a new emotion: anger. How could they be so . . . vengeful? She had always looked up to the Master Readers—and now she learned that the Council of Masters would rather have a suspected Reader killed than let him prove his innocence. The true intent of this expedition was to kill Lenardo and Torio—and now Melissa would be added to the list.

What did it matter?

//Have you Read enough?//

Melissa was startled to find Torio's presence nearby

—and to feel, when he contacted her, a despair to match her own. //How long—?//

//Long enough to learn what the Masters did to your teacher. To see that they will not trust you—you, who until yesterday were dutiful and obedient. I ran away, you know, because Portia failed me without a test. There's little wonder they wouldn't trust me, Melissa— but they had no reason but their own ingrown fears to mistrust you.//

//Why did Portia fail you?//

//I was Lenardo's student and friend. I . . . knew too much. She would first have married me off, to blunt my powers, but I doubt she would have stopped there. She could have found dangerous assignments for me, as she did for Magister Jason.//

//Because you know she failed in her duty to keep the government informed of your plot.//

//How did you know that?// Torio asked.

//Jason found out in Tiberium. He knew too much, too, because his one failing was insatiable curiosity. His questions brought suspicion on him.//

//Suspicion,// said Torio. //Distrust. Readers turning against Readers, using pretense—// His bitterness cut off. //What are you going to do now, Melissa?//

//That depends on what *you* are going to do. You and your Adept friends. What are you going to do to the Aventine army?//

//Turn it back before it reaches any of Wulfston's villages. The watchers have spread the word through the whole land now—look.//

Torio directed Melissa's attention beyond the infertile sandy plain on which the army was making camp to the first village in their path. Some thirty men and boys— and a few women, she noted—were arming themselves with swords, spears, bows, and even knives and pikes. The rest of the women, with their children, were packing to flee.

//They can't hold off an army of thousands!// Melissa protested.

//They'll have plenty of help before the army gets this far. Read.//

He guided her along the road to where a troop of over a hundred people marched toward the village—ordinary people, a little better armed than the first, following a white banner carrying a black wolf's head symbol.

//But where is Lord Wulfston's *army*?// Melissa asked.

//Those people *are* the army. Every man—and every woman who has particular skill with the bow—is a member of the Lord of the Land's army. Wulfston's father began the practice, when he achieved peace in his lands. There is no need to keep the able male population in a standing army, as Drakonius did. They are home with their families most of the time—that in itself has gained Wulfston their devotion. They will fight now to save their own homes and families from an aggressor. They may be outnumbered at first, until Lenardo and Aradia's troops get here—but which side do you think will fight harder?//

//With both Adepts and Readers on your side, does it matter?//

//*My* side? Melissa, will you not join us?//

// I am tempted,// she told him honestly. //I have been betrayed—but not by the Readers with the army. How could I guide someone to kill Magister Phoebe or Master Florian?//

//I understand. Come back to your body—I think I know a way to turn the army back without killing anyone.//

//Will Lord Wulfston—?//

//Gladly. We want a peace treaty with the empire, Melissa—not a conquest.//

As they retreated toward Wulfston's castle, Melissa Read more and more troops marching southward, well-armed now, and carrying wagonloads of shields and weapons. There were more wolf's head banners, and men in leather armor decorated with the same symbol.

//Why were the best-armed men not to the south,// Melissa asked, //where you might expect an attack from the empire?//

//We had the army clustered near where the fleet meant to land, although we didn't expect to need them at all.//

//And you didn't. We never knew they were there!//

//That was the idea—to demonstrate that one Adept, with the aid of a Reader and one minor Adept, could destroy the whole fleet if he so chose. The empire's generals are stubborn—they refused to learn in one lesson, so we will have to give them another.//

They were back to Wulfston's castle now—Melissa Read the Lord Adept sitting in the armchair in Torio's room, only his impatience clearly Readable. She slipped back into her own body, sat up, stretched—and felt for the first time hampered by gross physical form after the freedom of being out of her body. She realized that she had felt no fear tonight, and no great relief upon returning. If her powers were not improving, her confidence in them was.

She Read Torio also sit up and stretch. He told Wulfston, "Lenardo and Aradia are on the way. The Aventine army has made camp as you hoped they would—Wulfston, did you *intend* them to camp on that sandy plain?"

"Not necessarily—but where else could they bed down so many people, without splitting up. . . . They could have split up, of course. They have Readers."

Torio smiled. "You're learning to think like a Reader—and I'm learning to think like an Adept. How much more water can you and Rolf pour down on that plain in the next few hours?"

"We can probably keep it raining all night, but if we attack them there, our own people would have to fight in the mud."

"I don't think rain will do it," said Torio, getting up and going over to the table piled with books and scrolls. There was a map, similar to the one on the watchtower.

Melissa left her own room and went to Torio's. //Come in, Melissa,// he told her. Wulfston looked up as she entered, but said nothing.

"What are you going to do, Torio?" she asked.

"You Read that sandy mud the army was getting bogged down in."

"I know the area," said Wulfston. "It's just sand, no good for growing anything."

"*Deep* sand," said Torio. "If we can saturate it with water—" He could Read that Melissa had no idea of what he was getting at, and Wulfston offered no indication that he understood. "Quicksand!" he explained, picking up the map. He didn't look at it, but Read it, and said in annoyance, "But there is no source of water. I didn't Read far enough in any direction while we were there—but it doesn't matter. No lakes to spill into the plain with a simple avalanche."

A *"simple" avalanche?* Melissa thought, but remained silent.

"The sea is the closest source of water," Torio was saying, "but there is no way to move that much water to the plain over the intervening hills. Working against nature that way, you'd be worn out before you'd moved a tenth of what is needed."

"Quicksand?" asked the Lord Adept. "You know how to turn ordinary sand into quicksand?"

"Of course," said Torio. "It has to be deep sand, and it has to be saturated with water, that's all. When I Read the way that sand seemed to suck at the army trying to march across it. . . . But it's a bad idea anyway. If we *could* sink the army, how would we ever get them out? We would unleash another force of nature that we couldn't control."

"Wait," said Wulfston. "We don't want to sink the whole army. Think of it this way: *pools* of quicksand here and there. Under their best equipment—what did they bring along? A catapult? We concentrate the water under it—and it sinks. A battering ram? Down it goes! What do you think of that?"

"Lord Wulfston," Melissa whispered incredulously, "Can you *do* that?" It was obvious now—they were not out to kill anyone.

"I can do it," said Wulfston, "with a little help. Torio is the only Reader I have—there's not enough time for Lenardo to get here. The Aventine army will leave that plain in the morning. With fast horses we can be there before dawn. Melissa—are you going to report our plan to the Aventine Readers, so they start moving the army now?"

"It would do me no good to try," she replied. "Torio can tell you."

"They won't trust Melissa any more than they would me," Torio said. "She tried to warn them, and they wouldn't listen. That's why I went there before coming back to report to you, Wulfston—I thought Melissa might be a good enough Reader to contact them from here. I was right, but they rejected her."

"Then come along and watch," said the Adept.

//Torio,// asked Melissa as they went downstairs, //how did you ever come to think of quicksand? I never would have.//

Fastening on his sword, he replied, //For the same reason I can use a sword and you can't: Male Readers are trained to aid the army. When we're scouting terrain, quicksand is just one of the hazards we're to Read for.//

//Lord Wulfston doesn't wear a sword,// Melissa noticed.

//If he couldn't use his powers, he would be far too weak to use a sword.//

Rolf was waiting in the great hall, with several other men and women dressed in rough, sturdy garments. "Excellent!" said Wulfston as he looked them over. "We have a plan—Torio, is anyone from the Aventine army Reading us here?"

"Not that I can tell—but you are the hardest of all of us to Read. You explain the plan."

So Wulfston gathered the others around him while Torio and Melissa hung back.

"Do not Read," Torio cautioned. "Readers are too easy to locate. Wulfston is right that one of the Readers, out of body, could have found us since you and I returned. I'm taking the risk that it will take longer, as they don't know the territory, and I checked carefully to see that no one followed you and me."

"You did? I didn't notice. Apparently you do deserve the title you claim, Torio."

"The only title I'm claiming from now on is Lord Reader," he said grimly. Melissa looked at his face—and saw that his eyes were drifting, unfocused.

"*That* was why Master Florian thought I was confused when I told him about Rolf—you're blind, too!"

"Yes, but it makes little difference to a Reader. Wulfston thinks Rolf should find it easy to learn to Read for that reason, but I've been unable to teach him —or learn Adept tricks myself."

"Is it true, then—?"

"Yes. Lenardo learned it. Aradia learned to Read. If we had *them* with us tonight, we wouldn't need all of these other people."

"What can they do?" Melissa asked. "There are over a hundred Readers with the army. They are sure to pick up our plan from these nonReaders. Why are they being told?"

"They are minor Adepts," Torio explained. "Each has one talent—Rolf can control weather, Irmy can cause fires, several of them can move light objects. They will combine their powers and be almost as effective as another Lord Adept—maybe two."

"Their powers can be combined?"

"Yes. It's not like Reading. Not one of them could do more than move a pebble alone—but together they can lift a person . . . or gather water to pool in one area."

Melissa was fascinated. Readers worked together, of course, but their talents did not combine. The best

Reader in a group could Read for the others to his own
limits of distance or discrimination—but no further.

"I wonder," she said, "what it would be like to have
both powers?"

"So do I," said Torio, "and I am going to learn if it
takes the rest of my life!"

By this time Wulfston had explained the plan to the
minor Adepts, and they were ready to leave. Both Torio
and Melissa were free to Read again—and Melissa
quickly Read why it was safe for the minor Adepts to
know what they intended to do: All were as unReadable
as Lord Wulfston.

//When an Adept is braced to use his powers,// said
Torio, //he cannot be Read—nor can he Read, Lenardo
tells me. Somewhere in that restriction there is a clue to
the use of the two powers, but we haven't yet been able
to fathom it.//

Fine, fast horses were waiting in the courtyard, and
Hilda came running out with a warm cloak for Melissa.
No one questioned her riding with them; the Lord
Adept's word was law.

All along the road, troops marched southward.
Cheers went up as the Lord Adept passed with his en-
tourage. Melissa Read other groups of armed men moving southward, taking the best routes to converge just
north of the plain where the army was camped. She felt
no touch of any Reader but Torio, but there were sure
to be Readers watching them, out of body, as they rode
along the main road.

Near midnight they stopped at an inn, where they
were given fresh horses and where hot food was laid
ready for all of them—it took only minutes for the
group of Adepts to eat meat wrapped in bread; then
they picked up cheese and fruit to take with them, and
rode swiftly along the road again. Neither Melissa nor
Torio was hungry, but they tucked apples into their
cloaks for later.

Neither Reader could Read over the distance they yet
had to cover before the watcher's reports began, lights

blinking on the hilltops and runners and riders coming to them with messages: The Aventine army was breaking camp.

"They've Read our troops converging," said Wulfston. "They *have* to attack now, while they still outnumber the army directly before them. Torio, can you—?"

"No, my lord—it is still too far. I can stop here, though, leave my body, and stay in touch with you through Melissa."

Wulfston pondered a moment, then said, "No—I want you on the scene. Watcher," he added to the rider who had brought the latest message, "see if anyone can provide us with fresh horses again—we've got to ride faster!"

They pushed their mounts—and Melissa Read something strange happening to the animals. They did not seem to feel the tiredness in their legs, the ache of their overworked lungs— //Torio—the horses?//

//Wulfston's doing it. It's not good for them—he would never mistreat an animal, though. It's probably safe enough for a few miles.//

And in a few miles there were fresh horses—but only four riding horses, probably belonging to huntsmen. The rest were farm horses, strong but slow. Still, they were better than the tired-out animals they left to be cared for by Wulfston's people—with a warning that they needed to be walked slowly for a good long time to cool off after their effort.

Now Wulfston's party became strung out along the road, the minor Adepts consigned to the farm horses losing ground as the Lord of the Land galloped toward the battlefield. Torio and Melissa kept up, Rolf close behind.

At last they reached the point at which Torio could Read the rain-drenched plain. It was not raining where they were, but sharp cold winds were beginning to assault them, and Melissa could see the clouds ahead—a neat line across the horizon. She pulled her cloak tighter, and tried to stretch her body as she rode. She was going to be very sore in a few hours—like all Readers, she had been taught to ride at the Academy, but she had seldom had occasion to travel since being assigned to Gaeta, and her muscles were far out of practice for such a long ride.

Yet she wasn't tired. It was not long after Torio could Read the Aventine army that Melissa was able to do so for herself, rather than through his senses. They were too late—the battle had begun!

Dawn was breaking, gray through the rainclouds. The first units of the Aventine army had left the plain and were engaging Wulfston's men in the fields south of the first village.

"My lord!" Torio told Wulfston, "the fighting has started! The army is moving off the plain."

"We'll drive them back," said the Adept. "Show me where to strike, Torio." Wulfston unrolled a map, and Melissa saw again the technique for guiding non-Readers.

Torio pulled his horse up beside Wulfston's. "We're here," he pointed out on the map. "Here is where the armies are clashing—and they are already well intermingled."

"We'll have to get closer," said Wulfston, studying the map with a frown. "There is no high vantage point from which I can see the fighting."

Rolf caught up with them, his horse stopping with theirs. He listened as Torio said, "There are woods along the edges of the fields here—they don't show on the map. We can ride through there, and you can see what's happening fairly well."

"Good—let's move."

The other stragglers also caught up as they left off galloping along the road to cut across newly-plowed fields and into the trees. Here it didn't matter whether the horses were fast or slow; all were slowed to a walk by the underbrush. Rolf's horse balked, and Melissa caught up its reins. "I'll guide you," she said.

"Thank you," he said, his words polite but edged with bitterness. "They won't need my talent, anyway, until we get to the plain. Unless it's to keep it raining. You're Melissa, aren't you?"

"Yes."

"Can you tell me if the rain has stopped? At least I can keep that going, to hamper the enemy until my lord can reach them."

"It's only drizzling now," Melissa told him. "The clouds you brought together last night are nearly empty."

"But the clouds themselves are moisture," he replied. "This close, I can make them give up every drop—if I knew where they were. I . . . I'm lost, Melissa. We've been twisting and turning so I don't know which direction the plain is."

She pulled his horse up beside hers, and took his hand as she had Read Wulfston do. "That direction," she said, using his hand as a pointer. "The plain begins about four miles from here, and extends a good five miles."

"Thank you." He concentrated. She Read the clouds draw together again from the wide configuration they had scattered into during the night. The rain turned to a steady downpour.

"I told you where the plain was," she said. "How did you know where the *clouds* were?"

"I don't know. I mean, I always *know* where there are clouds, within a few miles, anyway. There's something about the air—I can't really describe it."

"Then why couldn't you have found your way just now by . . . feeling for that something that tells you where the clouds are?" She urged her horse forward, leading Rolf again.

"I . . . never thought of it," he replied. "But ordinarily it wouldn't help anyway—clouds move all the time. Just knowing where there are some clouds won't usually tell me where *I* am."

"But it will this morning. Keep focusing on those clouds."

"Focusing?"

It was a Reader's term. "Keep your attention on them. We're still twisting and turning—but are you lost now?"

"No," he said in wonder. "Thank you, Melissa!"

What she had used was a simple technique for teaching young Readers to sense the shape of the world about them—using whatever they found easiest to Read to locate other things.

Was Rolf Reading? He didn't feel like a Reader—but then he had no experience in verbalizing thoughts or other techniques usually taught to Readers as children. She had never heard of a Reader's being discovered through his ability to sense objects—but children almost always had that sense already when they were discovered, or developed it within a few weeks. It just wasn't very dramatic; even children whose parents were Readers were usually discovered when they answered an unspoken thought, or responded to somebody else's pain.

//Rolf!// she tried, projecting at the strongest level. He did not respond.

//It's no use,// came Torio's mental assurance. //I've *tried*, Melissa. He can't Read.//

Maybe you pushed him too hard, she thought, carefully not projecting to Torio. *And being blind, Rolf wants to Read so badly that he can't believe he can do it.* It was a common stumbling block, desire so strong that it produced frustration, while the frustration in turn prevented the budding Reader from recognizing when he *did* make progress.

Carefully avoiding the mention of Reading, Melissa asked, "What can you sense besides clouds?"

"Water," he replied. "Clouds *are* water, you know. I can go swimming and find my way to shore, because shore is where the water stops—and right this moment is the first time I've ever realized that that is how I do it. I can cause the air to move, to create winds—but again it has to do with water. Warm air carries more moisture; bring warm and cold together to get wind. Lord Wulfston has taught me a great deal about using my talent without wearing myself out—I'll never have his strength. But my single talent can be useful.''

"It certainly *is*," said Melissa. "Have you ever thought of using your sense of where moisture is to get around better?"

"I don't understand. Any blind person can hear or smell where the ocean is—but all but Torio will fall over knee-high rocks trying to get there."

"You do not sense the rocks because they contain no water?"

"Perhaps. I never thought about it."

"Do you bump into people, Rolf?"

"They usually move out of my way."

"But do you *ever*? If you come up behind someone?"

He pondered that. "No . . . I don't think I have for a long time. I fall over everything else, though."

"Dogs, cats, chickens?"

"Melissa, what are you really asking?"

"People and animals are mostly water—warm water. Have you tried sensing them that way?"

"Not deliberately," he replied. "I'll try it. Thank you, Melissa." He fell silent. Again Melissa tried to Read him, and again found nothing to suggest he was Reading. But what could his "sensing" be if not Reading?

The sounds of battle could be heard through the trees now; it was full daylight of an overcast day, but it had not rained where the two armies clashed, and dust rose to obscure the scene as they reached the edge of the woods and tried to peer into the melee.

Melissa and Torio together Read the intertwined armies—but new troops were coming in from the north to aid Wulfston's people, while to the south the Aventine army was bogged down in mud, making very slow progress across the sodden plain.

Wulfston dismounted and stood at the edge of the
woods as Torio described the battle. He held another
map now—no, Melissa Read, not a map. A wax tablet
scored into squares, which became the map of any area
a Reader was Reading for him. Melissa Read in fascina-
tion as Torio pointed to sections of the tablet, and they
became inscribed as he described them—woods, field,
edge of the plain, advancing troops. "But right through
this area," he said, running a finger down the center of
the grid, "both armies are fighting. If you throw thunderbolts in there, you're as likely to hit your own people
as the enemy."

"How many people?"

"Perhaps a hundred on each side—and both sides are
inflicting heavy casualties."

"We've got to stop it," said Wulfston. "I had hoped
to be here before they engaged. Now how do we—? I
have it! Jara! Mik! Come here. You have the power to
put people to sleep."

"Yes, my lord," almost in chorus, as the two minor
Adepts left their horses and joined the Lord of the
Land.

"We're going to put to sleep all the soldiers fighting
in this area—it doesn't matter which side they're on."
He handed the wax table to Torio, and the three Adepts
joined hands and concentrated. Melissa Read the effect—raised spears fell from limp fingers; swords clat-
tered to the ground; men crumpled and lay as they fell,
deeply asleep and totally helpless. The dust slowly settled over them.

"Now let's drive the Aventines back into the mud!"
cried Wulfston, mounting his horse and galloping
southeast. The rest of his party quickly followed.

A fresh contingent of Aventine soldiers were marching toward the scene of battle. Their Reader reported
what had happened ahead in dismay—and then, "Riders
coming toward us—I can't Read most of them—!"

A sheet of flame leaped out of the ground just in

front of the first rank of soldiers. They sprang back by reflex, bumping into the troops behind them.

But these were seasoned soldiers—their leader was shouting orders already. Archers stood and fired over the heads of the front ranks, toward the small band of riders—but the arrows were stopped as if they had hit a wall a few paces before the advancing band of riders.

Both Torio and Melissa told the Aventine Reader, //You can't fight us. Turn back. No one will be harmed if you will surrender.//

But of course at this point it was hopeless to ask for surrender. The army tried to keep coming, but again a wall of flame shot up before them. By now they were so close that Wulfston could shout across the gap between them, "Surrender now—or turn around and go home. We are not going to allow you to advance farther into our lands."

"Go on, Savage!" answered the Aventine officer, "use your tricks! You can only last so long—and then our army will take yours!"

"Keep that up, and soon you won't *have* an army!" Wulfston threatened, moving forward step by step. Several soldiers aimed their spears at him—but the wooden shafts of the weapons burst into flame in their hands!

Then flames were everywhere—spear handles, bows, arrow shafts, the wooden supply wagon at the rear of the troop—except for swords and knives, they were suddenly weaponless. And then men were screaming in pain and casting their swords and knives away—Melissa Read that they had become red hot!

That was enough—the young officer had the sense to order retreat before he had a rout to explain to his commander. They retreated with astonishing order—Melissa thought that under such circumstances, she would have fled at a dead run.

To the rear of the retreating troops, another unit was just dragging itself out of the mud onto the grass that provided firm footing. Half the men were trying to haul along a heavily-loaded supply wagon, its wheels mired to the hubs. They were out from under the rain here—Wulfston stopped where the scene came into view, concentrated . . . the sodden wagon covering peeled back, revealing food and weapons kept dry—which now burst into flame. The men leaped back by instinct. Melissa Read the soggy ground under the wagon suddenly become saturated—just in that spot, as the mud the men stood on became firmer, its accumulation of water gone elsewhere.

The flaming wagon sank, slowly but inexorably—in moments the last sparks sputtered out under the soupy mud.

"Excellent!" said Wulfston. "Did everyone see that? We want to sink weapons and supplies, *not people*! Fire talents, light anything dry. Water talents, encourage currents in the mud, and then concentrate the water under weapons and supply wagons. Jara and Mik—any Reader you see, put to sleep. Anybody in a white tunic. Make sure that none of you get far from someone who can deflect weapons."

While all this was going on, the Adepts were casually turning away a rain of spears and arrows—the Aventine army was not going to let itself be taken by a dozen savages! At least not without fighting back.

"Torio," Wulfston continued, "take Rolf with you and circle to the east—I'll take Melissa to the west. Keep in touch. Rolf, scatter those clouds before you do anything else—we don't want the rain anymore. It'll put out our fires. All right—form groups and spread out."

Melissa was not sure whether Wulfston took her with him because he trusted her, or because he did not. She was safe by his side, his skills easily turning away anything the army threw at them. But how long could he keep it up?

As if he Read her question, the Adept told her, "I can deflect arrows all day—but not if I must do really heavy work as well. Stay in touch with Torio and Rolf, Melissa. Rolf has more strength than any of my other water talents, but he's very limited compared to me. What I need is another fully-empowered Adept on the other side of this field—not a single-talented boy not yet come into his full powers. I wish my sister were here—but my father taught me long ago to work with what I have, not what I wish."

Both surprised and pleased by his openness, Melissa said, "Neither Torio nor I have reached our full potential yet, either."

"Nor I," he replied, "but I'm closer than you are—and you and Torio are what I have to work with."

"There are Adepts with greater powers than yours?" she asked.

"You should have seen my father in his prime. You *will* see my sister. Now, Melissa, show me where to concentrate the waters to do the most damage to weaponry . . . and morale."

They were out in the muddy plain themselves now, their horses slogging along at a slow but steady pace. Wulfston handed Melissa the wax tablet—and she saw that it was blank again, only the grid lines scoring it.

"That way," she pointed, "there is a catapult. They're having a terrible time with it, trying to get logs under it front to back, like a sledge."

"Show me the distance on the grid," said Wulfston. "If we are here, and this line is the edge of the army we can see from here, where is the catapult?"

As she showed him, the wax took on the impressions of everything she told him. "Are the men away from the machine?" he asked.

"Yes—they've got ropes on it and are hauling now."

"They're not going to get far."

Wulfston stared at the grid, concentrated—and Melissa Read the waters within the mud concentrate under the catapult. But it didn't sink—it moved forward more easily. The men found great purchase in the dryer ground.

"Lord Wulfston," Melissa said, "I'm afraid that was an error."

He stopped concentrating—the waters resumed their former configuration, and the catapult was bogged down again. "What happened?" he asked.

"The catapult is wood. So are the logs. It . . . floated."

He laughed. "My error, too. I should have thought of that. Find me something that will sink."

So Melissa Read for weapon racks carrying heavy swords and metal shields—found one still set up while a section of the army prepared to move out, and pointed it out to Wulfston. It began to sink—and she recognized another error, much more serious than the first. "Lord Wulfston! Stop! Soldiers are running into the quicksand to try to save their weapons!"

She Read more widely—and found the same thing happening in other places, where the water talents among Wulfston's minor Adepts were sinking weapons and wagons—not realizing the danger, people tried to save their weapons or supplies—and sank with them.

//It's quicksand!// Melissa projected to the army's Readers. //Read it! Don't let anyone run into it!// Torio was projecting the same message. The Readers tried—but in the uproar no one was paying attention! Fires burst out everywhere there was a dry bit of flammable material—for the rain had stopped entirely.

The sound of battle horns rang out across the plain. The army began to withdraw into a tight circle, forming a closed front against the enemy.

Wulfston's water talents had worked out a technique for creating quicksand in waves—waves of water sloshing back and forth through the field of mud, turning the ground firm one moment, treacherous the next. It was a good theory—no spot should have stayed liquid long enough to swallow anyone—but when the ground firmed people were caught. Sunk to the knees, they could not pull themselves out before the next wave surged through, sinking them farther. People panicked, struggled, were sucked in.

"Stop them!" Melissa cried. "Make them stop!"

"I can't," Wulfston replied, not yet realizing the havoc being created on the plain. Then a wave swelled beyond the boundaries of the Aventine army, turning the ground under Adept and Reader to quicksand—as their footing dissolved out from under them, their horses screamed and struggled, miring themselves. The wave receded as Wulfston gasped, "By the gods!" and concentrated on the thrashing horses. To Melissa's astonishment they became calm at once. The firm sand receded slightly from about their legs, and the animals climbed out. Melissa and Wulfston rode for the safety of the higher ground at the edge of the sandy plain.

"You're an Adept!" Melissa shouted at Wulfston. "Make them stop! People will die!"

On the other side of the plain, Torio and Rolf were in the same trouble—but Rolf was not a Lord Adept. While he tried to keep the water away, their already bogged-down horses struggled in terror. //Melissa—tell Wulfston it's happening again! We're killing them!// Torio projected.

//He knows,// she told him. "Lord Wulfston—Torio and Rolf—"

But Wulfston was concentrating on damping the waves the minor Adepts were creating. "Time the waves for me, Melissa—I can only do this for a short time. Find the water talents. I've got to stop them!"

Trying to divide her attention and Read for the minor Adepts at the same time that she was counting the waves of water sloshing slowly through the mud, Melissa felt as if her mind were being torn apart. Perhaps a Master Reader could do such a thing—but there was no Master Reader to do it! She counted the waves aloud, showing Wulfston on the tablet how they flowed. When he seemed to have one under control, she read the periphery of the field, searching for the minor Adepts creating the havoc—unReadable because they were using their powers!

Finally it occurred to her to trace the waves to their source. "There they are!" she cried, pointing to the grid map as she located the minor talents physically. Wulfston, tense and panting with effort, looked where she was pointing—and Melissa Read the group of water talents slump to the sand, asleep.

Only now could she remember that Torio and Rolf were in trouble. She found Torio—on foot, his horse stuck firmly in sand up to its withers. Rolf's horse had apparently gotten free, and carried the boy far away from Torio—yes, there he was, she Read with Torio, who was Reading his charge and following as fast as he could.

Rolf hauled on the reins, but his frightened horse refused to stop, pounding on until the muddy sand began to give way beneath its hoofs again—whereupon it halted in terror, catapulting Rolf over its head, into a pool of quicksand.

"Rolf!" Melissa cried idiotically—he was nearly two miles away from her. "Wulfston—help him!"

"How?" he asked, and she heard the fatigue in his voice. "Where is he?"

She grabbed the grid and tried to show him—but the configuration of the army they had been using to gauge his efforts had changed drastically. As she frantically tried to redefine the landmarks, Rolf was struggling and sinking!

Torio was running toward Rolf, but the mud dragged at his feet. Rolf, Readable now in panic, was completely disoriented. Some moment of logic came to him, though —for he became unReadable as the water receded from him, leaving him sunk to the chest in firm sand.

Melissa breathed a sigh of relief. Now he could just wait until Torio came to dig him out. But Rolf became Readable, tired and frightened—and the water came sloshing back as fast as he has pushed it away, to engulf him. He began to sink again. Torio was still too far away—and he had no rope, no tree limb, nothing with which to pull the boy out. And no Adept talent with which to save him.

Both Melissa and Torio could Read that Rolf could

save himself if he could reach the edge of the pool—the place where his horse had stopped and thrown him. He could hang on there and wait for Torio—maybe he could even climb out. But Rolf was lost. He did not know one direction from another. //Torio—shout to him!// Melissa told the young Reader.

//I have been—he can't hear me yet!//

Torio was wide open; through his ears Melissa could hear the din of the army, the horns, the shouting—he would have to be right on top of Rolf before the boy could hear him—and he was still several minutes away.

//Tell Rolf to use his powers!// Melissa said. //He can sense where the dry sand is—and he can cause the water to push him in that direction!//

But Torio could tell Rolf nothing at that moment—the nearby soldiers had spotted him running across the sand, and a volley of arrows whistled toward him. There was no Adept to protect him! He dived and rolled, miraculously coming up with no harm done except a covering of mud.

"Wulfston! They're shooting at Torio—and Rolf! Here!" Melissa pointed to the area on the grid map—a number of fires broke out nearby, but the archers were not touched—they were shooting again! "Here—archers!" Melissa exclaimed excitedly, pointing just to the east of where Wulfston's fires had struck. "Knock them out!"

And sure enough, the archers keeled over. //Run, Torio!// Melissa urged, but she could see that he would be too late.

//Rolf!// Melissa projected helplessly, //find the dry sand! The shore! Remember what you told me! Torio's coming to help you. Push the water away—Rolf!//

But Rolf was exhausted. His struggles had become feeble. He could barely hold his head above the mud that was sucking him down, down. . . .

Chapter Six

Torio found his feet again, struggling through the treacherous sand toward Rolf. The boy had inadvertently created his own trap, shoving the water away from him in a wave that of course came flooding back the moment he let go. Working against nature, Wulfston called it—the worst mistake an Adept could make, wearing out his strength instead of finding a way to accomplish what he wanted by making natural forces work *for* him.

"Rolf! Make it push you *this* way!" Torio shouted—but the boy still could not hear him over the din.

From the other side of the muddy plain, Melissa was trying to pinpoint one struggling boy for Wulfston, but the target was too small—he dared not shove the water at random, lest he wash it right over Rolf instead of away from him.

Meanwhile, Melissa kept up her hopeless broadcast to Rolf, //Don't give up! Torio's coming! Use your powers, Rolf—find the shore! The shore!//

Rolf managed to raise his arms to the surface of the quicksand—but the movement drove him farther under. Torio could feel his determination, overlaid with deep fatigue. Rolf would not give up, but he had little strength left.

The water was starting to distribute through the sand

naturally, now that no one was manipulating it. If Rolf could just stay afloat for a few more minutes, he would be in ordinary mud, not quicksand.

Rolf heaved himself around, facing Torio, but sinking another handspan in the process. "Hold still! I'm coming!" Torio shouted.

Rolf must have heard him this time—he became unReadable as he made one last effort. A feeble wave lifted him toward the dryer sand—flung him with arms and shoulders on the safe purchase, and then retreated before turning that dry sand to treacherous mud.

Torio pounded up, grabbed Rolf's hands, and tugged. Neither cared about the sand scraping their skin—Torio heaved with all his strength, Rolf almost a dead weight in his exhaustion. But finally he was free.

"You're all right," said Torio, breathing a silent prayer of thanks to all the gods that at least this time the boy placed in his charge was not hurt.

"Thank you," Rolf whispered, gasping for breath after his exertions. "Where's Melissa?"

"Melissa? With Wulfston."

"No. She was here, with you. I heard her. You were both shouting at me."

Too astonished to try to persuade Rolf of what he could hardly believe himself, Torio said, "Yes, you heard her, Rolf, but she's not here now. You've got to rest."

"Yes . . . rest," Rolf murmured, on the edge of the Adepts' deep recovery sleep.

Torio Read Melissa already anticipating his dilemma. "Torio's got Rolf out, Lord Wulfston—but Rolf is too tired to move. What should Torio do?"

"What's happening where they are?"

Torio Read with Melissa, dreading what he would find. He and Rolf were within easy range of the Aventine army, but the archers were still unconscious, and everyone else was busy digging out of the clinging mud—no longer quicksand. The surging waves had finally worn themselves out.

"Torio, can you carry Rolf?" Wulfston asked through Melissa.

When Torio tried to lift him, Rolf fought off his tiredness to insist, "I can walk . . . if you help." And, leaning heavily on Torio, he did. Rolf's horse hadn't gone far. Torio heaved the exhausted boy into the saddle, then climbed up behind him. Rolf leaned back against Torio and allowed himself to pass out.

Through Melissa, Wulfston directed Torio to ride to the group of unconscious water talents, and wake them. "Lord Wulfston's apologies," he told them. "He had no other way to stop you when you became *too* effective."

While this was going on, the last of the clouds drifted away, and the sun warmed the scene: a mud-covered army of thousands, immobilized by a dozen savages.

Wulfston and Melissa rode back to where the one true battle had taken place, and Wulfston's army marched onto the plain, dividing into two columns to surround the Aventines. No one approached closely. No one flung a spear or shot an arrow. The mired-down enemy were simply allowed to see a seemingly endless parade of armed men slowly surrounding them, while their Readers Read more and more troops marching in from the north, to the limit of their range.

Torio Read the dismay among the Aventine troops. Most of their weapons were gone, burnt up or sunk beneath the sand. They were soaked, mud-covered, and exhausted. Before them were fresh, well-armed soldiers . . . and if they attempted to fight them, might not the ground beneath their feet start swallowing them up again?

While the Readers reported to the officers, each unit was taking a head count . . . and discovering no fatalities! There were injuries, but no one had been killed except some who had gone into that first conventional skirmish.

Torio's heart swelled as he Read the news. //Melissa! Tell Wulfston this time we got it right! Nobody died!//

He felt Melissa's joy as she told Wulfston. Then the Lord Adept had her contact the Readers, and inform them that he would meet with the leaders of their army under a flag of truce. Torio, meanwhile, found a safe resting place for Rolf with some of the other minor Adepts, and joined Melissa at Wulfston's side.

There was suspicion as the generals marched forward, surrounded by as many of their men as could locate arms, but the officers were themselves unarmed. So were the Master Readers, Amicus and Corus, who accompanied them.

Commander of the entire army was Verinus, a tall, straight man approaching sixty, with dark eyes looking firmly at Wulfston as if defying him to attack. Mudsmeared he might be, but he wore full armor, including his helmet with its caked plume, and walked tall.

He was announced to Lord Wulfston, and then stepped forward to demand, "What truce do you offer us?"

"I am Lord Wulfston, whose lands you have invaded. I offer you hospitality. Move your people out of the mud onto the meadows, and rest for a time. Our people are already healing those who were injured in the battle this morning, but I regret to tell you that eighteen of your men were killed. Their bodies will be returned to you for whatever funeral rites you desire.

"In two days' time you will leave my lands. Your ships are at anchor some five miles to the southwest of this plain. You will board them and return to your empire."

Verinus blinked in amazement. When Wulfston said no more, he asked, "What do you demand of us in return?"

"Two things. First, you will carry a message to your Emperor: We will brook no more attacks across our borders. We are tired of war, but the next time you force us to defend ourselves we will not take such care merely to disarm you and let you live. Tell your Emperor to keep his army at home, and in return we will keep ours in our lands.

"Second, I have in my castle nearly fifty of your men who survived the shipwreck. My allies and I planned to trade these people later for a meeting with your Emperor. However, except for one ship's captain and two officers of your army, they are common soldiers and sailors, taking up space in my dungeons because I have no place else to keep them. Such a large number of hostages are a nuisance. I will trade them for two or three more . . . valuable ones."

Verinus said, "I will gladly pay for the release of my men with my own freedom, and I am sure my officers—"

"No," Wulfston interrupted him, "you are of no use to me. Your Readers may have reported that we had . . . some small difficulty in communicating while we were immobilizing your army. The severe scarcity on this side of the border is of Readers. I will take these two." He pointed to the Masters who had accompanied the Commander.

//Torio! Stop him!// Melissa warned. //He will be planting spies in his own castle!//

//Like you?// he replied cheerfully. //Wulfston knows what he's doing, Melissa. If these Readers report the truth, we will soon have that peace treaty!//

Masters Amicus and Corus were both fighting fear. "Commander Verinus," said Amicus, "the girl, Melissa, has been with these people only since she was washed overboard in the storm. Within a single day they twisted her mind and made her work for them. If you order it, Commander, I will stay—but you must warn the Council of Masters that nothing reported by hostage Readers is to be accepted as true."

Torio Read the man's horror increasing as he spoke.

He understood the blind terror of losing control of his own mind, and sought to reassure him. //Masters, you will find out quickly enough: No one will tamper with your minds.//

Oblivious to the silent communication, Wulfston said, "You must do any work I ask of you, Master Readers—with the exception of anything harmful to your empire."

"We will have no choice but to obey you," Master Corus said stiffly, refusing to expose his deep fear to this nonReader.

"Only if you give me your word, and only in matters in which I require your skills. No one will prevent your communicating with your homeland—and, the more quickly a meeting can be arranged with your Emperor, the more quickly you will go home."

//Go home as spies!// Master Corus realized.

//Never,// Master Amicus told him, and calm descended on both men.

It was Melissa who recognized the meaning of their sudden change in attitude. She stepped up beside Wulfston and whispered, "They feel just the way Magister Jason did when he decided to die rather than let you take him. They will find a way to kill themselves before they ever reach your castle."

"Suicide." Wulfston's dark skin blanched to gray at the thought—he might have been born Aventine, but he was savage through and through in his code of beliefs. For a savage, suicide was the ultimate defeat, the most dishonorable way to die. In the empire, however, it was considered an acceptable way to escape dishonor—or the forced action against their beliefs that these men feared.

"Your word, Master Readers, that you will not attempt to take your own lives. Torio—Melissa—what oath will bind them unconditionally?"

"By the Readers' Code," they chorused. "Make

them swear on their Oaths," added Torio. "No Master Reader would break a vow sworn on his Master's Oath."

The Readers turned to appeal to Verinus, but he said, "You have seen what they can do. For some reason they are letting us escape with our lives. What revenge will they take if we refuse their single demand?"

Despairing, the two Readers swore, and the parties separated. Wulfston was fighting deep tiredness; he would have stopped to sleep except that the watchers reported that Lenardo and Aradia had crossed into his lands, and were headed in the direction of the battle. "Torio—hasn't Lenardo Read us?" he asked. "Doesn't he know the battle is over?"

//Yes, I do,// Lenardo replied, and Melissa started. //I've been watching your arrangements, and since I agree with everything, I did not wish to interfere.//

Torio relayed to Wulfston, who said, "I hope I did the right thing in taking Readers."

//You certainly did no harm, and it may possibly do some good. I watched most of the . . . battle . . . if you want to call it that. Who thought of quicksand?//

//I did,// Torio told him. //It almost went wrong again—//

//But it didn't. You kept it under control. A good idea, Torio—I wish I'd thought of it.//

The captured Master Readers were trying to locate Lenardo—but he was far out of their range. What they could not know was that he was not out of body; since becoming a savage lord he had increased his range to unheard-of distances, and learned the trick of Reading without being Read. He had some other interesting abilities, too—but it would be best if Masters Amicus and Corus did not find out about them for the time being.

It was arranged that Lenardo and Aradia would divert to Wulfston's castle with their small train, and send the rest of their army home. Wulfston's army was

to care for the Aventine soldiers—and incidentally
guard against their attacking their captors. Supply
wagons were unloaded, and Wulfston commandeered
three to take him and the minor Adept talents home—
those who had not already collapsed were practically
asleep on their feet. Someone had dug Torio's horse out
of the mud, but he hadn't yet found out where it had
been taken. He was still riding Rolf's horse. The boy's
walking stick hung from the saddle. Torio laid it beside
the sleeping boy on one of the wagons, hoping he would
never need it again.

With Wulfston sound asleep, Torio was left in com-
mand. The trip home would take much longer than the
journey to the battlefield. He sent the wagons ahead,
and took Melissa and the other Readers to the field
hospital where the healers worked over those wounded
in the single battle.

Hevert, the best healer in Wulfston's land, had things
well under control when they arrived. Healing was one
of the many things the empire would benefit from if
they ever made peace with the savages. The four
Readers Read the fact that the wounded were healing
without medication, purely through the efforts of the
healers.

"My lord," Hevert said to Torio, "will you please
Read two injuries for me? This man seems to be
bleeding inside. I cannot stop it."

The man's ribcage had been crushed. Perhaps after he
had fallen from a lesser wound, one of the heavy supply
wagons had rolled over him. Whatever the cause, he was
critically injured.

The splintered ribs had been pulled back into place,
relieving pressure on lungs and heart, but the man's skin
appeared yellow—no color beneath his outdoor tan. His
lips were blue.

"Is it his spleen?" Hevert asked. "I worked on
that—"

"Not his spleen," Melissa answered. "You missed a

splinter of rib from his back. It's piercing his right lung.
Where is your surgery? We must—''

"Surgery?" Hevert was speaking hesitant Aventine
for Torio's benefit; this was obviously not a familiar
word. "You mean—cut into him? He is injured enough
already. Tell me where the rib is. I will move it back into
place."

Melissa understood at once—when Hevert handed
her a chart of the bones of the human body, she quickly
pointed out the rib that was broken. Hevert studied the
chart, knelt down and gently felt the ribs of the injured
man with his fingers, counting . . . and as he concentrated, the splinter of rib dislodged from the man's lung
and slid back into its proper place.

"He's bleeding more heavily!" Melissa said. "He'll
drown in his own blood!''

But in moments Hevert had the bleeding under control. When Melissa said, "That's it. He's healing," he
sat back on his heels, breathing heavily.

"Thank you, my lady," Hevert said. "You are as
good as Lord Torio at pointing out injuries."

"She's better," said Torio. "She's had medical training I haven't. Thank you, Melissa. Hevert, you said you
had another critical patient?''

"Not critical," replied the healer. "He'll live, but I
don't know if I've done the right thing." He got up, and
led them to another pallet where a man—hardly more
than a boy—in an Aventine tunic lay. His right arm
showed an ugly cut through the bicep. The bone had
been sliced through, although it was already beginning
to heal. Muscles and blood vessels were reunited—he
would keep his arm.

Torio could say nothing; he was too powerfully reminded of discovering Decius with a similar wound—although to the thigh rather than the upper arm. In the
empire, there had been nothing their best healers could
do but amputate.

If only we had had such powers!

"Sorcery!" said Master Corus.

"He will have his arm," Hevert said, ignoring the comment, "but will it do him any good? Will it be paralyzed, my lord, my lady?"

Torio said, "Melissa, I can do the fine discernment to Read the nerves—but I have not had medical training you have. I cannot tell whether they have been reunited in the proper patterns."

Melissa looked to the two Master Readers. "Help me, please, Masters."

"Aid you in abetting Adept sorcery?" asked Master Amicus.

"This man is an Aventine citizen," Melissa answered. "Our own healers could not have saved his arm at all—I certainly could not have, and I am a skilled surgeon. Think of his whole life ahead. Will he be left with an unfeeling, unmoving, useless arm? I will do my best—but I am only a Reader in training. You are Master Readers. You can Read deeper into those fine nerves than either Torio or I could."

"Which is the true betrayal," Torio asked, picking up something of the turmoil in the two Master Readers' minds, "aiding a healer to restore an Aventine soldier to full function, or denying health to a man who might have served again to protect his country, and preventing his even working to his full capacity as a citizen?"

The Master Readers looked at one another, and nodded. "We will help."

Hevert had successfully united most of the major nerve fibers—the ones that had shown in the cut flesh. But there were others, not easily seen, that he had missed. When the Readers were finished, though, the boy on the pallet had an arm that would heal to full function, as good as it had ever been. Through it all, he remained in healing sleep. Torio wondered if he would ever know that he had a savage healer and at least one renegade Reader to thank for a healthy arm.

To be sure that Hevert and the other healers had

missed nothing, the Readers Read the other injured men. "A fine job, Hevert," Torio said when they had finished. "I will report to Lord Wulfston that you have done well. Even the most badly injured will be ready to be moved by the time the men from the castle join them."

"Thank you, my lord."

Some of the men who had been less severely injured were waking, the Aventines confused, the savages used to such rapid healing. They got up and stretched, testing their bodies, and headed out to the food line, almost as hungry for food as to find out what had happened while they were in healing sleep. Torio and Melissa were also hungry; the two Master Readers joined them, although they ate little and said less, merely absorbing the peculiar scene as the savages made certain that the enemies who had attacked them were helped off the muddy plain and shown the small river where they could wash, then were fed and given places to rest.

Torio Read Melissa Reading for her friends among the Readers at the back of the army—they were still hours from moving off the plain, although progress was easier now as the sun dried the mud to a firmer surface.

//Magister Phoebe!// Melissa pleaded, //I know you can hear me!//

But no Reader would respond. Torio caught a thought—and he was sure Melissa did, too—*We must think of them as being dead*. There were tears behind the thought, and Melissa forced back her own tears, choking on her bread and cheese. She gulped some wine, and looked at Masters Amicus and Corus. "It's no use, child," Master Amicus said aloud. "We are cut off from them forever. I know you don't understand that it's better that way. I don't suppose I will, tomorrow."

Before they left the scene, Torio went to wash off himself—much of the exterior mud he had picked up rescuing Rolf had dried and brushed off, but sand had worked its way under his clothes, chafing him. Shivering, he stripped and washed out his clothes. It was spring, but not really warm enough to be comfortable naked. His silk shirt was almost dry, if badly wrinkled, by the time he had washed all the sand from his hair, brushed his tabard, and scraped his boots. Then he cleaned his sword—Lenardo's sword, originally. There had been no time for Torio to return for his the night they escaped from the empire . . . and now Lenardo no longer needed conventional weapons.

Torio's hose and undergarments were still soggy—he didn't really want to climb back into them, but he had nothing else to wear. Wishing for the thousandth time that he had some Adept talent, he shook out the garments, but succeeded only in spraying drops of water on himself.

"Let me help, me lord," said a savage soldier standing guard—and the water ran off the clothes as if they had been made of duck's feathers.

"Thank you," said Torio. "Your help is appreciated . . . ?"

"Huber, me lord."

"Thank you, Huber. I will remember your kindness."

Huber, a grizzled soldier who must have seen many a battle over the years, gave a gap-toothed grin. "And I'll remember this day, me lord, them empire soldiers stuck in the bog—! Things has changed since you Readers come. My family's got enough to eat, 'n' we're safe from attack by sea or land—hardly have to fight at all. You got no need to thank your people, me lord, for what little favors we can do you."

Warmed by the encounter, Torio pulled on his clothes and joined Melissa and the Master Readers again.

Horses were waiting when they were ready to ride. In a few hours they caught up with the wagons—and joined the Adepts on the pallets in them, for it was almost sunset, and Torio and Melissa had had no sleep the previous night, the Master Readers very little.

Torio woke once as the wagon stopped for a change of horses. The smell of roast meat filled the air, and the Adepts all got up to eat. Torio rolled over, covered himself with someone's abandoned cloak, and didn't wake again until dawn. Everybody was waking and stretching. Master Corus, who was in Torio's wagon, sat up and looked around glumly, not Reading.

"We'll be home within the hour," said Torio.

"You truly think you are at home here?"

"I'm sorry—you're here under protest, but you won't be mistreated. You haven't been so far, have you?"

"No. Several times during the night I thought of climbing out of the wagon—everyone was so sound asleep, and I don't think the driver would have noticed. But I thought, if you don't think it's necessary to bind us or guard us, you do not think we could escape if we tried."

"You're right," said Torio. "We have enough Readers to find you very quickly—but even if we had none, the watchers would find you. Ask Lord Lenardo to tell you about the time he tried to escape from Lady Aradia's castle."

"*Lord* Lenardo. We have heard strange tales about this renegade who now styles himself a savage lord."

"He *is* a savage lord, and so am I," Torio told him. "Here titles are earned according to one's powers, not one's politics."

"Oh, yes," said Master Corus, "I have heard that you believe you were mistreated by the Council of Masters."

"Not the Council. *You* had nothing to do with the decision, did you? I was never tested. Portia simply decided I was a failure—because I am Lenardo's friend."

"Portia does not base her decisions on such arbitrary matters. She refused you testing because you were not qualified."

"Oh? Would you care to test me, Master Corus? You are afraid even to open to Reading this morning. Why? You Read me yesterday."

The Master Reader was not much older than Lenardo, mid-thirties, Torio judged, "looking" at him for the first time. His sandy hair was receding, his fair skin sun- and wind-burned from the ocean voyage. His face was unprepossessing, eyes watery blue, nose and chin not particularly strong. Not the face of a man of action. His feet and the hem of his black-banded tunic were dirty, but the rest of his outfit had only occasional splashes of mud. He had not been one of the near-victims of the quicksand, obviously—nor had he waded in to try to rescue others.

"What are you afraid of?" Torio probed.

"We do not know . . . how you savages make traitors out of Readers. I feel no loyalty to you, no hatred for my homeland. I do not think anything was done to me while I slept. But now both you and your Lord Adept are awake—and I do not know what you may be planning."

"Nothing!" Torio said angrily. "We *wouldn't*, even if we could—and we can't."

Master Corus stared at him. "No . . . *you* can't. You haven't had the training. But Lenardo has."

"What training?"

//Torio.// It was Melissa, who had been Reading their conversation for some time, keeping a tight grip on her emotions. //Jason told me something before he died. I didn't understand it then—he was rambling so—but he said Readers treat patients whose sickness is in the mind . . . by making them believe what the healers want them to.//

//What?//

//I don't have the training, either. I had finished my first year at Gaeta—I would have had to be examined for Magister rank before going on to learn how to cure illness of the mind. And that is why. Only Readers in the top ranks are allowed to know that it is possible—//

//Melissa—you must know: Adepts *can* implant a suggestion in a person's mind. Wulfston says it's not successful if the person strongly disagrees with the suggestion. They *can't* change someone's loyalties. But you ought to know that they can do other things—like keeping someone in a room by making him think the door won't open. But even that won't work for long if he has a strong enough motivation for getting out.//

Master Corus, still closed against Reading, had been thinking over what to tell Torio. "There is a technique to cure mind sickness. It is used only when all else has failed, to control people violent toward themselves or others. Several Readers, together, can remove ideas from the person's mind—ugly memories, desire to hurt or be hurt—and replace them with positive thoughts. Magister Readers learn the method during final medical training. Lenardo could use the technique . . . for corrupt purposes."

As he listened, Torio was Reading Corus. //Melissa . . . // he observed in astonishment, //this man is lying!//

It was supposedly not possible for a Reader of Torio's age and rank to tell if a Master Reader were not speaking the truth . . . and yet Torio felt that what Master Corus said did not ring true. //I think he's not telling the *whole* truth,// he amended, //not that what he just told me isn't true. He knows some other use this technique is being put to—a use he feels guilty about.//

Aloud he said, "You will soon meet Lenardo. You felt the strength of his mind yesterday. Consider this, Master Corus: Misusing a Reader's powers weakens them. Lenardo's powers have increased a hundredfold. How could that happen if he were using them for corrupt purposes?"

That silenced Corus, and Melissa kept her thoughts to herself for the rest of the journey, too.

Lenardo, Aradia, and Julia were waiting for them in

the courtyard of Wulfston's castle. There were hugs of greeting all around—then the new arrivals scattered to change out of the clothes they had slept in, and the minor Adepts who lived nearby went home.

Within the hour, Wulfston, Torio, Rolf, Melissa, Lenardo, Aradia, and Masters Amicus and Corus were gathered for a sumptuous meal in the great hall. Torio enjoyed Reading the Master Readers' astonishment at the amount of food consumed by Wulfston, Rolf, and the delicate-appearing Aradia. From her powers, Torio had at first imagined an amazon until he had actually "looked" at her, discovering a pale, slender woman, hair like a cloud of sea-foam, only the firm gaze of her violet eyes and the set of her chin suggesting her vast strength.

Aradia was dressed today in her favorite purple—Torio had noticed that she wore that color whenever she met new people, except upon the most formal occasions, when she favored white.

Lenardo was dressed in dark green, his tabard as richly embroidered in gold as Wulfston's. No one wore crowns to breakfast, although Julia had confined her dark curls with the gold fillet that identified her as daughter and heir to a Lord of the Land.

The Master Readers wore clean tunics from their own packs, but they had not traveled in the scarlet robes that would show their rank—and make them immediate targets for enemy arrows. Their freshly cleaned wool traveling cloaks appeared very plain by contrast with the richly dressed assembly, for even Torio and Rolf had put on their best garments—Torio was learning from Wulfston the psychological value of appearances, and Rolf always seemed to know and do what Wulfston expected of him.

Torio had considered wearing his Magister Reader's robes; he no longer doubted his right to them. However, that outfit would acknowledge his inferior rank to the Master Readers. Dressed as a savage lord, he claimed equality. Therefore he had put on shirt and hose in a reddish brown that matched his hair, with a richly-embroidered tabard of dark greenish blue. It was close to the color of his eyes, which were now clear and healthy to all outward appearance, since one of Lenardo's healers had dissolved his cataracts in the mistaken belief that that would cure his blindness.

Melissa had not put on her Reader's tunic, either, although, knowing Wulfston's staff, Torio was sure it had been cleaned, mended, and placed in her room by now. She was dressed in a light blue silk dress, with a darker blue surcoat embroidered in silver. Her dark hair was smoothed back into a coiled braid at the nape of her neck, but wisps of curl fought their way out of the confinement, making a halo about her heart-shaped face. The same exposure to sun that had given Master Corus a red nose had turned Melissa's skin golden, and sprinkled a few freckles across her nose.

She's pretty, Torio thought—the first time in his life he had ever thought that of a woman.

The two Master Readers risked Reading now, although everyone spoke aloud for the benefit of the non-Readers. Torio had not had a chance to confront Rolf about what had happened on the battlefield—but the opportunity came when Master Amicus asked, "Lord Lenardo—" Torio caught his hesitation about what title to use, and the refusal to grant him that of Master Reader, "why did you bring a child with you to what you expected to be a battle?"

Julia gave Amicus a withering look, but Lenardo replied, "Julia is an exceptionally talented Reader. We would not ordinarily expose so young a child to potential danger, but we are grievously short of Readers of any age or ability."

"However," Torio interrupted, "there is now another Reader available—one completely loyal to Lord Wulfston."

"Who?" Wulfston asked, with a puzzled glance at Melissa.

//Tell them, Rolf,// Torio broadcast at the strongest intensity.

"Tell them what?" the boy asked in total surprise.

Even Wulfston, the only one at the table who could not Read it, immediately understood what had happened. He got up, went to Rolf, pulled him out of his chair and hugged him. "It's working! Torio—how did you do it? Can you teach me now?"

"I don't understand!" Rolf protested. "I didn't do anything."

//Yes you did!// Torio replied.

//Rolf, *listen*,// Lenardo added.

//Nobody's *talking*,// Julia told him.

"But . . . how did it happen?" Rolf asked in confusion. "Torio—how did you *know*? How did you know when I didn't?"

Torio explained, telling how Rolf had insisted he had heard Melissa's voice when she was miles away, on the other side of the battlefield. "Melissa, you gave Rolf the clue, when you suggested that he orient himself by using his ability to sense water. But Wulfston, you were right about motivation: Rolf opened to Reading to save his life."

The black Adept returned to his seat, lost in thought. Then he sighed. "I am surrounded by Readers, and I cannot reach any of you." His sense of isolation was palpable.

Aradia ran to Wulfston and hugged him tightly. "You will learn, my brother—I *know* you will. It takes time, that's all. But we have three people now with both powers—that proves that more can learn."

"Why don't you just—" Master Corus began, but Master Amicus interrupted him.

"Corus—no!"

Torio, Lenardo, Melissa, and Julia were all good

enough Readers to catch Corus' unspoken words—
implant the idea that he can Read in his mind—and echo
them to Aradia and Rolf.

"What did he say?" Wulfston asked, not missing the
tension among the Readers. When they all remained
silent, he leaned forward and demanded, "*Tell* me!"

Aradia remained behind him, her arms still around
him. "That we might . . . implant in your mind the
belief that you can Read," she said gently.

Wulfston put his hands over his sister's, as if for sup-
port. It was obvious that the idea was as abhorrent to
him as to any Reader, and yet, "My sister," he said, "I
trust you. Lenardo—you are as much family as Aradia.
I will be safe in your hands."

"No!" Lenardo and Aradia spoke as one.

"Do you remember how we worked together to save
Nerius' life?" Wulfston asked. "We could have killed
him, removing the tumor from his brain—but we risked
it, and gave him back his health. I am willing to risk—"

"Father was *dying*!" Aradia said. "The worst we
could have done would have been to kill him a few
weeks sooner. You are in no danger, little brother. All
you need to get what you want is patience."

"And you do not understand the danger," added
Lenardo. "In Nerius' case we were working with a
growth of specific location and dimensions. It was hard
work to explain to you, and even harder for you to
do—but it was physical. Wulfston, you *never* know
what will happen when you tamper with a person's
mind. We could do much worse than kill you. I will not
do it, Aradia will not—and thank the gods you are a
Lord Adept whose mind no one can tamper with if you
do not will it."

A strange combination of astonishment and guilt was
radiating from Masters Amicus and Corus. //They're
right,// Master Corus said. //We should never have
allowed Portia to start—//

//Stop! Stop Reading!// Master Amicus demanded,

grasping the other man's arm.

//What difference does it make now? We can't go home. What difference if these people twist our minds, or if the Council—//

Suddenly something happened that Torio had never Read before—Master Amicus' mind was grappling somehow with Master Corus', trying to prevent his thoughts— Searing pain jabbed through him. Melissa screamed and put her hands to her head. Rolf cried out hoarsely, and Julia gave out a child's wail of pain and fear.

"Wulfston!" Lenardo gasped. "Amicus! Knock him out!"

The Master Reader slumped in his chair, and the pain subsided to a shallow throbbing. Master Corus put his face in his hands and sobbed.

Aradia was leaning heavily on Wulfston, unReadable. She pulled herself up, walked to Master Corus, and laid her hands on his head. His pain stopped entirely, but dread fear replaced it—he froze as he sat, waiting. She began to Read again. Feeling his fear, she said, "I won't hurt you. No one will force you . . . but won't you tell us what you started to? Aloud, please, so my brother can hear."

He looked up at her, then at Lenardo. "I was afraid," he said dully, "of Portia and her inner circle of Masters. At first I thought they knew best—they were all older, have been Master Readers longer than I have. But this past year I voted with them because they hold the power. Portia can influence the Emperor—she is of his family, did you know?"

"I didn't know," said Lenardo. "But it should make no difference—the Emperor, the Senate, the Readers, all work for the best interest of the empire."

"That's what I thought—I really did. For a long time. I didn't question—"

"I understand," Lenardo assured him. "I was the same, until Portia sent me into the savage lands, and I discovered that things are not always as we have been led to believe. Tell us—when did you begin to question?''

The man blushed with shame. "I didn't. I knew what they were doing, and I made no effort to stop it."

"Who is 'they' and what did they do?" asked Torio.

"What they were going to do to you," he replied. "I've Read you. You are a Magister Reader—there is no question about it. You will be a Master when your powers are fully developed. But they—Portia and her inner circle—declared you failed. They'd have married you off—"

"To blunt my powers. I know."

"Wait," said Lenardo. "I 'knew' it, too, Torio. But I am married, and my powers are not blunted. Only at first—"

"If you had been married in a proper Readers' ceremony," said Master Corus, "your powers would not have returned."

Melissa gasped, but remained silent, keeping her thoughts to herself.

"What are you saying?" asked Aradia.

"Marriage—sex—does blunt one's powers. We do not fully understand it, but it seems to have to do with . . . bodily changes, the way one's powers change at puberty, and are blunted by illness. Pregnant women always have weakened powers—temporarily. But . . . those powers could return, and even grow—under the right circumstances."

"That is the way it happens with Adepts," said Wulfston. "At least most of the time."

"Father," said Aradia. "Lilith. And Lenardo and me, although I have not yet borne a child."

"But the Council of Masters wants to retain control over all Readers," said Master Corus. "There are so many Readers who will never attain the top ranks—but who might come close over the years, close enough to threaten the political power of the Masters—"

"Readers have no political power," said Torio. "We can't hold office—we can't even own property unless we're failed."

"The Council—or at least Portia's inner circle—may not hold public office," replied Corus, "but they wield power. They know the secrets of the Senators. They find out about business deals. It's . . . the way things have always been done, I was told. I took my share. It was easy . . . and the others told me it was my right. It wasn't. It was wrong—I can see how my powers have failed from misuse. I could not hide my feelings even from Torio."

"So," said Aradia to Lenardo, "it turns out your fine, upstanding Council of Masters are no less desirous of power than Adepts are, my husband."

Lenardo nodded. "They are simply less honest about it. But it makes no difference, Aradia—"

"No difference!" cried Melissa. "No difference that my best friend has lost her powers because they twisted her mind? No difference that Portia became so afraid of Master Jason that she sent him into danger, to die? No difference that everything we've always believed in is a *lie*?!"

At her outburst, Torio started to turn to Melissa—

And was in the midst of a crowd on the steps of the Senate in Tiberium, his mind screaming with other people's rage and fear as the earth heaved beneath his feet! The tremor lifted the stone slabs used as steps, toppling him—the world spun before his eyes—while inside the Senate he Read the roof cave in! Men screamed and tried to run. Solid stone fell on them. Across the forum, a reviewing stand filled with dignitaries collapsed, throwing people into the crowd—he recognized the golden robes of the Emperor!

Pain and fear filled the air, wrath playing counterpoint as he Read, both broadcasting and shouting, "Stop! Stop it! You'll kill everyone! You're destroying the whole city! Everyone will die!"

Chapter Seven

The scene cut off as abruptly as it had begun. Melissa found herself back at Lord Wulfston's table, gripping the edge, her heart pounding in terror. She looked around, Reading. Rolf was rubbing his eyes, his fear and shock overwhelmed by the sight he had never known before. Torio pulled the boy's hands away from his face, saying, "It wasn't you, Rolf." //But what was it?//

"Tiberium!" Master Corus exclaimed. "Another earthquake—destroyed!" A bitter laugh escaped him. "Now I have no home to return to."

"Was it?" asked Aradia. "Was it real? Lenardo— has it finally happened?"

"No," he answered. "It was my vision. But you all saw it this time? That's never happened before."

Wulfston looked around at their stricken faces. "Would someone please tell me what happened?"

"The earthquake again," said Lenardo. "The destruction of Tiberium. The same vision I've been having —except that it went on a few moments longer . . . and now I know *when*!"

"Summer Festival," said Torio. "The banners, the crowds, the Emperor in the reviewing stand. More people are in Tiberium then than on any other day of the year."

"We must stop it!" said Lenardo. "Two months—only two months to ease that fault."

I hope it kills the whole Council of Masters, Melissa thought privately.

"We'll go in again," said Wulfston. "We have to go deeper into the empire—"

"And what if we set off other quakes?" asked Torio. "We're working without enough information again. What if we set up the very disaster you foresee, my lord?"

Lenardo studied Torio, and smiled ruefully. "The right question, Lord Torio. Who has suggestions?"

"Your visions have always come true, Lenardo," said Aradia.

"Yes, but not always as I interpreted them. And I have never been able to prevent one."

"What we need," said Wulfston, "is a map of the entire length of the fault—but even you can't Read all the way to the southern section, Lenardo."

"I can if I go back into the empire. With the powers I now have, I will be safe for long enough to make your map, Wulfston. This time we will have every bit of information before we begin. When we are ready, we will spread our Adept talents the length of the empire. Just before the festival, people will be traveling all up and down the main road—a few more strangers won't be noticed."

"The problem," said Wulfston, "is Readers. We can gather several hundred people with varying degrees of Adept talent—but how do we coordinate them? Torio's quicksand almost became a disaster because I could not communicate with the water talents in the midst of the action. We need several hundred Readers, as well . . . and all the Readers we have are right here in this room."

Melissa glanced at Master Corus, and the still-unconscious Master Amicus beyond him. She had the beginning of an idea . . . but she knew Amicus' loyalties were still with Portia, while Corus appeared to be willing to do whatever seemed most expedient for his own safety—hardly someone they should trust with their plans.

Wulfston followed her gaze, and asked, "Lenardo, Torio, how certain is it that the Council of Masters will indeed disregard what these hostage Readers report to them?"

"Not certain at all, concerning something they can verify—such as renegade Readers entering the empire with groups of unReadable strangers," said Lenardo. "We have made a strategic error. I suggest we keep Master Amicus asleep, put Master Corus to sleep before he has an opportunity to report to the Masters left with the army—and then take them both north to Lilith's castle and hold them there until after the Summer Festival. Even out of body, they cannot communicate over such a distance."

"You don't have to knock me out," said Master Corus. "I will go willingly." His relief was obvious.

"Why?" asked Wulfston, and Lenardo frowned as he tried to Read the man. Only his emotions were Readable.

Melissa remembered something Jason had told her. " 'When the moon devours the sun, the earth will devour Tiberium.' Master Corus doesn't want to be there when it happens."

"When the moon devours the sun," Lenardo mused. "I've heard that before. Is there—?"

"An eclipse," said Melissa, "just before Summer Festival."

"Then we know we have the timing right," said Wulfston. "Now, what about Melissa? Torio?"

Melissa let Torio Read her. He reported, "She feels betrayed, Wulfston. Her faith in the Council of Master Readers and the Aventine government has been badly shaken. Let her see what we're doing. I think she will join us."

"Very well," said Wulfston. "Lenardo, Aradia?"

"I trust Torio's instincts," said Lenardo.

"And I trust Lenardo's," Aradia added.

"Torio," said Wulfston, "keep watch on Melissa. I must prepare for the funeral this afternoon. Lady Melissa, the bodies of those who were drowned in the storm are being returned with the prisoners to the Aventine army. Our own dead are being brought here, by those closest to them. It is our custom to allow each person to be spoken of by those who loved him, before he is returned to the elements. We will keep the body of Magister Jason here, for our ceremony—if you wish to speak for him?"

"Yes, thank you . . . my lord," Melissa got out around the lump in her throat.

"Before we make any further plans, though—" Wulfston glanced toward Master Corus, and he slumped, as unconscious as Amicus. The Lord Adept called for servants to remove the two men. "Now. Aradia? Lenardo?"

"What news of Lilith?" asked Aradia.

"The watchers reached her before she had gone far enough to make it worth her while to journey all this way," Wulfston replied. "She sends us her congratulations, but has returned home."

"Rightly so," said Aradia. "We will write to her of our new plan—I do not want the watchers sending the message, lest it be read by some of our outlying neighbors. They are frightened of our strength now—but think what opportunity we would give them if they knew both Lords Adept and minor talents were out of our lands at one time!"

Lenardo smiled fondly at his wife. "Trust Aradia to think in terms of power and vulnerability. She is right—we must not let the whole world know. Fortunately, we will not be moving armies; no one need know that our lands will temporarily be left without Adept defenses."

"There are other defenses," Rolf put in. "Even a

Lord Adept's army can be delayed by storms. You will not need my kind of talent with you."

"You forget, Rolf," said Torio, "we need you as a Reader."

"But I can't—"

//Can you hear me, Rolf?// Lenardo asked.

"Yes, but—"

"No 'buts.' That's good enough to act as relay to nonReaders. Wulfston, do you think if we threw a few more of our minor Adept talents into quicksand—?"

"I'd dive in myself, if I thought it would do any good. But Rolf is a special case—if he could see, he would have known which way to direct his Adept talent, and would not have had to Read."

"But *I* didn't learn it to save my life," said Aradia.

"No—someone else's," Lenardo replied. "You heard a man scream—and you arrived in time to save him. But the witnesses claimed he never made a sound. I didn't realize you were Reading until the next day—but we must all be watching for evidence like that. We *know* it's the same talent now." He stretched out his hand, and Melissa saw on his forearm the dragon's head brand of the traitor to the Aventine Empire. He became unReadable—and the heavy candlestick slid down the table and into his hand.

Melissa gasped. They had *said* he had learned Adept powers—but this was the first time she had seen it. He turned to her, Readable once more. "Yes, Lady Melissa, it works both ways. You *can* learn Adept powers. Rolf makes the evidence undeniable: Aradia and I are not some peculiar special case. It is one talent, not two."

"Then . . . we cripple ourselves," said Melissa. "Our own beliefs destroy our powers. But why—?"

"Melissa," said Torio, "what would have happened to you in the Aventine Empire if you had shown Adept tendencies?"

"That's not what I mean," she replied. "I *know* how

things are—but I don't understand *why*. If the Empire
had Adepts, trained like Readers and loyal to their
homeland, the savages would never have been able to
hurt us. And you—why would you prevent children
from Reading?''

"I almost got killed for it," said Julia.

"It's the same question," Melissa insisted. "Why not
use both talents?"

"You can't," said Aradia, "not to their fullest. I am
not a very good Reader—not even as good as Julia—
because I will not give up my Adept powers."

"What you just saw," added Lenardo, "is the limit
of my Adept ability. But Aradia and I are adults. My
daughter sometimes accuses me of discouraging her
from learning Adept powers, but that's not true. We do
not know what could be accomplished by someone who
exercised both talents from childhood. But after you
have learned to rely on one power, you are unwilling to
compromise it. The food you eat to keep up strength for
Adept functions dulls Reading—and *using* Adept power
weakens the body, if only temporarily. Sleep and food
restore it—but in the meantime Reading is as diminished
as if you were critically ill."

"And eating the cattle fodder Lenardo prescribes for
clear Reading," Aradia supplied, "weakens the body,
making it impossible to use Adept powers to their
fullest. I feel secure when I am at the peak of physical
strength. If I allow myself to become weak, my neighbors will attack and destroy me. Even since we formed
our alliance, not a year has passed without our being attacked by other Lords Adept. That is why Adept powers
are the ones we encourage. A Reader cannot protect
himself against Adept attack."

"Or anybody else's," Melissa said softly. "The
Emperor wants Readers, because he can control them.
He couldn't control Adepts. Lord Lenardo—you are a
Master Reader. Is it . . . deliberate?"

"Is what deliberate?"

"Does the Council of Masters know that Reading and Adept powers are the same? Is all our training designed to stifle our Adept powers?"

"No," he replied. "Master Clement has been a member of the Council for many years. He would know—and when I was sent into such danger here, he would have told me. No, Melissa, I think the division took place so long ago that it has passed from memory. There are not even legends, at least none that I know of."

"And that is strange in itself," said Aradia. "We have no stories linking Reading and Adept powers either. Nothing to say how they came to be divided."

"Perhaps we will find out one day," said Lenardo. "Meanwhile, though, we must discover how to reunite them. Torio and Melissa, spend all the time you can teaching Rolf to understand what he Reads. Aradia, write that letter to Lilith. Wulfston, please excuse me—"

"We all have things to do," Wulfston said as he rose from the table. "Julia, will you please come relay for me in case the Readers need to contact me?"

As they got up, Rolf automatically picked up his stick. Torio took it from him, saying, "You don't need that."

"But even if I *am* Reading, it's not vision," Rolf protested. "That was seeing—what happened when we all perceived Lord Lenardo's vision?"

"Yes," Torio replied.

"I understood what I felt and heard, but not that—other. It frightened me. I'm not sure I want to 'see'—I don't know how to interpret it."

"I don't know if you'll ever 'see,' Rolf," Torio told him honestly. " 'Visualizing' is what Readers call it, and it's an advanced skill. It takes concentration—I don't visualize unless I have a reason for it. Right now you must learn an easy form of Reading, sensing where objects are so you won't run into them."

Melissa watched them, both blind, Torio so secure,

Rolf uncertain and awkward. Rolf was not Reading now; he clung to Torio, fearful and disoriented. "Rolf," she said, "think of what you said yesterday. The way you sense water—you can sense other things—anything. You just turned toward me—you can sense where I am."

"I heard you."

//Now you're not hearing me.//

"Yes I am. —oh." //Can I do that, too?//

//Indeed you can,// Torio told him gleefully. //That's good—try it all, Rolf. We'll help you.//

They made it a game, Torio and Melissa moving about the room, making Rolf find them. They placed furniture in his way . . . and soon he found he could sense it and walk around it. In an hour, he was negotiating a veritable obstacle course, laughing and crying at once.

"That's enough for today," Torio said at last. "Let's go up to your room, Rolf, and I'll teach you a meditation exercise. You should end each lesson by lying down for a few minutes, completely relaxed, to absorb it all."

"Yes, my lord, my lady. And . . . thank you. I never dreamed it would be possible—" He started for the door, faultlessly turning in the right direction, but automatically putting his hands out.

"Not necessary," said Torio, touching Rolf's right hand. "You lead the way now."

"Yes, my lord."

Melissa watched them go. Then she turned, shoved a chair back into place, and picked up Rolf's discarded walking stick. Holding it on the palms of her hands, she willed it to rise in the air. Nothing happened. She tried imagining it sliding off the tips of her fingers—but it didn't budge except to quiver slightly as her muscles began to twitch. *Yet I know I have the power, locked inside me.*

With a sigh, Melissa started to leave the great hall, but stopped before a display of painted shields, symbols of the savage alliance. The blue lion she did not know, and had seen no banner bearing it. Apparently it was the symbol of the Lady Lilith.

She recognized Lord Wulfston's symbol, the black wolf's head on a field of white. Next to it hung a shield made from the same pattern, but with the wolf's head white on black and facing in the opposite direction. The Lady Aradia—brother and sister had chosen symbols that showed they were indeed alike, despite outward appearances.

The last symbol was audacity itself: the red dragon's head. Lord Lenardo, of course. What courage, she thought, to turn the brand meant to mark him with dishonor into the symbol of a savage Lord of the Land! The man impressed her, not least for his ability to adapt to a whole new life. She remembered Jason scolding her for changing her mind—but Jason had died rather than risk the *possibility* of change.

These people lived with change—they were actively attempting to change the world for the better, and changing themselves to do so. Unstifled by the rules of the Academy, even their Reading powers blossomed beyond the norm. It was shameful how Melissa's powers lagged behind Torio's. Julia was years beyond what would have been expected in the empire, and as for Lenardo—how had he Read the field of quicksand from a distance at which none of the Master Readers could locate him?

Curiously, without malicious intent, Melissa Read for Lenardo. He and Aradia were in one of the rooms upstairs, Lenardo seated in an armchair, relaxed, Aradia just fastening something over her hair.

But it was Lenardo who had provoked Melissa's curiosity . . . and she could not Read anything other than where he was. "Aradia," he said suddenly, "please go down to the great hall and find Melissa. Explain the funeral preparations to her."

Melissa burned with embarrassment at invading their

privacy, but Lenardo's attention was elsewhere. Aradia came downstairs, Reading, but unable to distinguish Melissa until she was halfway down the stairs. No, she was not a very good Reader, but she *was* one, and an Adept, too.

"Lady Melissa."

Aradia had changed clothes. She was now all in gray, her hair covered with an unadorned headdress, a veil beneath her chin so that her face looked out from a circle of gray cloth. "If you will come up to the wardrobe room, I will help you find appropriate garments for the funeral."

"Yes, my lady," Melissa replied, and followed Aradia upstairs, past the sleeping rooms, and into a large room where numerous garments hung on pegs. There were chests and shelves, too, but most were empty.

"My brother has been here only a year," said Aradia. "There is not much of a collection yet. We brought gray garments, for we expected a funeral . . . but not such a small one. Torio's idea was brilliant—there might have been no deaths at all if Wulfston had been able to reach the battlefield in time."

"That's really what you want, isn't it?" Melissa asked.

"Oh, yes! But power struggles are a way of life here. Human nature is still nature—you cannot work against it. But if we can show our enemies our strength without killing them, then their friends and families have no reason for vengeance. It will take a long time. We must always be prepared to fight. But Readers and Adepts together find fresh ideas. Create a storm to blow the enemy fleet away. Bog them down in quicksand. And hope that if we do such things often enough, they will stop attacking us."

"I fear you underestimate the Aventine Empire," said Melissa. "They think you seek to destroy them— and they intend to fight you to the last man."

Aradia sighed. "Then their Readers will start searching for us the moment we set off the fault again—and Read that our intention is to *prevent* destruction. Here." She lifted a brown dress off a peg and held it up against Melissa. "This should fit you. And here's a surcoat in gray. Earth colors and ash," she explained. "No bright colors, Lady Melissa."

Melissa took the garments, saying, "Why does everyone call me 'Lady Melissa'? No one calls Rolf a lord."

"Torio says you are qualified to be a Magister Reader," Aradia replied. "Our titles are based on one's powers, just as yours are. Rolf is not a fully-empowered Adept; he has only one talent. If he learns to Read well enough, Lenardo and Torio can test him—perhaps he will earn the right to a title and lands someday."

"Lands?"

Aradia laughed. "Do not be greedy, Melissa. All the lands we currently hold are spoken for, and we have no plans for conquest." She looked Melissa over from head to toe. "But you are young—and both Torio and my brother are of an age to be attracted. They have become best of friends, and work together excellently. If you were to find a true match with either of them, we would all be greatly pleased. But don't play games. If you attempt to gain power by using your female charms to turn them against one another, you will have me to deal with . . . and I am also a woman."

Melissa was dumbfounded. No such idea had entered her head—but then Aradia did not know of her love for Jason. She could not love another man. "I am a Reader," she said. "I have been taught never to think of marriage."

"But you are very adaptable, as we have all seen. Go get dressed, Melissa—but remember what I have told you."

Melissa thought about the conversation while she dressed, but once the funeral began she forgot it, suddenly enveloped in the grief she had put aside. In this strange land which she did not associate with him, Jason had seemed not to be dead, but back in Gaeta, where she would touch his mind once more if she ever went home.

But now, Reading his body with the others on the funeral pyre, she was forcibly reminded that he was gone. *If he had only known what they are doing here! If I had only known the healing techniques I saw a minor Adept use yesterday.* She would learn those techniques, she vowed—let that be an appropriate monument to Jason. As she Read the funeral preparations, she realized he would have no other.

The funeral pyre was built on a hill about a mile from Wulfston's castle. The cortege wound its way to the top, each person laying a symbolic stick of wood on the pyre. The flat rock surface of the hilltop could have accommodated a much larger pyre and many more mourners . . . and had, Melissa was sure. She followed Torio's lead, and Rolf followed her—placing his walking stick as his contribution.

Wulfston and Aradia spoke; the friends and relatives of those who had died each said something—and then it was Melissa's turn. For the first time she realized how little she knew about Jason! She could speak of him only as her teacher, with warmth and affection . . . but where was the personal feeling she had thought they shared?

Numb with surprise and a grief far more for what might have been than for what had been, Melissa watched as Wulfston, Lenardo, and Aradia sprinkled earth and water on the pyre, stood back—and the flames leaped skyward with a white heat.

When the flames subsided, only a scattering of ash stirred on the bare rock face. As if on signal, a cheer went up from the people gathered there, and they turned and began walking down the trail, laughing and talking, some even singing. Melissa stared, uncomprehending.

Rolf had gone on ahead, but Torio remained beside

Melissa. "They have mourned for death," he said. "Now they will have a feast to celebrate life."

"They?" she asked. "I thought you were one of them."

"I am, but there are some things I find strange. You have much more of the savage attitude than I have, Melissa."

He was not Reading; she had to guess from his tone of voice that he did not intend an insult. Before she could comment, Torio continued, "These people live for the moment. I thought yesterday that I was finally content here, when we stopped the Aventine army without a battle. But today here we are again, mourning our dead, having returned the Aventine dead to their own people."

"If we had reached the plain before that first battle, no one would have died," Melissa pointed out.

"What of those who died in the shipwrecks? Why couldn't I have thought to Read the condition of the ships before telling Wulfston to raise the storm?"

"Torio, you can't think of everything!"

"A Lord of the Land is responsible for all his people. How can I ever accept such responsibility?"

Melissa started forward, following the last of the mourners down the trail toward the castle. Torio took her arm. She was startled for a moment—until she realized that he was not Reading in order to keep from broadcasting their conversation to the other Readers.

Then she realized what Torio had said. "A Lord of the Land is responsible for all *his* people," she repeated. "You cannot be responsible for those who *attack* you, Torio."

"You do not blame me for Magister Jason's death?"

"Not anymore. I could blame myself—I Read you calling to all of us, offering help. I could have refused to let Jason die. I wish I had. But at that time how could I *know* that he was wrong about what you do to Readers? How could I guess that what he thought he 'knew' was twisted rumor? By all the gods, I wish I had come to you and let you save his life. I will never make that mistake again. Even if he had been right, if he were alive there would be the chance that we could fight you off, escape—''

"You sound like Aradia," said Torio. "She always says that life is all there is."

"Well, it's all we have right now, anyway."

Both Readers fell silent, nor did Torio begin to Read again, although Melissa did. He continued to let her guide him while he thought his private thoughts. But when they were almost back to the castle, he suddenly said, "Thank you, Melissa."

"You're welcome—but what did I do?"

"Made me understand what Lenardo has been telling me for years—we cannot change the past, but can only learn from it; we have the present, and we can change the future. Look at how we've changed Rolf's future, for example! Like you, I'll never make the same mistake again."

"You'll make new ones," she said. "So will I."

"I know," he replied, letting go of her arm as he opened to Reading, "but we won't let that stop us from doing the best we can!"

The next few days passed in a blur of activity. Travel plans were made, but it was uncertain as to who was going, or where. Melissa wasn't sure if they didn't know themselves, or if specific plans were being kept from her. Torio was busy much of the time, and so training their newest Reader fell to Melissa.

Rolf's Reading showed no marked improvement, but as his ability to interpret what he Read grew, so did his confidence. One morning at their lesson time, Melissa could not find him in the castle. When she Read outside, though, she found him—running. By the time she went down to the courtyard he came pounding in, breathless —but with the strength left to pick her up and whirl her around, laughing. //I'm so happy!// he told her. //Lady Melissa, I never dared to run in my life before! How can I ever repay you?//

//I didn't do it, Rolf—you did. It's such a beautiful day—let's not go back inside.//

They left the castle and the village and wandered into the fields nearby, Melissa having Rolf test his range. It was still less than a quarter of a mile for inanimate objects—he'd have been failed just about now if that were his range after a lifetime in an Academy. Considering the short time he had been Reading, though, he might yet develop a useful range of a mile or more.

Melissa took him along the edge of a newly planted field to an area some men were clearing. "How many people?" she asked him.

"Four—no, five. And four horses."

"The people—male, female, ages, sizes?"

"Oh, Lady Melissa, I can't tell that from this distance! I'm only now starting to sort out the people I know from a few paces away, unless I hear their footsteps or they speak or think to me."

"Then can you tell me what the people are doing?"

He concentrated, Melissa deliberately not Reading so that he could not Read through her. "I can't make sense of it," Rolf confessed. "They are digging? But what? Now they're trying to lift something—and digging some more."

"They're clearing some big rocks out of a field, so they can cultivate it," Melissa explained. "They've got lots of them in the wagon already, and that's why there are four horses—it is really *heavy*. They have to dig some more around the boulder they're working on before they can lift it. There are five big, strong men. I haven't seen many like that around here, except in the army."

"They were probably in Drakonius' army," said Rolf. "He sent his officers to our villages every so often, and took away all healthy boys over fourteen. In the army they got good food, and healers to work on them. The people in my village were glad I'm blind—the army didn't take me, so they had someone to control the weather. What are the men doing now, Melissa?''

"They're trying to lift a boulder. It's too heavy for them—they shouldn't—'' She shouted, "Hey! You'll hurt your backs! Let me get an Adept to—''

The five men, straining, had lifted the rock to waist height, their muscles bulging as they staggered toward the wagon—but Melissa had distracted them. Two looked over their shoulders in her direction, and she realized that they did not understand her. "Rolf, tell them—''

One of the distracted men turned his ankle on the uneven ground, throwing the others off balance. They lurched, trying desperately to hold on, unable to drop the boulder without dropping it *on* themselves—but their muscles were giving out. A second man's leg gave even as the first was scrabbling to regain his hold—both went down, the rock on top of them!

The other three men were forced to let go, and the boulder crushed one man's arm, the other's chest. Screams of pain filled the air—then the man whose chest was crushed fell silent, unconscious.

Melissa rushed to where the three uninjured men were dragging the boulder off the others. "Hold him!" she said, pointing to the man with the broken arm. "He'll be all right if he doesn't move it." When they stared blankly, she said, "Rolf—translate!"

Rolf spoke to the men in the savage language. One of them soothed the conscious man, while Melissa bent over the unconscious one.

"We need a healer," she said, then "No, Rolf!" as the boy started away. "Send one of these men, and you help me!"

//Lord Lenardo!// she broadcast, //Torio! Lady Aradia!// But she could not Read for a response as she concentrated on the injured man.

Rolf knelt beside Melissa as one of the men ran off toward the castle. "Rolf, this man is bleeding into his left lung. Stop it."

"I'm not a healer. I can only control water—"

"Blood *is* mostly water! Read for it, then stop it."

She Read with him, showing him where the flow was. Rolf went unReadable, and the blood stopped. Melissa sighed with relief—the man would survive until an Adept reached them. But even as she relaxed, he began going into shock. His heart raced—then suddenly stopped. "Rolf—his heart!"

"What?" Rolf's concentration broke; blood flowed sluggishly into the lung again.

"Don't stop!" Melissa cried, realizing she would have to try to pump the man's heart from outside his body. But splinters of broken ribs jabbed inward—she Read that if she tried pressing on his breast bone, she would drive one into his heart. It was a miracle that it had not gone in and killed him.

But he was a dead man now if she could not make his heart pump blood again, make him breathe—

The patients who had died in her care at Gaeta seemed to stare up at her from the man's unconscious face. For a moment he was Jason, cold in her arms. She *knew* the power was in her, if only she could reach it. She Read back toward the castle—but the man Rolf had sent for help was only now entering the courtyard as Torio hurried down the stairs to see what was wrong. *They won't be here in time.*

She Read the man's heart, saw that it was uninjured, and tried to envision it pumping normally. Nothing happened. *No—I can't Read at the same time,* she remembered, stopped Reading, concentrated—something inside her twisted, and she gasped in fear. She forced concentration, and tried again, laying her head against the man's bloody chest to try to hear what she dared not Read. As she concentrated on envisioning—pushing—squeezing—the man's heart, the twisting feel-

ing came again, and with it the reward of a faint *lub-dub*
from inside the man's chest. In a moment there came
another—she tried to straighten up, felt impossible
weakness, and fainted dead away.

Melissa came to lying on the ground with Rolf, Torio,
and Aradia bending over her. Automatically she tried—

"I can't Read!" she cried, putting her hands to her
head.

Aradia took her hands. "It's temporary," she said in
a reassuring voice. "Relax, Melissa. You just overdid
it."

"The injured man!" She tried to sit up, but Aradia
pushed her back. "He's fine—already in healing sleep.
Rolf tells me—"

"You did it, Lady Melissa!" Rolf said excitedly.
"You really did start his heart! I Read you do it!"

"You used too much energy," Aradia explained.
"It's a common problem. But you saved that man's
life—I would never have reached him in time. Do you
think you can walk now? A nap and a meal, and you'll
be good as new."

Melissa found that she could Read faintly. As soon as
she had that relief, excitement buoyed her up. "I don't
want to sleep! I want to learn more!"

Julia came running up, followed more sedately by
Wulfston. "Oh, that's not fair!" the little girl cried.
"Why can't *I* learn it?"

"No one is preventing you, Julia," Wulfston said in a
warning voice, and the child subsided from her threatening tantrum. "Congratulations, Lady Melissa," he
added, not allowing the slightest twinge of envy to mar
his words.

Melissa was sitting up now, feeling normal enough—
except that she could not Read even to the castle. Aradia
noticed her testing herself. //Your powers will return to
normal with a night's sleep—but using Adept power will
temporarily reduce your Reading ability.//

//If it's temporary, it's worth it,// she told her, and added aloud, "When can I learn more?"

"After food and rest," said Wulfston.

Despite her protests that she felt fine and wanted to try more Adept tricks before she forgot how, Aradia took Melissa upstairs and made her lie down. "Sleep if you can," the Lady Adept told her, "and at lunch eat what Wulfston and I tell you to—never mind what my husband says."

Melissa forced down about half the huge slab of roast meat Aradia insisted she have for lunch. Born of Readers, she had never eaten meat, even before her powers had developed. The taste and texture were strange . . . and she had to remind herself not to think that this had been a baby lamb, or she could eat none of it. She half expected to be sick, but she wasn't—she was fascinated by the work Wulfston did in the rock-riddled field the men had been trying to clear, splitting the rocks into smaller pieces so they would not have to strain themselves again.

Like Rolf's Reading ability, her Adept power was small, but Lord Wulfston carefully taught her how to use it to best effect without draining herself. "Look for ways to work *with* nature," he told her. "You can bring a whole mountain down by crumbling one bit of clay at its base—gravity will do the rest. If you *must* kill a man, to keep him from killing you, stop his heart. Don't try to push him back with the force of your mind."

To split rocks, Melissa Read the natural stress lines in the boulders for Wulfston, making his job easier and finding that she could split one or two herself. The next day she had a lesson in healing—but with horses, not people.

"Drakonius again," explained Wulfston. "He took everything from his people. Farm horses became draft horses for his army. We haven't nearly enough horses in this land, and so every animal is being pressed into service for farming, even those not built for it. And in hunting season, the plow horses are saddled and ridden. It will take years to breed enough animals so that each can serve its proper purpose."

Melissa Read the first horse for Wulfston, pointing out exactly where the muscles and tendons were badly bruised. He stroked and talked to the animal, then placed his hands over the injured area . . . and warmth poured into it. The mare snorted and tried to pull away, but the Adept spoke to her softly, and she stood still, allowing the healing.

Melissa could Read that the blood flow increased to the injury, but not much more. She found her powers limited, either by the energy she had been expending, or by the poisons clogging her blood from the meat she had eaten. She began to understand why it was so difficult to be both Adept and Reader.

When Wulfston encouraged her to try to heal the second, less badly injured, horse, Melissa put all her effort into the task. She Read the strain, placed her hands as Wulfston had, and envisioned the same increased blood flow to the injury, tried to feel the healing warmth, stopped Reading while she kept up the belief that it would happen—and felt the same sudden inner weakness she had before. Again she couldn't Read, but this time she didn't faint. The horse shied away from her, but she was leaning against him, breathless. Wulfston put his arm around her, and she let go of the horse, which danced a step or two away. "Steady, now," said Wulfston—she didn't know whether to her or to the animal.

The horse twisted his head and nosed at the point on his shoulder where the strain was. "I think it worked," said Melissa, able to stand on her own feet again. Her Reading was coming back now, faintly at first, but at least she could sense the healing warmth in the horse's shoulder. "Yes—it did. I can do it! Thank you, my lord!"

Melissa was suddenly conscious that Wulfston was

still holding her. Aradia's warning came back to her,
and she pulled away, startled. Wulston let her go easily,
but Melissa cautioned herself to reinstate her Reader's
distance from people.

Then she recalled Torio taking her arm, Rolf swing-
ing her around. There was none of the reticence she had
grown up with. The touching she had seen going on here
was that of a family . . . one she was not a member of,
but, she realized, very much wanted to be. She Read the
horses glowing with that strange heat, and thought of
the man whose life she had saved yesterday. *I am a
healer now—and here, where I learned it, is where I
belong.*

A few days later, Lenardo, Aradia, and Julia left
Wulfston's castle to return to their own home in Zendi.
Melissa continued her lessons with Rolf and Wulfston,
while the three of them increased their efforts to teach
Torio to use Adept powers. He was as frustrated as
Wulfston. Neither could seem to make the break-
through, even though they now knew it had to be possi-
ble.

Wulfston's lands were being put in order for his leaving them for a few weeks. Going with them would be a
few healers, and every minor Adept he had who could
move objects with his mind. Melissa was not told the
details, but she knew plans were afoot for smuggling
several hundred minor Adepts, and their handful of
Readers, into the Aventine Empire.

"Why won't the Council of Masters warn the
Emperor about that fault?" Melissa asked Torio.
"They must know it can go off at any time."

"They know the fault is there, but where do you
move the government without still being on the fault
line? It runs right down the middle of the empire. Move
to the coast, and a major quake could still drown the
government in a tidal wave."

"Do they know about Lenardo's vision? You have

friends in the empire. Have you told them, so they will be sure not to be in Tiberium at Summer Festival?"

"They have been warned," he said grimly, but would tell her nothing more.

Melissa longed to warn everyone at Gaeta—but her teachers and colleagues would not listen to her if she did try. Alethia and Rodrigo, she was sure, would not go to Summer Festival. And even out of body, she could not Read that far. If she could, she would risk losing contact with her body. She had no wish to die.

So she continued to learn how to use the small Adept power she had acquired, to help alleviate the fault and prevent disaster. By the time they were ready to travel to Zendi, where Adepts from all over the alliance were gathering, Melissa felt confident in her powers.

The city of Zendi had once belonged to the Aventine Empire, and was the kind of civilized community she was accustomed to. The streets were cobbled and clean; fountains played in the intersections; a major feature of the forum was a huge bath-house with every luxury. Melissa had been to Tiberium once, and had found it grand and exciting. Zendi had that same air.

Wulfston told her the story of how Aradia had tested Lenardo's right to be a savage lord by giving him this battle-ravaged city full of fearful, distrustful people. Despite having no Adept powers at the time, he had escaped assassination attempts, rescued Julia, and won the love and respect of his people.

"I didn't think he could do it," Wulfston admitted. "I thought they'd kill him within the month. If you had seen this place a year ago, Lady Melissa, you would have said the best thing to do was burn it down and start over! But look at it now. My sister knew who understood city people." The Lord Adept chuckled warmly at the memory. "By midsummer, Aradia and I were still winning the confidence of our people—and Lenardo was throwing a festival!"

Lenardo's house was luxurious but empty. There was

enough furniture for his guests, but no more—no clutter, no statues to obscure the beautiful mosaics on the walls, no displays of captured treasures.

There Melissa met the Lady Lilith and her son, Lord Ivorn, both fully empowered Adepts with no Reading ability. Ivorn, who was about twelve, cornered Melissa and Rolf at the first opportunity, insisting on an explanation of how they had exchanged powers. However, they could no more explain to him than they could to anyone else.

If Lilith felt the same frustration her son did, she did not show it. She was a placidly elegant woman, taller than Aradia, with dark hair and piercing dark eyes in a rather pale face. When she spoke, though, she commanded attention.

Melissa did not see much of Lenardo the first two days she was in Zendi—he greeted his guests, then disappeared until dinner. The next day he appeared at breakfast, and not again until the evening meal. Something was wrong. . . . Melissa could feel the increasing tension, but no one told her its cause.

But on the third day they were just getting up from luncheon—again without Lenardo—when one of the servants came in to announce, "There are two people very insistent upon seeing Lord Lenardo, my lady. They say their names are Clement and Decius."

Both Aradia and Torio practically ran from the room. By the time Melissa and the others followed them to the entry hall, Aradia had almost reached Lenardo's room. Torio was hugging a very old man in dusty traveling clothes, crying, "Oh, Master Clement, we were so *worried* about you! Lenardo couldn't find you anywhere!"

Then he turned to the other figure, a boy a little older than Lord Ivorn, who threw himself on Torio despite the fact that the movement hurt him. The flash of pain drew Melissa's eyes to the boy's left leg, a peg leg which irritated the stump to which it was fastened. "Decius,"

Torio was saying, "how did you manage such a long journey? Oh, please, come inside, both of you. Why have you come? What happened? We have heard nothing of you in five days!"

The old man was also in pain—when he walked, his back and hips ached with rheumatism. He should never have pushed himself to a long journey.

As people parted to let them pass, Torio realized that introductions were required. The old man was Master Clement of the Adigia Academy, where both Lenardo and Torio had grown up. Decius was one of the students there. By the time they had been seated at the table, and Torio had reeled off introductions of all the people staring at them, Aradia was back with Lenardo.

"Master Clement!" exclaimed Lenardo. "No, don't get up," as he bent to hug the old man. "And Decius —how are you, son? Why are you here? I had left my body and was Reading all over the empire for you—and here you are in my own land! Why didn't you let us know? We would have met you at the border. You didn't walk—?"

"No, no," replied Master Clement, with a twinkle in his bright brown eyes. "I'm not as decrepit as you think, son, but I'm not senile, either. We rode. Your grooms took our horses outside."

"Even so, it's a terribly long journey. How did you get across the border?"

"We set fire to the trees Torio left plugging the wall in the woods," Decius replied. "It took a while, but then we could take our horses through."

"But why?" asked Lenardo.

Master Clement looked around at the other people lining the long table. "You may speak freely," said Lenardo. "If anyone here were spying for the empire, I think I would have discovered it by now."

"I'm sure you would," the old man replied. "However, will your allies not think that *I* might be here to spy?"

"No, Master Clement," Aradia replied for them all. "Please tell us why you have made this long, hard journey."

"Because I have the information you need—and no longer a place in the empire."

"What happened?" Lenardo asked.

"Portia has been suspicious of me since you escaped," Master Clement replied. "When the Adigia Academy was moved to Tiberium, I naturally took my place on the Council of Masters. But I am not part of Portia's inner circle. I have never been interested in politics—a mistake a good number of us have made over the years, Lenardo, leaving Portia and her cronies to concoct whatever schemes they pleased. Now she has gone too far, and is trying to prevent the Emperor from taking away her power. Rumors were already spreading throughout the empire, before this latest fiasco, that Readers were turning traitor. As to your blowing the fleet away, and then sinking the army on dry land—"

"It wasn't dry," Torio put in.

The old man smiled. "You're right, son. It's funny—to you. But sometimes it is better to kill someone than to make a fool of him—and you made fools of the entire Aventine army. Thereby, you made a fool of the Emperor. He is not pleased. Nor are the people, who have been told you defeated the army in battle. They are terrified, and crying out for the Emperor to protect them."

"Master Clement," Lord Wulfston put in, "we did not want to kill people who were doing nothing more than their duty to their homeland."

"And now they must do it again," said Master Clement. "The Emperor has declared all-out war, by land, with the army marching northward in full force along the border."

"But that's futile!" said Torio.

"The people expect the Emperor to attack before their enemies recoup the losses the empire claims. You did not help matters by taking two master Readers hostage.''

"That was a mistake," said Wulfston. "I thought if they saw what we are trying to do here—"

"Those two? Amicus is one of Portia's cronies and Corus will move any way the wind blows. What have you done with them? Killed them?"

"Of course not!" Lilith answered. "They are safely locked up in my castle far to the north, under heavy guard. Despite their unsavory personalities, we may be able to trade them for concessions in a peace treaty."

"There will be no treaty now," said Master Clement. "Portia could not prove that I have been in contact with you. She dared not create factions in the Council of Masters by accusing me of spying. So suddenly there was a villa available, three days' ride to the south, for the Adigia Academy—and we were told one evening to move out of Tiberium in the morning. I was Read every moment we were packing, and until we were well outside the walls in the morning—I had no opportunity to contact you, Lenardo."

"But if Portia suspects you—"

"If she had known for certain that you and I were in contact, she would have called other Masters to witness—and had me executed for treason. But she and her inner circle have become so corrupt that I doubt they can Read beyond the ends of their noses. Portia simply wanted to be rid of me—and she wouldn't send me north, where I might be tempted either to join you or report to you. So I calmly rode one day to the south with the rest of the Academy—and on one of the mountain passes Decius and I fell over a cliff."

"What?!" exclaimed Aradia.

"Oh, a dozen Readers Read it happen—or think they did," Master Clement replied. "Lenardo, I have observed that trick of yours often enough, to make Readers Read something that is not really happening. Decius and I were bringing up the rear. Actually, we never entered the treacherous pass—but those ahead Read us start out onto the trail, my horse slip, and Decius' go over, too, as he attempted to rescue me. I did not like to do such a thing to the boys who loved us . . . but I could not ask them to lie, and I could not take a whole Academy of children across the border. Since Torio left, Decius was our best young Reader—and therefore most susceptible to Portia's wrath.'' He pressed his fingers to his closed eyes as he said, ''I hope we can somehow create a safe place for the other boys by the time they are grown up enough to be in danger from jealous Readers.''

''We will,'' Lenardo said softly. ''You are tired, Master. After you have rested we will talk—''

''No—there's not enough time. The reason I had to come is that I have Read the whole length of the earthquake fault. We must get all the people you will use to disarm it into the empire before the Emperor masses the army at the borders. I don't know how to prevent them from being trapped, though—there is so little time. Men are being conscripted throughout the land. In only fifteen days, the march will begin, from Tiberium. There will be a grand parade, with the Emperor reviewing the troops in the forum as they set out on the glorious campaign—''

''Fifteen days!'' exclaimed Lenardo. ''The Emperor on a reviewing stand in the forum?''

''No!'' gasped Torio. ''We thought we had over a month yet!''

''What?'' asked Master Clement as he and Decius looked around at the faces staring in surprise and horror.

''I thought it was the Summer Festival,'' exclaimed Lenardo, ''but it could be the day the Emperor reviews the troops. The earthquake! In only fifteen days!''

Chapter Eight

Torio sat in the early morning sunshine in Lenardo's courtyard, the calm eye in the storm of activity going on within the household and throughout the city of Zendi. Despite the hour, Torio was by no means the first one up; Cook's crew had already been cleaning up after other early risers when he had eaten breakfast almost an hour ago. Now he was studying the map of the earthquake fault.

The map was not in the courtyard, but drawn across a series of wax tablets laid end to end down the middle of the table in the dining hall. Torio had no need to be in the room to Read it. Besides, he had it memorized.

The dining hall was becoming crowded now, people who had already eaten staying to study the map while new people arrived, hungry and eager to join the activity. Cook's assistants shooed the newcomers to trestle tables along the edges of the hall. Torio frowned at his break in concentration, and returned to studying the map.

A familiar mind touched gently at the edge of Torio's consciousness, not intruding. //I am in the courtyard, Master Clement.//

The old man hardly appeared the same person as yesterday. It was not merely that he was rested, and dressed in the imposing scarlet robes of a Master

173

Reader. He moved differently, freely. It was the first time in Torio's memory that he had Read his teacher without the chronic ache of rheumatism.

Master Clement said, "I brought no Master's robes, but these were laid out in my room when I woke."

"They're Lenardo's," Torio explained. "He had his seamstress hem them up for you."

"My clothes may have a mundane explanation, but I don't. I am not surprised that I overslept—I was on the road for five days, with very little rest. Yet not only am I not stiff and sore today—I feel twenty years younger! Where is your sword, Torio? I think I'll get back into practice. Did you know I was once accounted as fine a swordsman as you are?"

Although the old man was teasing now, Torio knew that in a few days he might actually be capable of wielding a sword again. So he replied, "I know Master. I would be honored to practice with you . . . until the day we no longer need swords."

"As long as people are people, that day will never— Oh. You mean until all Readers master Adept powers, Torio?"

"It is obviously possible," replied Torio, "although I have made no progress whatsoever."

"Aye—it is a frightening prospect. Yet think of being able to heal people as you were healed." He touched Torio's shoulder. "Even as simple a thing as easing my rheumatism is a blessing. I did not realize how much pain I had grown used to, until I found it gone."

"We'll heal more than the pain," said Torio. "Each night our healers will set your body to healing again until the swollen joints are back to normal, all restrictions gone. It will take several more nights—but we need you awake in the daytime to help with our plans."

The old Reader stared at his twisted hands. "Is it possible—?"

"Any of the Lords Adept can do it."

"This I *must* learn," said Master Clement.

"Melissa is learning it very quickly. She studied surgery at Gaeta—and is only too happy to abandon it in favor of Adept techniques."

"Melissa I met last night, and Rolf, who has learned to Read. Are there any others?"

"None but Lenardo and Aradia. What we need at this moment are more Readers—you and Decius increase our number by a third!"

Decius joined them in the courtyard. Wakened by the increasing noise level in the house, the boy had thrown on his clothes but not bothered to fasten on his artificial leg. He was using the crutch he preferred to the peg leg most of the time. He rubbed his eyes and yawned, then tried to apologize, but Master Clement said, "You have nothing to apologize for, son—you've certainly earned your rest after that long journey."

Back at the Academy, Torio had been greatly relieved to observe Decius' adjustment to his injury—once over his shock, the boy had taken it as a challenge, relearning everything he had ever done, including riding a horse. The only skill he had been unable to recover was swordsmanship. At Decius' insistence, Torio had worked with him as soon as he was fitted with the artificial leg—but the rapid weight shifts and lunges of swordplay irritated the stump of his leg more than any other activity, and he could not stand the long hours of practice.

As Master Clement went on ahead, Torio told Decius, "Go eat breakfast, then put your leg on and I'll give you a lesson in swordplay. I'll bet you haven't practiced since I left the Academy."

"There's no teacher, with you and Master Lenardo gone," Decius replied. "But I can't wear my leg today, Torio. I've had it on for five days, to balance me on a horse and so I could walk if necessary and not have one arm busy with a crutch. I'm too sore—"

"Are you? Did you Read yourself this morning, Decius?"

The boy Read the stump of his leg, then asked, "How did you do *that*?" as he discovered the bruises and blisters healed, and the scar tissue smoothed over permanently.

"I didn't do it, but I helped Lord Wulfston, after you were asleep. Did you notice how light Master Clement's steps are today? Lenardo and Aradia worked on him."

"This is wonderful!" said Decius. Then, "Torio—you don't have to convince me that I belong here. I trust Master Clement—when he said to come with him, I came."

"That's how I got here, with Master Lenardo—you'll have to learn to call him Lord Lenardo now. Read around you, Decius. Things may be far from perfect here, but nobody will try to stop you from being everything you can."

"Uh . . . you haven't learned—?"

"No—but Lenardo has. Melissa has. Aradia and Rolf have also learned to Read. Maybe you'll be a Lord Adept, Decius."

The boy considered that. "Could I grow a new leg?"

"No more than I could grow new eyes," Torio replied, "but you can learn to heal wounds, or to defend yourself so you don't need a sword."

"I'll learn," said Decius. "Why haven't you learned, Torio? You're no older than Melissa."

That was an interesting point. Rolf and Melissa were close to the same age—young, still in the growth of their powers. Lenardo was a Master Reader, but young enough that he could expect his powers to grow for a few more years; Aradia was Lenardo's age, Wulfston a few years younger. Torio filed the thought for later examination, and while Decius followed Master Clement to the kitchen to assuage the ravaging hunger brought on by healing, he waited for Melissa, for they had an appointment to go over the fault map before noon.

The group of Adepts and Readers was now too large to work as a unit; they were working individually and in small groups, studying the map, attempting to decide where to apply pressure to allow those precariously balanced rock edges under the earth to settle into a stable position without wreaking destruction in the land above.

Master Clement had made the map by the dangerous procedure of leaving his body to travel the length of the fault, to distances beyond the safe range of even a Master Reader. That was probably the final blow to Portia's trust; he had spent hours out of body, he told them, instead of just the few minutes at a time required to contact Lenardo. He guessed that Portia had been unable to contact him during that long mental journey, and decided it was too suspicious to allow to go unpunished.

This he had told them while directing Lenardo, Aradia, and Wulfston to create the physical map in the wax tablets. "It is fortunate," he added, "that I have many friends among the Masters. It is even more fortunate Portia has no Adept powers—else my heart might simply have stopped, and who would have questioned heart failure in an old man? But if she wanted to kill me, Portia would have had to send someone who would then have been dangerous to her."

"Do you think Portia morally capable of such an act?" Lenardo had asked.

"Six Master Readers have died in the past year," Master Clement replied grimly. "How much Portia had to do with that fact I cannot say, but she made a very serious error in keeping secret your mission to stop Galen. She has taken one action after another to cover her mistake—and since it was discovered, she is in panic. She sends people she fears into dangerous situations, hoping to be rid of them. Those in Portia's inner circle are closing ranks with her to protect themselves."

How long, Torio wondered, could the Readers hope to keep the corruption at their center a secret? According to Master Clement, most Masters of Academies, living far from the center of government, were only now discovering the true situation in Tiberium. They still hoped to clean their own house—there was talk of unseating Portia—but if she Read their threats there was no telling what she might do.

"Once it becomes public," Master Clement had said sadly, "there is no hope that Readers will be allowed to continue self-government. Our first priorities must be to prevent the destruction of the empire, and stop the war —but next we must bring the best young Readers out of the empire, before either Portia's schemes destroy them or the government virtually enslaves them."

Torio was alone in the courtyard, lost in thought, when Melissa came to find him. "I thought you never stopped Reading when you were awake," she said, sitting down next to him. "I couldn't get your attention."

"I'm sorry. I was wondering what will happen to all the Readers in the empire once the corruption in the Council becomes public knowledge."

"Politics," she said. "I never took an interest in it—but I doubt much will happen. Senators are often corrupt—and all that happens is that when someone gets caught he's unseated. The whole Senate isn't broken up."

"Senators are expected to seek power. Readers are not," said Torio. "Melissa, did you ever hear the legend of the first Reader?"

"Of course. Nobody's supposed to know it, and everybody does. But it's just a legend, Torio—a horror story children tell to frighten each other."

"A horror story? Or a cautionary tale? If nonReaders had their way, Readers *would* be imprisoned, maimed, tortured to force them to work for those in power. We are simply more civilized about it. Our dungeons are the Academies—any child who shows Reading ability is taken from his family, by force if necessary, and locked up in an Academy until he is no longer dangerous."

"And the greater his powers," Melissa said in wonder, "the longer he remains there. Talk about twisting minds! Look at what we believe."

"Aye," said Torio. "A lifetime in the Academy, in isolation from nonReaders, is the ideal, granted only to those in the top ranks . . . keeping those with greatest power away from the temptation to use it. Readers are forbidden to hold office, and discouraged from taking an interest in politics. And those who cannot resist the lure of power—"

"Must seek it in devious ways," said Melissa, "as Portia has. Torio, we are maimed, as surely as if they crippled us physically."

"More so," he said thoughtfully. "Look at Decius. There is little his physical disability keeps him from—it didn't prevent his escaping."

"Nor you," she said, touching his face with her soft hand. "But Torio, you should see, and Decius should have two good legs. We are crippled by having half our powers denied us."

"No longer," he replied. "We know the truth now—and the more people who know it, the more they will encourage the rest of their powers. As you have."

As Melissa dropped her hand from his face, Torio caught it in his. When she pulled back, he said, "I'm sorry—"

"No," she replied, "don't apologize. *I'm* sorry, Torio. I'm not used to the way people touch each other here. I'm not sure what it means."

"It means friendship," he replied; it was not the time to suggest that it might mean more. "But right now, if we don't study that map as we're supposed to, we'll have a great deal to apologize for!"

The plan was for the group of Readers and Adepts to spend the day studying the map, and in the evening share suggestions for distributing their Readers so that every Adept could hear, or at least see one.

But that was not possible. Eight Readers could not be stretched almost the length of the empire. They could use watchers, but flashing lights were too likely to be spotted. Moreover, it took precious time for a watcher to read a signal and pass it on—time they would not have while trying to control immense forces of nature.

A frustrated assembly gathered around Lenardo's table that evening, after a meal at which even the Adepts had eaten little. "In some areas" Rolf pointed out, "the fault line runs almost under the main road through the empire. Those of us with lesser powers have to be *close*, or we can do nothing. I know I'm going as a Reader, but I know the limitations of minor Adept talents."

"We must have people right along the road," said Aradia. "And here, where the land is flat for long stretches, where do we place watchers?"

"At least the troop movements will obscure the fact that so many strangers are wandering along the roads," said Master Clement.

"But half the minor Adepts are women," said Melissa. "We can't disguise them as soldiers."

"What about dressing all the women as Readers?" Torio suggested.

"No," said Melissa, "not in white—they'd be sure to be caught out by other Readers. But ordinary clothes and *badges*—the Sign of the Dark Moon!" And as she spoke the words, all the other Readers around the table felt Melissa's inspiration. "That's it! That's where we can get other Readers! The Path of the Dark Moon!"

"What?" asked Lenardo and Master Clement together.

"You Master Readers—you pay no attention to your old friends who were failed," she replied, "but they're all over the empire, working as Readers in minor capacities."

"But child," said Master Clement, "why would they help us? That would be betraying their own people."

"I have a close friend," said Melissa. "Alethia won't betray me, even if she refuses to help. Let me try."

"Where is she?" asked Torio.

"Gaeta. I have never gone so far out of body—"

"Torio," said Lenardo, "can you guide Melissa safely, or shall I?"

"I've Read Gaeta with you," Torio replied, "and Melissa knows it well. And it's on the coast—I can always follow the shore back to familiar territory."

"Then go ahead, while we consider alternatives. Even if we find enough Readers to act as relays, only a few of us can Read the stresses within the ground. How can we place those few to cover the most territory?"

Torio went to his room, Melissa to hers. In moments they were out of body, "floating" above Lenardo's city. When Melissa began to drift southwest Torio asked, //Don't you know how to get quickly to somewhere you know well?//

//No—I've only recently become comfortable out of body at all. It's incredible that you are so much more skilled than I am, when you haven't had as much training.//

//But I have—Lenardo hasn't let me forget my lessons, and I have had to put my skills to use in life, not classroom exercises. Concentrate on Gaeta as you know it—some familiar spot. Imagine yourself there. Visualize it—//

An image grew in Melissa's mind of a pier jutting out into the sea, waves lapping on the rocks beneath. And then they were "there," "on" the pier. //Alethia's house is just up the hill,// Melissa told Torio.

Torio "followed" Melissa past several people who did not know they were there, to a neat walled cottage where a little boy played in the garden. Inside, an infant slept in a cradle while a yong woman put away the supper things and prepared the crib for her older child. She worked slowly, misery in her every move.

//Alethia—what's wrong?//

//Melissa? It can't be! They said you were dead, and now they've taken Rodrigo—//

//I'm not dead, and please don't project so strongly.

We must have privacy. I wish you could leave your body.//

//You know I could never learn that.//

//You may, someday. But who took Rodrigo?//

//The army.// Alethia sat dejectedly in a wooden chair. //They've taken all the Readers they didn't before—many of the healers from the hospital, too. I'm so frightened—you were reported dead, Melissa.//

//Were Masters Amicus and Corus listed as dead, too?//

//Yes.//

//Well, they're alive. Magister Jason died in the ship-wreck—//

//Shipwreck? What shipwreck?// Alethia was hope-lessly confused.

//Alethia,// said Melissa, //hasn't any of the truth come down the Path of the Dark Moon?//

//I don't know what's true. There is some insane story that the army was trapped in quicksand, and hun-dreds of helpless men slaughtered by the savages.//

//The quicksand is true; the slaughter is not.// Melissa quickly sketched what had really happened.

//The Emperor claims there was a great battle,// said Alethia. //We were very narrowly defeated, and killed many of the savages. Now we are building an even big-ger army to strike before the enemy can recoup their losses. The Council of Masters reports the same thing. The only mention of quicksand came down the Path of the Dark Moon. But Melissa—have you escaped from the savages? Do you need help?//

//I am with friends. We need your help, Alethia.//

//We?//

//Magister Torio of the Adigia Academy is here with me now, or I would not dare travel so far out of body.//

//Magister—? There was a Torio killed trying to leave the empire, and brought back to life by savage sorcery. Melissa—// They could feel Alethia's dread.

//No, I am not a ghost,// Melissa told her friend.

//Neither is Torio. The savages cannot raise the dead, but they have healing powers we never dreamed of. Alethia, I've never lied to you—and while what comes down the Path of the Dark Moon may be exaggerated or embellished, it is basically true. Isn't it?//

Reluctantly, Alethia agreed.

//If there had been the great battle the government claims, what would be happening to Gaeta now?//

Alethia considered. //The hospital!// she realized. //Some of the wounded would be brought here—the ones they could not cure in the other hospitals. Magister Phoebe and some other Readers returned—but they brought no injured soldiers. How could there have been such a battle?//

//There wasn't,// Melissa assured her. Then, while Alethia was willing to listen, she asked, //Will Rodrigo be in Tiberium when the Emperor reviews the troops?//

//Yes—he is training with a unit in Cassino now, but they will march to Tiberium next week.//

Reading Melissa working delicately on her friend, Torio did not interfere. Everything hinged on Alethia's trust.

Melissa began, //There is no way to tell you this gently . . . but unless you help us, Rodrigo could die in Tiberium, before he ever sees a battle.//

//No!//

//Alethia, don't shut me out! We can prevent it!//

//If the savages attack Tiberium, what can *I* do?//

//Not the savages,// said Melissa. //An earthquake. The very day the troops gather in Tiberium, the city will be destroyed.//

//Why haven't you gone to the Council of Masters?//

//They have declared me dead, although they know better. Alethia, you are our only hope—you and others on the Path of the Dark Moon.//

Alethia got up and walked to the cradle, picked up her baby, then went to the door and looked out at the

little boy playing in the last rays of the evening sun.
//You saved my son's life. You were midwife when I
bore my daughter. Now you claim my husband's life is
in danger—but what can I *do*, Melissa?//

//What I am asking is very dangerous. You could be
tried as a traitor.//

//But to save my husband's life . . . ? Melissa, why
would the savages want to save Tiberium? If our government were destroyed, wouldn't it be easier for the
savages to take over the empire? Answer that, Melissa,
and I will help you, I swear it.//

//They don't *want* the empire. Drakonius, the Lord
Adept who drove our borders back, is dead. The present
Lords Adept seek peace. If you could see their lands,
their people, you would understand, Alethia.//

//Perhaps. But I can't. I do know they caused an
earthquake in Gaeta in which you were almost killed.//

//They were setting off all those minor tremors to
prevent a major quake. They didn't know there was a
fault under Gaeta—because they *don't have enough
Readers*. They had to stop their efforts after that, lest
they create such havoc again.//

//Alethia,// Torio broke in, //you have a safeguard,
you know—you will all be Reading us. Our lives will be
in your hands: You can turn us in to the authorities at
any moment you think we have betrayed you.//

//We have to trust you,// added Melissa. //You and
everyone you can trust along the Path of the Dark
Moon will determine all our fates.//

They left Alethia to think over their request. It was
the next day before they dared contact her again.

//I've done it!// she told them. //The word is passing—and Melissa, what I have learned in the past few
hours—oh, my dear friend, how ignorant I have
been!//

//What happened?// Melissa asked in astonishment.

//There are Magister Readers on the Path now, torn
from their Academies and declared failures after years

of healing or teaching. Most have been in despair, married off, their powers blunted—but those to whom it happened months ago say some of their powers have returned—and several of them went out of body to Read the fault lines. It's all true! There *is* a dangerously unstable fault; there *is* a connection with the stabilized fault under Gaeta; and the Council of Masters have warned no one! And the quicksand—Readers who were there have confirmed it. The Path of the Dark Moon is peopled with Readers betrayed by the Masters.//

//Will they trust us?// asked Torio.

//Only because we need your Adepts as much as you need our Readers. And we outnumber you. It is as you said, Magister Torio: If you attempt to betray us, we can betray you. Your Adepts might escape . . . but you cannot count on their being able to rescue all of you.//

Torio was astonished at the disillusionment among the Readers he and Lenardo and Master Clement contacted over the next few days. Whatever came of all this, one certainty would be a rebellion of the minor Readers against the rule of the Council of Masters—after they saved their homeland.

With hundreds of members of the Path of the Dark Moon to help them, entering the empire became easy. Torio and Lenardo cut their hair, and Lenardo and Wulfston shaved their beards; the seamstresses prepared empire-style clothing for everyone.

Wulfston and Torio wore the Sign of the Dark Moon, for Torio feared to wear Magister's robes lest he be identified if his blindness were discovered. Wulfston worried about trying to pass for a Reader, but young, healthy men could not otherwise explain why they were not in the army.

As they had the farthest to go, they were the first to leave. Wulfston was their second strongest Adept; his position was at the far end of the fault line, to draw the worst tremors away from the center of population toward the uninhabited hills. With them rode several minor Adepts, to be stationed along the southernmost section of the fault. With a bit of Adept help, they climbed the wall a few miles to the west of Adigia.

Pepyi, one of Aradia's retainers, took their horses back to Zendi, and the small group of savages met with the members of the Path of the Dark Moon waiting to be their guides. Each minor Adept paired with a Reader, they set off just before dawn. By full daylight, all were on the main road to Tiberium, spaced several miles apart.

Torio and Wulfston did not talk much along the way, as Torio was trying to Read without being Read. He could not do Lenardo's effortless trick; he had to concentrate on not allowing stray thoughts or emotions to enter his mind, and hope that he did not get caught accidentally Reading a better Reader. The miasma of excitement, worry, and fear they rode through was enough to conceal his whereabouts if he cut off in time—but it also prevented contact with their other Readers.

On the way into Tiberium they rode with the crowd. At night they slept in the fields, wrapped in their cloaks, just as everyone else was doing—the few inns were full and had taken the opportunity to raise their prices far above what failed Readers could afford. Wulfston, naturally gregarious, fell in with family groups around the campfires each evening, setting Torio's nerves on edge. But he spoke the Aventine language fluently and without accent, and his badge suggested to nonReaders only that he was to be trusted. He was exotic enough to be asked about his background, but he simply told the truth.

The one problem was that the tiny community Wulfston had been born in was in the north, near Adigia—therefore he had to claim to have been sent to that Academy. Inevitably, someone from Adigia was in a group they talked with. "I don't remember a black child among the Readers."

"Oh, I didn't last long," Wulfston laughed. "I guess

I'm one of the worst Readers in the empire—that's why I'm assigned to help out the shepherds in the southern hills so better Readers can guide the army.''

The genuine frustration in Wulfston's laughter came through to the nonReaders listening to him; Torio felt their sympathy, and wished again that he could teach the Adept to Read.

Once they passed Tiberium, they were bucking the crowds moving toward the capital. Even the lesser roads were crowded, and their progress was slow. Wulfston had to risk taking off his badge and buying a meat meal at an inn each day, lest his Adept powers be blunted by the vegetarian diet he had to assume while posing as a Reader.

Finally they reached their destination, winding up a mountainous trail far from the roads, and made camp. Lenardo would contact them when everyone was in position. It was two days before the Emperor's review; they intended to ease the fault one day before.

But in the morning, when Lenardo's mind finally touched Torio's, he reported, //Some of the Readers were not able to get away from their responsibilities so soon. All are on their way now. I will contact you at dawn—it will still be hours before the review.//

Wulfston took the delay with equanimity, studying the map once more, eating another meal, and then going into the deep, strengthening sleep Torio had seen so often, leaving the young Reader to idle away the day and put himself to sleep that night with one of a Reader's basic exercises.

Both men woke at dawn without prompting. Soon Lenardo was "there" in Torio's head. So was Aradia, in rapport with her husband and thus able to Read whatever he could. Soon Julia joined them. The three were in Tiberium—had, in fact, helped themselves to the villa occupied until a short time ago by the Adigia Academy, and spent the night in comfort. Aradia's powers would control the central fault, with Lilith to the north and Wulfston to the south to draw the effects of the shifting underground rock plates away from beneath the capital.

Soon Lenardo drew Master Clement, who was just south of Adigia with Lilith, into rapport. Decius and Lord Ivorn were halfway between Adigia and Tiberium, Rolf and Arkus, another minor Adept, closer to the city. Melissa had met Alethia, who insisted on taking part in the project, a day's journey south of Tiberium.

Spread between these familiar figures were hundreds of minor Adepts and failed Readers, two or three pairs to every mile. Lenardo slowly drew the Readers into rapport, all sharing his tremendous range and power. It was not additive, as Adept powers were—if anything happened to Lenardo, communication would be broken. Neither Torio nor Master Clement could Read over the vast distance between them without going out of body, and in the midst of a crisis the time that would take. . . .

Torio refused to think about it. There was no reason for anything to go wrong. They were working with complete information and plenty of Readers. They were here, in position. *That* was the hard part. Getting out of the empire again would be the next difficulty—but the Adepts could use their powers on the retreat as they had not dared to while sneaking in.

Wulfston held the map—this one paper for easy carrying—and listened to Torio describe what was happening. "Lenardo and Aradia are leaving the villa now for the forum; Julia is joining some minor Adepts at the north gate of Tiberium." Both Torio and Wulfston had objected to having Lenardo and Aradia at the scene of the potential destruction, but Aradia's limited Reading made it necessary that she *see* what was happening. If she had to use the full force of her Adept powers she would blank out her Reading—Lenardo would have to guide her.

The rapport grew in intensity as more and more minds joined in. Hundreds of Readers along the fault from north to south, almost a hundred in and around

Tiberium alone, knew a dual existence: their own and Lenardo's. Torio had never known anything like it before; he wondered if anyone had.

Lenardo maintained control. Reading with him, they saw through his eyes, felt the warmth of the morning sun in the city streets he trod, smelled the street vendors' pastries, heard the hawkers' cries. The reviewing stand was ready in the forum, the banner with the golden sun, the Emperor's standard, waving above it. Some people were already gathering, while soldiers kept them from staking claim to a spot in the parade route.

Lenardo and Aradia blended into the crowd, Lenardo Reading the Senate building, recalling that in his vision there were senators inside—and indeed, at this very moment men were taking their places. Now? Torio felt the cold knot in Lenardo's stomach—would they be there during the review? Would his vision come true, no matter what he did?

But he reassured himself, and all those in rapport with him, that this was simply proof that they had the right day. They must set off the quake now, carefully controlled, before the Emperor could take his place, before the troops began to march—

Lenardo and Aradia sat down on the Senate steps, inconspicuous in the crowd. Lenardo Read to the Palace, found the Emperor's honor guard already assembled in the main hall, the Emperor dressed in his royal robes— but at this moment in private conference with Portia. She was regal in the scarlet robes of a Master Reader, but on her breast she wore a golden medallion with the sign of the royal family.

"The Senate is this very day debating whether to take away my power," she told the Emperor. "You must stop them, nephew. NonReaders cannot govern Readers."

"Let me deal with one matter at a time," he replied. "Now don't worry—if what you have Read about the earthquake proves true, the family will owe you our lives, my dear Portia. If Tiberium falls—"

"The eclipse is less than a month away. Leave well before. These things are never accurate to the day, but the prophecy certainly means this summer of the eclipse."

"Then," he said, turning away from her, "the senators spending their summer debating what to do about your Readers will no longer be a problem to either of us . . . will they?" And with that he stalked out the door.

Portia followed the Emperor, calm and dignified, a rare public appearance. As she began to Read, Lenardo trembled, wondering if he could hold rapport with the other Readers and still prevent Portia from Reading him. He could. She showed no sign that she Read him—nor did another Master Reader waiting for her, to whom she whispered after her careful check for intruding Readers, "We have nothing to worry about, Marina. Our friends will all be away from Tiberium, and the Emperor will reward us for saving his life."

Torio understood now why Master Clement said Portia's powers were weakened. Both she and the other woman had stopped Reading, trusting their powers as Master Readers that they were not being Read. They were obviously not aware of what they had lost—not distance or discernment or the ability to perform a Master's functions, but the sensitivity to other minds that should have told them they were being Read.

"We must warn all the other Readers—and the common people, too," said Marina. "Portia, you would not let thousands of people die—!"

"There are certain people," Portia explained, "that the Emperor would rather be rid of. A natural catastrophe—"

"But Readers. We must get all the Readers away—"

"Don't be foolish! Do you want to start a panic? The Readers we fail are not true Readers, Marina. They don't understand their powers, and we must weaken them lest they misuse them. Nobody we care about will die. Now no more—there are too many Readers about today."

The incredible shock through the assembled Readers forced Lenardo to drop rapport lest he broadcast it to Portia and Marina. Torio, who had been relaying numbly to Wulfston, was alone in his head again, with an ache in his soul. Wulfston waited anxiously. "All the Readers Read what Portia said," Torio explained. "Lenardo had to drop rapport."

Forcibly composing himself, Torio Read out toward the Reader/Adept pair only a mile away, well within his range, and met fury. //They destroy our powers! By the gods, Portia will pay for this! Old crone—//

//Hush—Bevius, we don't have time for anger!// Torio said. //Overthrow Portia *later*—you certainly have enough witnesses. But right now, think of all the Readers in Tiberium. Are you going to let them die?//

It took several more minutes for Torio to calm Bevius down; then they waited for Lenardo to re-establish rapport. Finally it came, but there were gaps in the chain where some Readers were still too angry to concentrate. Rolf, intending only to help, broadcast, //No Reader or Adept used more than half his powers until now. I am an Adept—but I have learned to Read. You will discover Adept powers—//

Melissa joined in, //Rolf is right. You have done as much to blunt your powers as Portia, by never questioning what was told you. True—anyone who questioned was exiled. But look at Lenardo. Help us now—and we will help you unlock *all* your powers!//

There was a sudden pause, then //Show us,// from a hundred minds at once. Melissa looked around, picked up a small stone, and set it on the ground before her. She concentrated—blank to Reading, but Alethia watched her for the assembly. The stone tilted, toppled, rolled as if down hill—on perfectly flat ground! She resumed Reading, breathing hard, and broadcast into the astonished mental silence, her intensity growing as her powers returned, //You can all learn it. Help us this once—you will change the world!//

//We can have such powers?//

//You *do* have them,// Lenardo told them, //but we are still trying to discover how to teach Readers to use them. Try to calm the people who are still upset. We must ease that fault *now*!//

By the time complete rapport was established, the ceremony in the forum had begun. The Emperor mounted the platform in his golden robes—people cheered as more sun-adorned banners unfurled. The honor guard turned and took their places before the platform. Instead of the heads of the parties in the Senate, who were still deep in debate, Portia and Marina flanked the Emperor. Very clever of Portia, Torio realized: she had used the very debate which sought to reduce her influence to make it appear to the citizens of the empire that she and the other Master Readers were the Emperor's most trusted counselors.

When he felt his thought picked up by other Readers, Torio repressed his feelings lest he spark off their harsh anger again. Lenardo was concentrating on the fault beneath Tiberium, carefully Reading the configuration, the depth, the way the edges leaned and the direction they would slip. The natural inclination would lead to a collapse directly under the city—almost directly under the forum—and kill thousands of people. They must prevent that.

//Everyone concentrate,// Lenardo told them. //Readers, get your Adept partners chanting in unison —when I give the signal, cue your partner on your number.//

It had all been worked out from Master Clement's map—each pair must draw the stresses away from Tiberium on cue, so that the whole fault would settle gently into stability, instead of toppling the capital city into a chasm. Aradia had the job of directing the rock surfaces beneath the city itself, letting the plates of stone settle horizontally across the incipient chasm to form a secure foundation unlikely to budge for many generations. Now she Read with Lenardo, and nodded. //Go ahead.//

Everyone concentrated. Aradia dropped out of the rapport. Torio grasped Wulfston's hands, taking up the chant Adepts used to form their circles of power. Their effort would come later, but they were in rapport with the others already as the potential forces beneath the city . . . moved. All the tremendous power Aradia commanded could do no more than shift one portion of one rock surface, but they had carefully researched that one spot to bring the whole thing tumbling from its precarious equilibrium.

Such forces were ponderously slow, far slower than their rhythmic chanting. The Readers Read the movement beneath the earth long before anything could be felt on the surface. Underground cliffs realigned—a low rumble growled through the city, but in the forum it was drowned in drumbeats and cheers as the Emperor stepped to the front of the reviewing platform.

Aradia Read for a moment with Lenardo, studying what she had started, gauging the pressure to make the surfaces fall into the desired horizontal position. Then she was unReadable again, the shift continuing as the Adepts all around the city exerted their strength to draw energy away from that center.

There was a shift and lurch in the floor of the forum. A minor tremor shook the army's banners, and cries of fear went up here and there. It lasted only moments, though, and was quickly dismissed as another of those annoying—

//GET OUT OF THE FORUM!//

Where it came from, Torio could not have said—it was the mental voice of one of the Readers in the rapport, using Lenardo's power to broadcast outward, breaking their secrecy to reach other Readers in danger.

Then others took it up. //RUN! THE CITY WILL FALL! ALL READERS—RUN FOR YOUR LIVES!//

At this strategic moment, Lenardo dared not break

the rapport— //Stop that!// he told them. //The city will *not* fall if you work with your partners—//

But many of the failed Readers were *not* working with their Adept partners now. Alethia broadcast, //RODRIGO—RUN! GET AWAY FROM THE FORUM!// Soon all the Readers with friends or relatives in Tiberium were trying to warn them.

There was no stopping the forces Aradia had set in motion. "Draw the—stresses—this way—Wulfston!" Torio said in the rhythm of their chanting, but it was too soon—the slow-moving wave of underground motion was still miles away. Then, realizing the Adept would waste precious strength that might be needed later, he broke the rhythm. "Stop! You can't do anything yet. The gods help us—it's all gone wrong!"

"What—?"

"The Readers—they're warning their friends! They've abandoned their Adept partners—no one knows what to do. If we were only *there*—"

"Aradia? Lenardo?"

"Still on the Senate steps—Aradia can't hold those forces by herself. The quake is getting worse—it's going to happen, Wulfston!"

Julia was shouting, "Stop! Don't go in there!" as both Readers and minor Adepts abandoned their posts around the city to surge through the gates.

//Stay back!// Lenardo broadcast as Aradia Read with him once more, her first weariness evident. But as soon as she had reconnoitered, she went back to applying her strength to the fault.

"By the gods—she's doing it, Wulfston!" Torio cried. "Aradia is guiding the stresses—" He fell back into the chant of nonsense syllables, in preparation for their effort.

But failed Readers were converging on the forum, adding their own vision to the rapport—and hatred flowed outward as they saw the reviewing stand, the Emperor, Portia, the assembled army. . . .

The resulting emotion was hopeless to repress. Lenardo could not stop it from being broadcast by the hundreds of failed Readers in Tiberium, nor could he break the rapport. It had taken on a life of its own! Readers in the upper ranks gasped as the anger of the failed Readers poured over them. On the reviewing platform, the Emperor was launching into his opening remarks, about leading the army himself this time—a perfect excuse to get out of Tiberium. Behind him, Portia stiffened as hatred filled the air. Marina cringed. Everyone else on the platform was a nonReader, as were the soldiers drawn up all around them.

//Bring down Tiberium!//

//Destroy them all!//

While Aradia struggled with the forces beneath the earth, the Readers in the rapport joined minds in one all-powerful desire: to destroy the people who had betrayed them!

Torio felt Melissa drawn into the raging hatred, her small power directed at the reviewing stand—it shook! The rapport rippled as angry Readers guided their Adept partners, using them for revenge—hate—it shifted and twisted, the ugliest sensation Torio had ever known, trying to drag him into it.

//No!// he cried, not knowing he had shouted aloud until Wulfston grasped his shoulders and shook him.

"Torio! Come out of it! Stop Reading!"

But he couldn't. The Readers continued the chant, swaying in rhythm, guiding their mind-blind Adept partners to do their bidding.

"South now—stronger—

"Push it—harder—

"Once more—harder—"

The rhythm of a gigantic heartbeat shook the land as the nonsense syllables turned to words, directions—

"Northward—lower—

"That's it!—harder—"

//No! No!// Torio broadcast, meeting Master Clement's dismay at Readers using Adepts as tools of vengeance.

Even the old Master could not shut himself out of the raging rapport. With Torio, he observed in horror the assault on the Senate, the wooden platform full of dignitaries—it was Lenardo's vision all over again as he was tossed away from Aradia, a tremor heaving the steps into vertical slabs. Inside the building the roof caved in. Men screamed and tried to run. Solid stone fell on them. Across the forum the reviewing stand collapsed, banners bearing the golden sun toppling with slow grace onto the writhing, injured people.

Portia was in the rapport, her mind screaming, //I will not allow this!// at the same time that impossible pain lanced through her fragile body and Torio Read that her back was broken. //No! You cannot do this to me!// she raged, and left her shattered body behind, her presence in them all, mad, hideous, wanting to hurt them—

//Lenardo!// she challenged, grappling with his mind as Master Amicus had done with Master Corus'. //You will pay for this! You are mine, Lenardo— mine!//

Torio realized sickly that Portia sought to take Lenardo over, to possess his mind and control his powers!

Distracted by trying to find Aradia, flung to his knees as he tried to stand on the heaving steps, Lenardo had only half his attention on Portia's raging presence. He screamed and clapped his hands to his head as she created pain to weaken his defenses.

//Portia!// Torio sent at full intensity, //let him alone!//

It was enough—Lenardo's concentration shut Portia out. She turned on Torio. //Then you, blind fool! I can use you even more easily, boy. You should be dead anyway!//

Corrupt Portia might be, but Torio knew he was no match for her powers. He didn't even know what she meant to do, let alone how to fight it! He hadn't known the ruling of another's mind was possible until he had Read Amicus try it.

Portia's thwarted power-lust gripped him—he was helpless before it, cringing away into some dark corner of his mind, while she—

//No, Portia.// It was Master Clement's calm presence, coherent amid the chaos. //You never meant to hurt anyone. Let Torio go. Come and rest, Portia—// The old man's strong, clear mind created a haven of blessed relief, dissolving Portia's rapport with Torio.

But Portia refused to be calmed. //Traitor! You and Lenardo and all the others! You will pay for this! Traitors all! You will never destroy my powers!// And her presence was gone, as she moved into one of the other planes of existence.

//Master Clement—no!// Both Torio and Lenardo were too late with their entreaty—the old man had followed her.

Lenardo dared not pursue him, and Torio could not —the pandemonium of mental activity blocked any sense of where his teacher might have gone. A small tremor moved the hillside he was sitting on, and he realized, "Now, Wulfston! Draw the stresses *now*!"

This time the Adept's efforts had the desired effect— they were tossed and heaved, but the fault under Tiberium was being relieved. Beneath the forum, the rock plates settled into a horizontal bridge over the deep chasm. There were cracks in the forum floor. The Senate had fallen in, killing everyone inside. Soldiers picking themselves up from among their dead and wounded companions hauled the remains of the reviewing stand off the bodies beneath—and found the Emperor on the very bottom, crushed to death. So was his wife—and his two sons, who had been ready to lead units of the army, were dead as well.

While nonReaders ran from the scene of destruction or tried to locate their dead or injured companions, Readers wearing the Sign of the Dark Moon swarmed into the forum, tearing down the banners bearing the golden sun, shouting, "It is time that Readers ruled!"

Lenardo located Aradia, badly injured, bones broken

—he stopped Reading to concentrate his own small healing power, and what was left of the rapport collapsed, leaving Torio once more alone within himself.

Wulfston was still gripping Torio's shoulders—pain penetrated and he shook the Adept off. "The rapport is broken," he said raggedly. "Lenardo is concentrating on Aradia—he's not going to think of us for a while."

"Let's go!" said Wulfston, reaching for their already-packed gear. "Come *on*, Torio—they need us!" But he staggered as he rose, and Torio took his arm.

"Lie down. I'll go out of body and—"

"There's no time! Aradia is unconscious, Lilith hours away—Lenardo has no fully-empowered Adepts with him. I'm all right, Torio. I haven't used half my energy."

Because he was as anxious as Wulfston, Torio helped saddle the horses and they set off for Tiberium. It had taken more than two days to get here, when they were avoiding calling attention to themselves. Now they galloped, obtaining fresh horses every few hours by the simple expedient of stealing them—twice leaving men who tried to stop them crumpled in sudden sleep.

They met people fleeing the destruction in the capital city. Everyone knew the Emperor was dead. The closer they got to Tiberium, the more fear permeated the air—by early morning the word was out that the Senate had been destroyed as well, and no one knew who was running the empire. Torio Read garbled opinions of what had happened—but very few knew the savages had anything to do with it or even realized that there were Adepts among them.

As they approached the city, though, Torio did not find the destruction he feared. Terror and hatred had faded into empty anxiety. The city itself stood without serious structural damage. The closer they got, the more surprised Torio became; while some people huddled fearfully in their homes, many others were out cleaning up debris. Soldiers kept order—a few buildings had been looted, but they were already boarded up.

Here people were indeed aware of Adepts—and terrified of them. They did not know who among the strangers could kill them "with a look," and they did not wish to find out. Everyone also knew that the royal family and the senators were dead—there was no government except that of the savages, who were known to have Readers now. There were stray thoughts of rebellion, but none serious—the army had surrendered and was now in the service of their captors.

Torio Read Arkus directing units of Aventine soldiers, Helmuth—nonReader and nonAdept but ever Lenardo's most reliable henchman—sending other soldiers to draft a work crew to clear the streets blocked by the collapse of the Senate building. He was in the forum, where the debris was already cleared away, the gaps in the cobbles bridged with sturdy planking. Unable to locate Lenardo or Aradia, Torio led Wulfston to the forum, where Helmuth told them, "They're at the Adigia Academy building, my lords. All is under control here."

Wulfston looked around, bleary-eyed with lack of sleep, and laughed. "Why did I worry? We gave Lenardo a city of savages, with no Lords Adept to help him —after what he accomplished in Zendi, why expect less here?"

But Torio worried as he rode toward the villa that had housed his Academy for the past year—for he should have been greeted by Lenardo's vigorous mind. Instead, it was Melissa who told him, // Lord Lenardo is sleeping—at last. He exhausted his strength healing Aradia and others, but when Lady Lilith arrived we finally got him to rest.//

Torio relayed this information to Wulfston before they entered the building. The students' bedrooms were filled with injured people in healing sleep, some waking now, bewildered, to be fed and sent home. By the time Wulfston was reassured that his sister would soon be well, and fed the meal he had been too concerned to stop for during the night, a bed was prepared for him.

Relaxation of tension had Torio nodding over his breakfast, too. Since everything was under control. . . .

But before he could find an empty bed Decius came for him, weeping. "Please, Torio—come and see if you can do anything for Master Clement!"

The old Reader lay in his own bed, physically unhurt. His body was there; his mind was not. Lilith sat beside him, pale, her eyes sunken into dark circles. Julia sprawled nearby, eyes red with crying. "Torio! Tell them they've got to wake Father! He's the only one can help!"

"Lenardo is exhausted," Lilith said. "His Reading powers are greatly impaired—when he told me that, I did not tell him about Master Clement."

But Torio was staring at his teacher's still form. "You moved him!"

"Yes," Lilith agreed. "I did not know I should have left him where he fell—when he fainted, I thought it was exhaustion, or his heart, or a stroke. Torio, there was no other Reader to tell me what he had done."

Torio sat on the edge of the bed, Reading the serene face of the old Master. Despite its age, his body was now healthy; it breathed; its heart beat. But it was uninhabited. Master Clement was elsewhere, lost among the planes of existence.

Melissa hovered in the doorway. "Torio, can you do anything?"

"How long did you wait before you moved him?" Torio asked Lilith.

"Nearly three hours. I cannot Read—I thought I had put him into healing sleep."

"Then it makes no difference that you moved him," said Torio bitterly. "No Reader dare stay so long on the planes beyond—he was lost long before you moved his body."

"But he said he was out of body for hours when he made the map," Julia protested.

"Out of body, but in our world. You'll understand when you are old enough to try it, Julia. Lilith, do not blame yourself. It is Portia who has claimed one last victim.''

''Portia's dead,'' said Julia. ''She didn't come back either, and her body died. She didn't understand, Torio —none of us did till I Read her medallion. Father made me—I didn't want to touch it.''

Torio remembered the child's special talent for Reading items people had worn or kept close to them. ''What did you learn?'' he asked.

''The Dark Moon devoured the sun of the royal family. She never thought about what was on that medal— the sun, like on the Emperor's banners. She was so proud of being of royal blood—the Emperor's grandfather's aunt. That's why she knew all about politics— she wasn't s'posed to be a Reader. There's never been another one in the royal family. She had to have power —so she worked her way to Master of Masters.''

Torio nodded. ''She couldn't stand not to rule.''

The little girl added, ''When I felt into the past, though, she was . . . nice. She didn't mean to hurt anybody. She liked helping people with her Reading, for a long, long time.''

Torio went to the child and hugged her. ''I'm glad to hear that, Julia. I suppose we will have another funeral tomorrow. Will you say that for Portia, please?''

There was indeed a funeral the next day, in the savage tradition. However, it was not the cleansing ceremony Torio had become used to—for the one man he and Lenardo and Decius mourned the most was not dead.

Master Clement's body might live for many days yet —the Adepts would not allow it to die. Wulfston and Aradia insisted, ''Life is all we have. If we had allowed our father to die when we thought his tumor was hopeless, Lenardo could not have helped us heal him.'' And Lenardo, although he knew as well as Torio that it was hopeless, planned to try searching the planes of existence as soon as he recovered his powers.

At the funeral, curious Aventine citizens ringed the

forum to hear their conquerors eulogize the people they had just killed—at least that was how they saw it. They didn't understand, but they wept as the bodies of the entire Senate, the royal family, several Master Readers, and a number of soldiers went up in the white-hot flame of the funeral pyre. Their whole way of life was burning away, and they didn't know what would replace it.

Torio walked with Melissa back to the villa. They had not carried funeral garments with them, of course, and so both were dressed today in Reader's garb, Melissa in a plain white tunic, Torio in the same white edged in black that Lenardo wore.

In the streets of Tiberium, the sight of a male and a female Reader walking side by side drew stares. In a mixture of protectiveness, possessiveness, and defiance, Torio took Melissa's arm.

She looked up at him with a shy smile, but said nothing. Neither did any of their friends—and when they reached the villa, Torio led her to the courtyard. One side was open to a hallway off which were several sleeping rooms—but occupants of two of those rooms were, indeed, sleeping, and the other rooms, including Torio's, were empty.

A fountain formed a pool in the courtyard—the younger boys at the Academy used to play here, splashing in the shallow water. Flowering shrubs created alcoves for several benches hidden from the view of anyone passing in the hallway. It was to one of these that Torio led Melissa.

They sat in silence for a time, until Melissa asked, "Torio . . . what's wrong?"

"Wrong? Except for Master Clement, nothing, really. I don't know what's going to happen next, Melissa. That . . . that doesn't bother you, does it?"

"If knowing what's going to happen means having flashes like Lenardo's," she replied, "then I don't want to know."

"That wasn't what I meant—but that disturbs me, too. All our efforts—the earthquake at Gaeta that nearly killed you, and led me to lie to Portia—the storm, the quicksand—in the end everything happened just as Lenardo foresaw it. If we had done nothing—''

"The earthquake would have happened anyway," Melissa said. "It would have been much worse, though, Torio—what happened was Lenardo's vision, not the prophecy."

"What do you mean?"

"The prophecy said the earth would devour Tiberium. It didn't. You Read what happened: If Aradia and the other Adepts hadn't been able to draw some of the stress away from beneath the city, this whole area would have caved in. There would be no city standing here today—there would be nothing but a hole in the ground."

He pondered that. He had himself Read the possibility of total collapse, and yet the city stood. "So perhaps our meddling did some good after all. I want to think it did."

"Of course it did! I'd have done the same things you did, Torio—anybody would. What sane person would not try to prevent the deaths of thousands of people if he had it in his power?"

He turned to her, appearing to look at her as he had taught himself to do as a boy. She was studying his face. "You forgive me for Gaeta?"

"There is nothing to forgive. You were trying to prevent the major quake—and I have certainly seen enough since that night to know that there are limitations even to the powers of Readers and Adepts working together. But I'm not afraid anymore. I was always afraid to test my powers . . . until I crossed the border. Until I met you."

She closed her eyes, her face turned up to his. For privacy in this villa full of Readers, Melissa was not Reading. Torio had been Reading only enough to find his way. Now he stopped, but found no difficulty placing his arms around Melissa, drawing her close, meeting her lips with his.

Torio had never kissed a woman before—but he

quickly found the way to shift their position so they could comfortably indulge in a prolonged embrace. His heart was pounding, but he refused to let his mind wonder where this might lead. He simply enjoyed the moment.

When they broke off kissing, Melissa remained in Torio's arms. Her head fit neatly against his shoulder, so that he could rest his cheek against her hair, breathing in its fragrance. Still . . . "I'm not sure we should be doing this," he said with little conviction.

"I am," Melissa replied. "I'm . . . not sure where it will lead for us, Torio, but it's not wrong for Readers to touch each other."

He felt her turn her face up again, and there was no reluctance in his response. But in the midst of their kiss, he heard the sound of footsteps. Torio began to Read just in time to find Wulfston turning away in great embarrassment at having walked in on their private moment.

"Wulfston—don't go." Both Torio and Melissa spoke, almost in unison.

The Adept halted, flustered. "I'm sorry. I was just going to sit out here for a while. I didn't know anyone was—" He essayed a rueful smile that didn't quite succeed. "Until I can learn to Read, I'll try to be more alert . . . or louder."

Melissa and Torio were sitting side by side on the bench now, a hand's span apart. "We were discussing what happened here in Tiberium," said Melissa.

"And at Gaeta," said Torio. "Wulfston, you and Aradia always say that you work with nature."

Wulfston smiled. "That seems to be what you were doing."

Torio felt himself blushing, but forced himself to go on. "But there are times when you work against it."

Wulfston accepted Torio's serious tone and sat down on a bench opposite the couple. "We worked against nature to prevent the destruction of Tiberium."

"Exactly!" said Torio. "And Melissa just pointed

out to me that we succeeded. The earth did *not* swallow the city!"

"True," Wulfston agreed. "We achieved part of what we intended. But we have to take responsibility for all the things that happened that we didn't intend—the political damage we created will be much harder to repair than the earthquake damage."

"And the shambles we've left the Readers in," added Melissa.

"Not just those who joined us," said Torio. "What about those not involved in our plan? There are thousands of young Readers in training, hundreds of Magister Readers, scattered Masters who were not part of Portia's circle. They are not our enemies, and yet they certainly have no reason to trust us."

"After the way the Readers used them," said Melissa, "the Adepts won't trust them again soon, either. What do we do, my lord?"

"What you have done, Melissa," Wulfston replied. "Learn one another's powers. Then learn the right way to use them together. Gaeta happened because we didn't have enough geological information; we can take care that that kind of error never happens again now that we have many Readers to gather information for us."

"But Tiberium—" said Torio.

"*Human* nature," said Wulfston. "I don't know if we'll ever learn to judge it accurately—but we must try. If we don't want one war after another, we must understand and trust each other. It won't be easy, but it's the only answer."

Not everyone agreed with Wulfston, as became evident at dinner that evening. Everyone was awake now, Aradia well enough to be up for the day, although she would do more healing in the night. She opened the session by turning to her husband to say, "Well, Lenardo, like it or not, it seems we now have an empire to rule."

"Have we? We didn't come here as conquerors, Aradia."

"But it was foretold—'In the day of the white wolf

and the red dragon, there will be peace throughout the world.' The empire tried to breach that peace,'' she said.

Lilith agreed. ''We can't walk away and leave these people to fight out a government among themselves. The Senate is gone, the royal family is gone. They'll end up with a military dictatorship.''

''What about the Readers?'' asked Decius. ''I'm surprised that the members of the Path of the Dark Moon have not yet challenged our right to remain here. I've seen Alethia and her husband, but where are the others?''

Melissa explained, ''They've gone into hiding, out of shame. They misused their powers, Decius—they sought vengeance. They killed Portia and the Emperor and the Senate—I almost joined them, the emotion was so strong. When I realized what I was doing I stopped—but there was no stopping that group mind. When the rapport was gone—most of the Readers suddenly could not Read. Everyone who joined the killing spree has lost some Reading ability—some are mind-blind. I do not think we need fear an uprising along the Path of the Dark Moon, unless we treat them so badly that they are willing to sacrifice what little power they have left.''

''We will not treat anyone badly,'' said Wulfston, ''but we have no advantage here as we had in lands Drakonius controlled. The Aventine government did not mistreat its citizens; we cannot win their loyalty with simple kindness.''

''Why not let the people form a new government?'' asked Torio. ''Let them elect a new Senate.''

''Encourage them to hold elections and *then* walk away?'' asked Lenardo. ''That might be a solution.''

''Not without a strong ruler,'' said Aradia. ''Lenardo, haven't you learned yet that human nature is much more unpredictable and dangerous than the nature of wind and fire, earth and water? We prevented an earthquake from devastating this land—but *people* destroyed it just as effectively, by destroying *people*.''

Torio noticed how different Aradia's view of human nature was from her brother's. Nonetheless, he agreed with both of them on one point: "We have started something we must finish. Just over a year ago, Drakonius caused the earthquake at Adigia. He made the fault under the empire unstable—and walked away. We had to finish what he started. I started a war with my lie to Portia—the idea that we can raise the dead created such fear that the empire sent an army against us."

"Torio is right," said Melissa. "He didn't walk away —he discovered a way to prevent a real war, and saved many lives. We finished the earthquakes; the fault is stabilized. Now the Aventine army has surrendered to us again, but the people here are leaderless, just as unstable as that fault used to be. Should we end one kind of instability only to create another?"

Lenardo looked around the table. "I think I am outnumbered," he said.

Aradia smiled her wolf-like grin. "Now you know how I felt when you and Wulfston and Lilith opposed my idea of forming an empire last summer."

"Apparently your visions are as true as mine, Aradia—as you said, we now have an empire, whether we want it or not. What is the use of such visions if there is nothing we can do to prevent their coming true?"

"Lenardo," said Wulfston, "your vision came true— *your vision*, not the total destruction of Tiberium."

"Yes," said Julia, "*that* is what was foretold, Father, and we prevented it."

"Remember what you told me?" said Torio. "Master your powers and you will master your fears. You fear your visions—but they are one of your powers."

Lenardo stared at Torio for a long moment. "Again the teacher learns from his student. You are right, Torio—I must stop fearing my visions. Then I may stop misinterpreting them."

"Readers must accept all their powers," said Melissa.

"We must win the confidence of the strong Readers left in the empire who were not part of Portia's circle," said Torio. "If they haven't guessed by now what Portia was doing, other Readers will tell them under Oath of Truth."

"Portia," said Aradia with a shudder. "I understand her, perhaps better than any of the rest of you. Because of her powers, she was denied power. That is not healthy. Readers must be given power, openly—or they will breed more Portias, silently festering and secretly manipulating, turning their strength toward hurting instead of healing."

"You are right, Aradia," said Lenardo. "If Portia had been openly allowed to exercise power, she would have been content and other Readers would have had the same right. Any extreme move would have been countered—because it would have been public. We must change the whole attitude of and toward Readers."

"So we go on meddling," said Torio.

"Every form of government is meddling, in a way," said Aradia. "And anyway, I think you agree with us, Torio."

"I do," he replied. "I don't want to go back to the Academy. I'm a part of the changes we've made—and the ones yet to come."

Melissa put her hand over his. "So am I," she said.

"And I," said Decius, taking Melissa's left hand. Wulfston took Torio's right hand, his right to Aradia, who joined with Lenardo . . . Julia . . . Ivorn . . . Rolf . . . Lilith . . . and back to Decius.

Torio felt the power in that circle of Adepts and Readers—perhaps the greatest assembly of power ever gathered in one room. It tingled through his body and mind, controlled by trust and good will. They would disagree again, he knew, but at that moment all were in a rapport of acceptance. *This is the way Adepts and Readers are supposed to act together!*

The sensation of leashed power and trust was too welcome, too soothing, to be broken at once. They basked in it, healing their anxieties, their strained nerves, their guilt, grief, and sorrow. He felt the minds of all the Readers in the circle, the emotions of Wulfston, Ivorn, and Lilith—wishing the three Adepts might break through—

But only their emotional strength supported the circle. Torio's thoughts turned with those of the other Readers—as if it were one mind rather than seven—to Master Clement; their sorrow at his loss; their fear for him, lost on the planes of existence; their hopeless yearning that somehow he might yet return. The thought seemed to take form, drawing energy from those with Adept power—even the three mind-blind who could not comprehend what was happening, remained still, silent, participating.

Like a glowing beacon, the thought rose above the circle, a moment's memorial to a man who had touched all their lives—if some only briefly. The force of Lenardo's immeasurable mental power concentrated the emanation until it seemed unbearable—they would have to let it go—but no one wanted to leave the rapport as memory washed over them like the mind of the gentle old man himself, as if for one moment he were actually there with them—a brief touch, and then—

Lenardo suddenly started, gasped, and leaped from his chair, shattering the rapport. Torio jumped up and followed him, not believing what he Read. Despite his handicap, Decius was on Torio's heels when they entered the room where they had left Master Clement's body. The old man was sitting up, Reading about him in amazement. Then his three students were on him. "Master Clement!" "We thought you were dead!" "You were gone so long—"

"So long? Yes—it must have been hours," the Master Reader replied. "I was on a plane where time is different—I thought I was gone only minutes. But I was lost."

"It was *two days*!" said Torio. "Master Clement, we had no hope you could return."

"Portia?" asked Lenardo. "Her body died. Is she—?"

"I lost her," said Master Clement. "I meant only to calm and comfort her. She fled from me into the emptiness of one of the planes beyond." He sighed. "She was once a good woman, Lenardo. This recent power-madness—"

"Yes, we know," said Torio. "We praised her good memory today, Master Clement. But we thought we had lost you."

"I thought so, too," said the old man. "I could not find my way back. The emptiness of the plane I was on drew at me . . . I could not find my way. I wanted to fill that emptiness, or escape it—but there was no place to turn! If I allowed myself to be drawn away, I knew I could never return to you—"

By this time all ten people who had formed the circle at the table were crowded into the small room. He looked at them, Read them, and shook his head in disbelief. "There was a . . . a beacon in the emptiness. It seemed . . . not as you do now, with all your separate personalities, but like one mind with the power of many —much greater than any rapport of Readers."

Tears were running down Torio's face. "We found our way to each other," he said, "Readers and Adepts together. It's *right*, Master Clement—it has to be right for us to work together!"

"Of course it's right," said Master Clement. "I would never have left the empire if I were not sure of that."

The old man looked around the group again, and smiled. "You are all so young—you have many years to build a new way of life. I have heard what you call it, my dear friends—and I thank the gods and all of you that I shall now live to see the beginning of your new way of life: your Savage Empire!"

Jean Lorrah has a Ph.D. in Medieval British Literature. She is Professor of English at Murray State University in Kentucky. Her first professional publications were non-fiction; her fiction was published in fanzines for years before her first professional novel appeared in 1980. She maintains a close relationship with sf fandom, appearing at conventions and engaging in as much fannish activity as time will allow. On occasion, she has the opportunity to combine her two loves of teaching and writing by teaching creative writing.